W9-BVV-233

THE
QUARTER
STORM

ALSO BY
VERONICA G. HENRY

Bacchanal

THE
QUARTER STORM

VERONICA G. HENRY

This is a work of fiction. Names, characters, organizations, places, events, and incidents are either products of the author's imagination or are used fictitiously. Any resemblance to actual persons, living or dead, or actual events is purely coincidental.

Text copyright © 2022 by Veronica Henry
All rights reserved.

No part of this book may be reproduced, or stored in a retrieval system, or transmitted in any form or by any means, electronic, mechanical, photocopying, recording, or otherwise, without express written permission of the publisher.

Published by 47North, Seattle

www.apub.com

Amazon, the Amazon logo, and 47North are trademarks of Amazon.com, Inc., or its affiliates.

ISBN-13: 9781542033916
ISBN-10: 1542033918

Cover design by Faceout Studio, Lindy Martin

Printed in the United States of America

For Eric,
my partner in life and our nomadic travels.
Amor fati

CHAPTER ONE

The mind could conjure all kinds of fanciful scenarios to assuage the guilt of a poor choice of last words. In my favored delusion, my mother and I were chatting it up while she window-shopped at Oakwood Center over in Terrytown. That place was for her what my backyard *peristil* was to me: a sanctuary. Had Bondye been merciful, the background noise of bustling shoppers would have spared her, my vitriol quieted to a few sharp words uttered under my breath. But God wasn't always available to answer a servant's whims. In the end, the hurricane swallowed the apology I'd held off delivering until the next day and took a sizable chunk of the city with it.

Papa had once again been the stubborn root of what I hadn't known at the time would be our final conflict. He'd always sat wedged between us like a parapet in a grisly, decades-long conflict. My father's singular focus was that his daughter continue the unbroken line of Vodou priests and priestesses dating back to Benin. Manman wanted a different life for me. Though she lost in the end, their fights on the matter were a thing of legend.

And now the only thing I had left of her was a fragment of a text message that I had saved on a phone long since inoperable. Three cryptic letters that taunted me whenever I closed my eyes: *N O P.*

I found lost things for people all the time. Misplaced keys, money buried in backyard graves, a pet that had run off in search of a happier home. Even helped the police find my stolen car once. The water-gazing bowl's magic always uncovered many secrets. But I hadn't dared to look into those waters in service to myself in a long time. Their stubborn silence both judgment and sentence. Longing, though rarer those last few years, sometimes overwhelmed my efforts at self-preservation.

It was time to try again.

The altar to my patron, Erzulie, sat on a small table in a corner of the living room facing the front door. Both warning and welcome to all who entered. I lit the candles: fat round yellows, tall skinny reds and purples, a profusion of colorful strings of beads interwoven between them all.

The small space was completed with an image of Erzulie's *vèvè*: an intricately sketched heart filled with stars and curlicues sprouting from the tips and corners. With no expendable cash for luxuries, a spritz of my homemade concoction served as a perfume offering.

The water-gazing bowl, unused but for this purpose, rested at the center of a low table atop a white tablecloth. A thumbprint on the plain sterling-silver rim caught my attention. It was stalling, but I whipped out a purified cloth and polished away the imperfection.

A flutter of anxiety stilled my hands.

When I saw myself reflected in the gleam, I knelt, planting my knees atop the golden cushion.

The dubious muck that came out of your typical New Orleans faucet had never touched this bowl unaltered. The version I now splashed in had been boiled three times, run through a sieve, and blessed with the words of my religion. My heart swelled with hope and constricted with the disappointment of so many failed attempts. I knew better than to put myself through this again. But what kind of daughter gave up on her mother?

I lowered my head, clasped my hands together, and whispered, *"Revele."*

Ripples played across the water's surface as if stirred by a trail of unseen pebbles. Bubbling pinpricks simmered along the bottom. Invisible to all but me, water vapor rose and birthed liquid droplets. When a parade of dime-size azure clouds floated aloft, all was ready.

A current of unease warned me to turn away while I still could. It foretold the pain of the reopened wound that awaited me on the other side of another failure. But I couldn't stop now.

The spell worked best if you had a fairly narrow idea of where you wanted to search. All I had were shadows and guesses. Instead, lashes fluttering closed, I replayed memories of my manman. The bouquet of fine lines on her forehead and at the corners of her oval eyes; her walk, more of a sashay; her perpetually purple fingernails. The times when, through my childhood eyes, I had imagined she and Papa were a happy couple.

But she was never happy with my practice, had tried to drag me away from it and from Papa on several occasions, only to be found and brought back home. We finally left Haiti together as a family, bundling up our things and hastening onto an airplane headed for the place where her only friend had settled. My new and permanent home, New Orleans. I was eight years old.

I opened my eyes to slits, afraid that anything more would make the truth that much harder to bear. The clouds had cleared but the gazing bowl was a void, like the deserted lot where my mother's yellow house had once stood.

The curses on my tongue smartly gave way to effusive thanks to Erzulie and the other *lwa* for their presence and gifts. A Vodou priestess's thoughts were never hers alone: she learned to share them and her life with the gods and goddesses, for them to do with as they saw fit. The deafening pitch of a raging river slammed against my eardrums and quickly faded away. Erzulie had detected my insolence and reminded me that I lived only to *sèvi lwa yo*—to serve the lwa, and to serve her.

Even with the goddess Erzulie raging through me, I hadn't been strong enough to stop the hurricane's destruction.

I was left to wonder if the hurricane's devastating waters had swept Manman away, clutching nothing but my disrespect, unable to grasp my regret. Or if Papa was right, and she'd jumped at the chance to disappear from both our lives and had boarded a plane to her forever.

Those first weeks after the storm were a blur of sleepless nights, dead-end phone calls, and wreckage. I exhausted the traditional methods, starting with what remained of the local police, and then turned to the tools of my trade as a *mambo* priestess. Neither yielded me so much as one of my mother's broken fingernails.

In the intervening years, I'd cursed and cried, walked the city till I had blisters on top of my blisters, and badgered people who now turned away from me as I passed by. But my manman remained an enigma. Not quite a ghost and not the villain Papa imagined her to be.

No matter what my father said, I knew Manman hadn't run out on us. In my darker moments, I sometimes wondered if he'd been hiding her from me all these years. He was a powerful *houngan* in his own right, after all. But though he was angry at her, a little embarrassed even, the truth was he would never hurt me that way.

I stood and blew out the candles. Despite what everyone around me whispered, and what the police had stamped on their file, I knew she wasn't dead. I just needed to find her. And one day, I would.

CHAPTER TWO

When we first left Haiti, I was so homesick I feigned every manner of malady I could conjure. Anything that would allow me to ditch school, where the other kids teased me about my accent. At one point, I came home, tossed my backpack down, and told my parents in no uncertain terms that I was going back to Haiti, with or without them. Manman took me in her arms, kissed my tearstained cheeks, and told me that home is where the heart is.

These days, my heart belonged to Tremé and a traditional blue and white New Orleans shotgun built in 1906 and patched up every year since. After an embarrassingly short stint as a marketing research assistant, I'd set up my healing practice about a dozen steps from the back porch to my garage turned temple Vodoun, at least on the days I didn't attend to clients in their homes.

Today, I was getting ready for a new client to come to me. Pink lip gloss in a shade that actually looked good against browner skin tones. A longish skirt that, to my eye, added inches to the modest height I shared with Papa. A little liner to bring out the oval eyes I got from Manman. Slid on a white headband to help lay the edges from my fresh twistout, and I was ready.

I always awaited my customers out back on the canary-yellow bench in front of my shop, and I'd been delighting in the soul-mellowing music of blue jay and sparrow birdsong interlaced with my neighbor's flugelhorn rehearsal for a full hour when a car door slammed.

When she'd called to make an appointment for a spirit-doll ritual, I'd told the youthful voice on the other end of the line the same thing I told all first-time customers: don't go traipsing up to my front door (delivered with a level of professional tact, mind you). "Follow the impossible-to-miss path of blue and white paving stones that curve alongside the wood-slatted fence," I always told them.

My back never forgave me for the hours spent hunched over, setting and resetting each stone. There was even a sign nailed to the fence above the first paver, yellow backing with royal-blue lettering artfully scripted onto the wood: LE PETIT TEMPLE VODOUN 1791.

And to some these things were all but invisible.

Repeat customers made up the bulk of my practice. Newcomer traffic had fallen to a trickle over the last year. Tourists and locals alike increasingly drawn to the larger, fancier shops dispensing their fancifully bogus Hollywood brand of voodoo magic.

Better them than me. These days, my patience for those unwilling to learn was in critically short supply, much like the food in my kitchen cupboards.

As was my practice with all first-timers, I'd had her repeat the directions back to me. But the attention span required to listen, I mean *really* listen, required a depth of concentration that was laid to rest alongside good manners in a New Orleans jazz funeral, complete with a second line, sometime after the internet became more social than scientific.

I could've pretended that the only reason my shop was in my backyard instead of in the heart of Uptown or the French Quarter was a matter of convenience and virtue. But *vodouisants* like me didn't have much call for pretense. Investments in hard work and thrift had thus far yielded returns in the forms of a deep fatigue and a closet full of dated clothes. My life remained stubbornly fixed on a tightrope between broke and bankrupt. Goodbye, dream of a glitzy Dumaine Street storefront; hello, comfortably converted garage.

I stood outside, arms crossed, foot tapping, and listened to the banging on my front door for as long as I could before I marched down the stone walkway to the front of the house. And there she stood with her frail behind, straining on tiptoe, trying to peer through the stained glass at the top of my door.

I was surprised to see a white girl.

Not to say I didn't have white clients. New Orleans had changed enough in the decade after the hurricane that people from all races and nationalities were as unremarkable as an afternoon rain shower. But white believers willing to come out to Tremé, where gentrification had been razed like dandelions in a prize-winning rose garden, were rare as the days when the heady aroma of a simmering roux didn't waft through the neighborhood.

"Over here!" I called, and she turned. She trotted down the steps and came toward me with a sheepish smile at the corners of her wide mouth. Her toes curved in to such a degree that I half expected her to trip over her own feet.

"Reina?" Her breath hitched; then she started again. "I mean Mambo Dumond?" The black sweater buttoned to the neck was on the thicker side for the unseasonably warm spring weather. And she must have sacrificed a whole jar of Vaseline to the effort of sliding into the jeans entombing her slim frame. I winced. It was as if she were already punishing herself for whatever had brought her to my door.

"That's what they tell me." I would have preferred it if she'd gone back to the curb and taken the pavers, not the shortcut across my grass, but I kept that to myself. "Sophie Thibault?"

I extended my hand and was struck by how young the girl was. High school was in her past—college, too, perhaps—but her thirtieth birthday was likely years away. She had a strong handshake and limp brown hair that was in need of a good washing. Her only makeup was a slash of near-black lipstick. No point in asking where she got her perfectly arched eyebrows done; such luxuries didn't align with my current lack of resources.

"Yes, ma'am." Sophie was raised by someone who valued manners. You could call me a cynic, but people I met for the first time started out with a negative balance. They earned their way onto the positive side based on their actions. Little Sophie had earned a plus one.

"Follow me." I led my new client down the paver-lined walkway, past the canary bench. My shop was small but comfortable and well stocked. If my father ever ventured out of the Louisiana swampland for a visit, I think he would have approved. Among other things, Haitian deities were always particular about colors. Erzulie favored gold and yellow and blue and pink. So, for her, I'd painted my door and bench a dazzling yellow just shy of obnoxious.

Azaleas and bougainvillea were woven into a rounded trellis in a flood of color covering the wall. Potted lavender and honeysuckle rested on either side of the door, the soothing aroma a steadfast companion on evenings before the mosquitoes descended. They'd been gifts from customers who paid for services with the kindness in their hearts instead of cash.

Inside, I gestured toward a chair at the table, draped appropriately in a freshly laundered white tablecloth. Sophie perched herself on the edge of her seat while I padded across the polished concrete floor that I hoped would someday be covered in a nice bamboo wood and lit some sandalwood incense.

"This isn't like those shops in the Quarter. This is kind of like what you call a real hounfor, right?" Sophie asked and then slapped her forehead. "That's why you told me to come to the back. Of course—you work here and not your house."

"That's right." Huh—she knew a little about the practice. A plus two. "But it's pronounced more like 'hoon-for.'"

"What's so important about the year 1791?"

Few people asked that question. I had an answer prepared for those who did, one that didn't include the crucial role the lwa had played in Haiti's celebrated slave uprising. Spirits liked to keep their secrets, you know.

"Haiti." I handed her my tablet and asked her to enter her contact and credit card information while I dimmed the lights and lit the white candle at the center of the table and a few on the shelves that stood in place of artwork on almost every available wall. "Toussaint Louverture led a successful slave revolt. Look it up."

I wasn't one for much small talk while I set up, and luckily, Sophie wasn't either. She nodded her acceptance of my explanation and leaned forward, forearms on the table, fiddling with a silver, filigreed ring on her left thumb. She glanced over at the polished metal machete encased in glass hanging on the wall, a gift from my father that, unlike its twin in his peristil, had never tasted blood. He'd started training me in the ancient art of *tire manchèt* at the ripe old age of three.

At the back of the room, I traced the outline of Erzulie's *vèvè* painted on the wall above the sink. Among other things, my Erzulie was a spirit of love, and though some might have taken creative license, a heart was always at the center of her emblem.

"Geri." I invited her into the space.

With that part done, I took a seat opposite my new client. Without thinking, I touched the divot on the edge of the table where my mother had damaged the wood while helping me bring it inside. She intruded on my thoughts at the strangest of times.

Though it was at least ten degrees cooler inside than out, Sophie removed her sweater, revealing a T-shirt from Southern University, my alma mater.

I glanced over her information on the tablet, raised an eyebrow. I knew that address. Another peristil, a storefront in the French Quarter, with a small apartment upstairs. I'd considered renting the space myself. Now another vodouisant ran it. A competent one, at that. Why would this girl venture out here when services could be had right where she lived?

Tentatively, I urged my water sense outward. One of the three realms of my water magic, evolution of the physical variety, granted me the ability to heal, and to sense distress. Like a spiritual hygrometer, I measured, tasted the moisture in Sophie's body. It was a rapturous liberty I took without permission, a fact that wasn't lost on me. Drawing water from a living thing was always dangerous. But sometimes I used the measurements I gathered in service to my clients. Using too much or too little water each came with their own hazards. No alcohol, no elevated stress hormones in Sophie's blood. At least she was well hydrated. I still offered her a bottle of water, which she declined.

Time to get down to business. "Whenever you're ready to begin," I said.

Sophie scooted back off the edge of her seat and sat up bone straight. She didn't speak immediately, and I was happy to wait. I charged by the hour for certain charms and rituals, after all. My schedule for that day—and the next, for that matter—was clear as a saint's conscience. So I let Sophie sit there and fill the easy silence, fiddling with her thumb ring for as long as she wanted. She pulled it off, then on, then off once more before she set it on the table.

Finally, she met my eyes. I was surprised by the intensity of this little wisp of a girl's gaze. "I need a poppet, a spirit doll," she said and then added, "I think."

Another lovesick child. A young woman wearing the pitiful expression Sophie wore always meant a love spell. I withheld the sigh that wanted badly to escape my throat. "Tell me what you're looking for, and I'll tell you if you need a poppet or something else."

Sophie looked around the room, and I got the distinct impression she was trying to decide how much of her story to tell me. "This room feels, I don't know . . ." She rubbed her hands up and down her arms. "Spiritual. I can feel it more here than . . ."

She didn't finish her sentence. More spiritual than the shop downstairs from where she lived, perhaps? Was that why she'd chosen to come to me? I guessed if the boyfriend or husband lived there, too, it might have been a little too close to home.

"It's my boyfriend." She placed her hands flat on the tablecloth. Her short nails were painted a bright red. Sophie was a study in contrasts. "I need him to love me. To stay with me."

The college degree crammed in a box at the back of my closet proclaimed me an expert in marketing, but to my clientele I was a seasoned psychotherapist, training be damned.

"'Need' is a strong word. Since you're here, I'm guessing something has happened that has given you the inclination that your feelings for him aren't mutual. Sometimes, endings are just the beginning you need. Toying with the natural order of things can have unexpected consequences. You sure that's what you want?"

Typically, at this point, there would be tears. Some denials. A fit or tantrum. Sophie Thibault smiled. A wicked sight, more a tooth baring than anything. And the goddess Erzulie roiled, tugging at the water in my body, turning it ice cold. She didn't trust the girl. Goose bumps erupted along my arms. I needed a sweater, maybe a pair of gloves, but didn't dare get up in the middle of the consultation. That would've been untoward.

"Men don't know what they want." Sophie suddenly sounded twenty years older. And people said *I* had an old soul. "We have to show them. Guide them. Only problem is, other women always get in the way of the work you're trying to put in."

I didn't point out that I, too, was a woman. Or that perhaps the other woman who was interfering with her boyfriend may have had the same thoughts about her. But that other woman wasn't paying for the andouille sausage that would go into tonight's jambalaya. "The question you have to ask yourself," I said, "is if this man wants to be somewhere else, do you truly want to compel him—"

"Yes," Sophie said without hesitation.

"You have to consider how you'll feel." Little Sophie was going to get the speech whether she wanted it or not. "Compelling a man to stay with you sounds good until you realize that without the compulsion, he might be somewhere else. I've got to tell you that many of my clients feel that it isn't worth it in the end. As long as you're paying me, I have the right to give you my advice. Far as I'm concerned, sitting in that chair, you've already solicited it. And if you want my advice, I'd say let the man move on if he wants."

Sophie studied her nails, then thrummed her fingers against the table. She'd still have to pay my consultation fee, even without the poppet. That would at least get me some whitefish. When she finally answered, I wasn't surprised.

"What do I need for the poppet?"

"The Law of Contact dictates that we need something connected to your boyfriend. I construct the poppet from simple fabric." I indicated the bales of cloth that I used for such things poking out of a basket in the corner. "That is, if you want me to construct it from scratch. Or you can buy one of the premade and I can fill it in later."

Sophie's eyes traveled to the wall on her right that held rows of premade poppets. She turned back to me and shook her head. "No, I want to have one made from scratch."

Smart girl. "We'll make a follow-up appointment. I need a personal article from your boyfriend. Hair, a nail clipping, or something like that."

Sophie tilted her head and watched me for a moment. Had she changed her mind? Then she pulled her purse over her head, rummaged around inside, and removed a small silken pouch. She pushed it over toward me with the tip of her index finger. She'd already known.

I undid the tie and looked inside. A few strands of straight blond hair sat nestled atop a pile of dirt. My heart raced, but outwardly I remained calm. What type of spell was this girl hoping for?

"The dirt?" I asked to see if she'd tell me.

"It's from his plant. It's about the only thing he tends to in the apartment. He loves that plant more than me. Waters it, clips back the leaves, even sings to it when he plays his guitar. Figured you needed something personal, and for him, it doesn't get much more personal than his snake plant."

From a plant, huh? I didn't voice my suspicion that she wanted something more nefarious. Hell, maybe I shouldn't have even been suspicious. "You want to wait or come back?"

Sophie slipped her phone from her purse. "I'll wait."

That there was more to this girl than met the eye was a given. That it was none of my business allowed me to cast the thought out of my mind and focus on my work. I took the emerald-green fabric Sophie had selected, retreated to my workspace, and drew the blue curtain behind me.

Poppets could run the gamut from straightforward to convoluted. The variety my new client needed fell on the relatively simple end of that spectrum. Everything began with the initial construction. Some in the priesthood used wax, or clay. Unless specifically requested, however, I preferred the natural feel of a hardy quilting fabric.

I premade poppet husks in what could only be called a vaguely human shape: a head and torso, two arms and two legs. I stitched the two halves together, leaving one side open so that the doll could be customized according to need.

Next came the stuffing. My go-to was Spanish moss, but cotton would do in a pinch. In a small glass bowl, I tossed in ground Adam and Eve root, a teaspoon or so of crushed rose petal, and a pinch of sugar. After mixing this up with my fingers, I added the hair that Sophie had given me. I left out the dirt. Could have been from a grave for all I knew. As I sprinkled the mixture onto the moss, I searched my mind for just the right psalm and whispered the words: *For the director of music. With stringed instruments. A psalm. A song. May God be gracious to us and bless us and make his face shine on us.*

At this stage, most mambos and houngans would consider their work finished. Not so for those blessed to carry the lwa with them—the Beninites. Parables suggested we were more commonplace in ancient Benin, but over the centuries, our numbers had dwindled. And here in New Orleans at least, there were only two: Lucien Alexander and me.

It wasn't something we advertised, but for those with an eye to see it, it was there. That made my, our, healing practices altogether different. Erzulie was the goddess of rivers, and that river wine, my sangswe, flowed through my veins. With my father's help and some dicey trial and error, I'd discovered the three realms her touch had gifted.

Evolution was foremost. It made me a unique healer, because even a drop of sangswe wine enhanced my spells. If the humidity was just right, I could draw on that moisture to cure most cuts and scrapes with a touch. A delicately balanced amount of that same moisture ripened fruit; too much, though, and you ended up with a putrefied mess.

Currents ruled the sea, and they allowed me to channel and guide water. If I caught myself outside without an umbrella, I could redirect that water away from me. And it gave me the ability to do one thing you didn't play with: conjure physical manifestations of the lwa.

Change, emotional or form, was the enchanter, and the realm, I'd had the least success in cultivating so far. With the right combination of herbs and roots, a skilled practitioner could affect the mind.

For this part of the ritual, I held my hands over the bowl, palms up, fingers cupped but relaxed. My palm creases reacted. The darkened lines swelled, rippled, throbbed. With a gentle urging, the wine-dark water from my body oozed out. The sensation akin to being sliced open with a razor blade.

My sangswe wine dripped into the bowl. The herbs undulated and hissed as the water temperature eased upward. The mixture coiled around the edge of the circumference, completing the circuit three times before crawling up my fingers and settling on my hands. The mass solidified, hardening like a swampy shell. And then, the mixture cracked and splintered, sloughed off back into the bowl.

With effort, I closed the flow and relished the warmth until it had turned hot enough to evoke a sweat. After stuffing the dried contents into the poppet, I finished up the stitching, taking care to sew a few cowrie shells on the legs and three silver buttons on the left side of the poppet's chest. A zigzag stitch for the mouth and pinpricks for the eyes.

It was beautiful.

Sophie set her phone aside when I came back to the table and looked up at me with expectant eyes. It was time to charge the poppet. I grabbed a white candle from the mantel and lit it. As I took a seat, I set the candle on the table and slipped a tiny white gown over the figure. "What's your boyfriend's name?"

The look on Sophie's face told me that she was surprised by the question and hoped to not have to reveal the name. She paused a moment before, barely above a whisper, saying, "Virgil."

I mouthed a prayer and touched the poppet's head with anointing oil, breathing life into my creation. The poppet trembled in my hand and then inhaled a long, deep breath, holding it in for a few seconds, exhaling, and settling back to itself. I thanked the lwa silently. Then I removed the white robe and gave the Virgil poppet to Sophie.

The girl was positively wide eyed and, at first, didn't seem to want any part of her creation. This wasn't unusual. Folks asked for things and didn't realize the implications until all was done. It was time for my cautionary speech.

"Now, you don't toss this in your purse and leave it there," I began. "This is a love spell, so you have to nurture it. Tell it you love it and want its love back. Give it offerings of sweet things. Keep it safe and secluded. Then let it do its job."

Sophie considered my words, her expression blank, and then asked me a question, chilling because of the flatness in her tone and gaze: "And what if I don't want it anymore? I mean, the poppet or Virgil?"

"That's another spell altogether. Requires some different ingredients too." And another price.

Sophie thanked me and paid a tip in cash, which I appreciated. I'd taken loaves of bread, plates of food, and unwanted advice on my love life as payment. And for the people in Tremé, I'd continue to do so and to serve them as I served the lwa.

I wondered if the girl was really sure what she wanted. That dirt was an interesting addition that told me she'd listened in on a service or two in her time. Sometimes, depending on where the dirt came from, particularly someplace like a cemetery, they wanted something altogether different than love. But whether or not she knew it, my new client wouldn't be able to do any of that with the spells I wove.

And despite what some people might have thought, I didn't use my magic to harm people—unless they tried to harm me first. That made it self-defense.

Erzulie murmured her skepticism about my understanding of self-defense in the form of a watery brushstroke against the bones. I ignored her and set about cleaning up the place. I hoped Sophie Thibault would find real love, not the kind that people paid for.

As I made to remove the tablecloth for washing, I noticed the thumb ring sitting right where Sophie had left it. I doubted she would return for it, but I knew where to find her.

Voodoo Real. I had been more than a little envious when I'd heard that a new mambo from Houston had set up shop there. I'd met her once and seen her a handful of other times at the occasional vodouisant gatherings. Salimah . . . Salimah Grenade. Couldn't help but wonder what she'd done with the place.

Envy, curiosity, or a noble sense of goodwill. Probably a mix of all of them. Either way, I'd drop off the ring tomorrow and assess the competition.

CHAPTER THREE

The new vodouisant had been in the coveted Dumaine Street spot for a little more than a year. I'd seen her last at a public Manje Yanm ritual. These days, the observance commemorated more of a ceremonial tradition than the real harvest of the yams.

You couldn't beat the shop's prime French Quarter location. Within walking distance for some customers, a short trolley ride for others. But the tourist traffic? The money would defy logic. And the apartment upstairs? That was an extra dash of powdered sugar sprinkled on a fresh-from-the-fryer beignet. And I would have gladly rented the space myself if I'd had the price-gouged security deposit.

But the Quarter's tourist perks came at a cost. A steady stream of high-paying customers offset by an avalanche of nonsense demands from people who had watched too much bad television. And the rent was too high. I could handle myself against the petty thefts and vandalism, but who needed it?

I rounded the corner at Royal Street and was unsurprised to see police cars. They were as frequent a sight in these parts as hungover partygoers. Only as I got closer did I realize the police and a swarm of anxious onlookers were outside Mambo Grenade's place. The unsettled feeling clogging the air wasn't the normal us-versus-them type of tension either. My mind said to turn around, go back home, and I mean right this minute.

I wove forward into the crowd's midst.

Foot patrol had cordoned off the entrance, creating a ten-foot barrier in front of the shop. Blaring lights portended an ambulance wedged up on the curb, right below the **VOODOO REAL** sign. Humph. Vodou, Vodoun, Vodun—either was acceptable. I'd told the new mambo that I did not approve of the Americanized spelling. She'd noted my concern with a chuckle full of mirth and invited me to name my own shop whatever I wanted but to not trouble myself about hers.

The smell of patchouli incense wafted from the open door and mixed in with the Quarter's abiding perfume of beer and piss and fried foods. It was enough to make you sick if you weren't used to the combination.

I saw the mambo's cousin, her lone employee, leaning against the brick wall dabbing at his face with a piece of gauze a paramedic had handed him after a quick pat on the shoulder. There was no blood on it. Where was Salimah? I elbowed my way through the crowd, trying to recall the dude's name. He'd hovered over her shoulder the entire time during my first visit, and Salimah hadn't hidden her irritation.

"Mambo Dumond," he said when he saw me. At least one of us was good with names. He wore a squirrel's jittery wide-eyed expression.

"What happened?" I searched his face, as if the distress there could paint the picture for me. "Is Mambo Grenade all right?"

He squeezed his eyes shut. His hand trembled. "She all right, but some bad business has jumped off."

I waited for the rest of the story, but the boy seemed suddenly incapable of speech. He'd need some coaxing. I wished to hell I could remember his name. "Is somebody hurt?"

He shook his head but then said, "The man that stayed upstairs sometimes." He gestured at the second-story window with his chin.

"I think he's dead, but the cops ain't letting nobody up there. Salimah found him and called Houngan Alexander."

Now why would Salimah have called Lucien? What could that arrogant Lower Nine houngan have to do with this? At that moment, a paramedic stumbled out of the storefront, her face a kaleidoscope of blue, red, and purple. To say that she was shaken was to say that a beheaded chicken was a bit agitated. I figured Salimah must have still been inside.

The man that stayed upstairs sometimes. My breath caught. I unzipped my purse's side pocket and fingered the thumb ring. A gnawing sense of dread told me the dead man had to be none other than my new client Sophie's boyfriend. The one she'd needed the poppet for. Had she come home and stumbled on something? Done something stupid?

"What about the girl?" I asked. "Is she up there too?"

He swallowed. "Ain't seen her since last night."

While I struggled to digest the implications of Sophie's oddly timed visit, I saw something that sent another unwelcome jolt of anxiety down my back. A cavalcade of police cars—this wasn't your average traffic stop, after all. At their center, an unmarked navy-blue sedan, siren blaring on the dashboard. The sprinter-slim figure of Detective Roman Frost climbing out of the car. Neither tall nor short. An ostentatious dresser with a plain face. But on those blessed occasions when he chose to show it, a smile that a dentist might use to showcase their handiwork.

Seeing him tore open my chest cavity, spilling my heart to the pavement, where I imagined it loped over and lapped at his feet.

I took a step backward, hoping to disappear into the crowd. The bastard's gaze locked onto mine.

He seemed to take in the three prematurely gray hairs poking out from beneath my headscarf, the grease spot on my skirt, and the chipped polish on my fingernails all in one glance. I stopped my retreat. To leave now would be like running away from a mad dog: he'd close the distance between us, gliding past bystanders like hurdles on a racetrack.

He conferred with a tall, lanky officer whose gun belt seemed poised to slide down past his hips and made a beeline straight for me.

I plastered what I hoped was an unaffected expression on my face, lifted my chin, and waited.

"Rashad Grenade?" Roman directed the question to Salimah's cousin and took another opportunity to give me the once-over.

"Yes." Rashad, whose name I now recalled, had gone even more wide eyed, looking all around, as if even though the detective had called him by name, he might be speaking to someone else.

"You know the drill, my man. We've got questions—you give us some answers." By "we," Roman meant himself and his partner, Alton Darby. Darby played the good cop in their clichéd good-cop bad-cop scenarios. Though he was the nicer of the two, I still didn't trust him. I'd seen him blindly follow Roman's lead without question too many times.

Rashad looked at me with a sort of plea in his eyes as Darby led him away by the arm. I had nothing to offer the boy but my own relief that he had been dragged off instead of me. Detective Darby nodded at me from where he'd just stowed Rashad in the back seat of the car. Roman Frost, the man I had shared a life and (at least some of the time) a home with, hadn't even said hello. I wilted like a two-week-old bouquet and nudged my raw nerves back behind the fortifications I'd erected, licking their festering wounds.

But what bothered me even more was that I'd had a chance to learn only one thing—Sophie's boyfriend had met his maker, hours after she'd come to me for a poppet. Annoying the police, I lingered long enough to ask a few others in the crowd for the lowdown, but they either didn't know or weren't saying.

"Let's go," a police officer said, waving at the crowd to disperse. "Move it. The show's over." But the crowd was unmoved, an anthropomorphic glacier forged on chaos. There was lots of shoving, lots of grumbling.

And then the air shifted. A turning point of sorts where those of us attuned to such things knew when the small reserve of patience the cops had in the face of any tragedy had waned. That time was now. It started with a yelp coming from somewhere behind me. A rush of blue surged toward the sound, batons raised, fists balled.

Was it a prelude to destruction?

Lips curled into sneers. Mumbling about the right to assembly. Taunts and goading. A few shoves, a brandishing of handcuffs. The energy was taut. But like ice dropped into a heated pool, the crowd began to break up. I took the hint. I spotted a wedge of a path out of the chaos, lifted my skirt and hastened back the way I'd come.

Sophie had bigger problems than a lost thumb ring. Whether by her own hand or someone else's was the question. I'd have to find out what happened from Mambo Salimah another time.

∽

"Reina!" A voice brutalized by years of black-market cigarettes snared me as I rounded the corner of Saint Philip and North Tonti. And there was my house, easily within sprinting distance. Ms. Lucy rarely stopped me to ask after my health or to pass the time with idle chitchat. No, I always came out on the losing end of these encounters, and they would entail one of three things: a lengthy complaint about one of my customers, a not-so-subtle encouragement to abandon my wicked ways and join her church, or, on occasion, a begrudging demand for help.

Maybe if I just kept walking.

"I know you heard me!" Ms. Lucy barked, already on an irreversible intercept course.

I looked up and feigned surprise.

"Ms. Lucy." I closed the distance between us and reached out a hand to steady the older woman. My neighbor's visage was a memoir of a life lived in excess. Widow to a Big Chief of one of the city's most infamous Mardi Gras gangs, she wasn't used to being ignored. I suspected the cigarettes and age and the lwa knew what else had conspired to transform the fluid stride she'd had when I met her a decade ago into this jerky shuffle. Anything more demanding was too taxing on her lungs. "Catch your breath now. You don't need to be running. I can come to you."

"I ain't dead yet!" Ms. Lucy straightened suddenly, and it was like she shed twenty years in the movement. I checked the air around her, almost certain she'd invoked a youth charm, but I knew better.

I suppressed a sigh. I was so tired I couldn't even summon up the energy to be annoyed. "Yes, ma'am," I said, and then waited for the neighborhood gossip to catch her breath without further comment. With one hand on her ample hip and another on her chest, she gulped down a few breaths.

Ms. Lucy's bluster didn't fool me, though; deep down, she was just lonely. Her son had chosen not to succeed his father as Big Chief and had moved to Houston a couple of years before. His infrequent visits had coincided with her decline: the less he visited, the worse she got. I'd mentioned this observation once—just once. The dress-down she'd given me had been so resolute I dared not broach the subject again. The woman alternately loved and feared me.

A full minute later, she said, "You heard about Salimah?"

Spend enough time with people, and some common themes would emerge. One was that it was easier to get information when someone thought they were the first to tell you. "Salimah . . ." I painted on a bewildered expression.

"You know, Mambo Grenade over at Voodoo Real in the Quarter. Opened the shop after that po'boy place shut down? Going on maybe a year now? You know who I'm talking about?" With Ms. Lucy there was never a paucity for the particulars. And though she gifted the other priestess the honorific "Mambo," she'd never done so for me. Must've been a Haitian thing. Salimah was a New Orleans girl, born and raised in Tremé, with only a short stint in Houston. While all these years later, to some I was still "that Haitian girl"—sometimes worse, depending on who was doing the talking.

"Yes, I know who you mean," I said. "What about her?"

"Child, the police got her." She dragged out the *p* and the *o*. "Don't know what for but hear tell they sniffed out some weed in there." She paused. "Or maybe it was some of that new yeyo. You know her mama was on some bad stuff, got hooked up with this Spy Boy and carried her narrow behind off to Baton Rouge when she wasn't nothing but a teenager. Her grandmama brought her back, though. Anyway, what you gon' do about it?"

My neighbor's gossip was hit or miss. Mostly miss. So, while she stood there glaring at me with her arms crossed, I pieced together the more likely scenario. Rashad had said that something had happened to Sophie's boyfriend. And since he hadn't been rushed off in an ambulance, that meant he was dead. Salimah had called the police and been arrested shortly thereafter.

I was speechless. The police thought Salimah was involved? Impossible. Vodouisants didn't kill people. And either way, what did Ms. Lucy think I was going to do about it? I intended to stay as far away from Detective Roman Frost and the NOPD as I could. My mind churned.

I only realized I had been staring blankly at Ms. Lucy when she snapped her fingers in my face.

"Am I talking to myself? Cat got your tongue or something, girl? You act like you didn't just hear me say the cops got one of us, one of *you*, locked up. And you gone mute like I'm passing time talking about the weather or some such nonsense."

No, she would never do such a thing.

I exhaled. "I heard you. I just don't know what you expect me to do about it. I'm not a lawyer. I don't have any friends down at the police station. And I barely know Salimah."

"Humph," Ms. Lucy huffed. "You supposed to be some big Vodou priestess or whatever you call yourself."

"I call myself Mambo Reina Dumond, and so do most other people."

"Watch your tongue, now. I can still put a whoopin' on your fresh behind."

The old woman seemed to have gotten herself so riled up at the thought that she fell into an awful coughing fit. I patted her back, amazed that she let me do so, until she calmed down.

"Breathe," I cooed, rubbing her back.

After a few deep breaths, she gathered herself. "Seeing who your ex-man is, seem like you could do something to help that girl. But I guess you more concerned about making a buck and talking with them spirits or demons or whoever you always lighting them damn candles for. A fire hazard, if you ask me."

Ms. Lucy turned around and shuffled off across the street. I was glaring at her back, imagining myself running up and tackling her, when the older woman spun around and said, "Be that way then."

She coughed, lumbered back the few steps over to her house, and disappeared inside.

CHAPTER FOUR

After making sure Ms. Lucy had gotten back inside, I turned and gazed up at my house. Painted a muted royal blue, like the color from the Haitian flag. White trim and yellow accent pieces here and there, for my mistress, Erzulie.

My house.

Well, to be fair, according to the lease-purchase agreement I'd signed three years earlier, it would be my house in a little over a decade. Where was that agreement anyway? Roman had promised to review it for me but had never gotten around to it.

Though Papa and my friend Darryl had balked, skeptical as always, there was no shame for me in this arrangement. No big down payment that I didn't have, and what I paid in rent went toward the purchase. My practice had been established long enough that qualifying for a mortgage now, despite my fluctuating coffers, shouldn't have been an issue. Soon, I'd be a homeowner in my favorite neighborhood.

I climbed the three steps up to the front porch, leaned against a pillar, and crossed my arms. The weather was a careless perfection. Cool enough for a light jacket during the day and warm enough to enjoy the porch in the evenings. Everything spring crisp, not yet summer sluggish.

My mind whirled with the possibilities of what had happened to Sophie's boyfriend—Virgil, if I recalled correctly. And had it happened while she was with me or afterward? What about before? And why would the police suspect Salimah Grenade? The poppet I'd made for Sophie could have been lying around, but then again, the man was killed in an apartment above a Voodoo shop. No, that likely had nothing to do with it.

None of my concern.

It was early still, about three in the afternoon. The unmistakable aroma of roasting meats lovingly nurtured on an open grill wafted in on a sensory-laden breeze like a Mardi Gras streamer.

Johnnie's barbecue was what you'd call "New Orleans famous," which was only slightly less impressive than world famous. Rumor was that on weekends, his dinners outsold Dooky Chase's and Willie Mae's restaurants combined. His son was the budding flugelhorn prodigy. My nose and stomach led me in my neighbor's direction, but I couldn't get Ms. Lucy's words out of my mind. Dinner would wait.

I considered the fact that this could all be a strange coincidence while I admired the palms and live oaks replanted after the storm. Single and double shotgun houses with their floor-to-ceiling windows. Porches crowded with indoor and outdoor furniture, because in Tremé, they were interchangeable. Manicured lawns lined with potted plants and flower beds already birthing blooms. From somewhere nearby, the screech of a trumpet player for whom I feared even two lifetimes of practice wouldn't be enough to master the instrument.

The rest of the country counted Christmas as the most wonderful time of the year, but in Louisiana, Mardi Gras wore that crown.

Our city had gone from refuge for African descendants and birthplace of the music that spawned everything that followed to a lawless shell filled with people who knew nothing of her history, or her cultural nobility. But somewhere in the midst of its long, cold winter of violence and political graft, we remembered who we were. That here, deep in the earth, lay our redemption.

Hurricane Katrina had sought to erase it all.

As I turned away, my mind clouded over again with two thoughts: what to include in a new tincture for Ms. Lucy's cough, and the unwelcome possibility that my new client was involved in her boyfriend's death.

I wiped the red haint dust from my feet on the doormat and opened the door with relief. I kicked off my shoes and left them where they lay tangled with another pair, mere inches from the shoe rack hanging on the inside of the closet door.

I was immediately greeted not by the cat I'd been thinking of getting for years but by the smell of leftover jambalaya.

I loved cooking (or, according to various sources, *trying* to cook) but hated lingering food smells. I made a beeline for the kitchen, ignoring the mess of junk mail and the catalogs piled on the dining table that I perused religiously but never managed to buy anything from. I cracked the window over the kitchen sink.

After securing a cold glass of water from the fridge, I plopped down at the dinette, pulled off my headscarf, and put my feet up in the other chair. If what Ms. Lucy had said was true, I at least owed it to myself to find out what had happened inside Voodoo Real, and I knew exactly where to go for that information. I downed the water in a few gulps and shuffled off to my bedroom.

It was time to see my friend Darryl "Sweet Belly" Boudreaux. I checked the canister on my antique dresser where I kept all manner of sweets—one lone strawberry hard candy. On the way, I'd need to replenish my stock.

⌒

The Lemon Drop stood defiantly dug in at the corner of North Rampart and Saint Louis, like a smudge of blue in an otherwise slate-gray sky. New businesses had mushroomed all around the building. Prime real estate that, in worse times, had served as a warning to tourists, the barrier between the

French Quarter and Tremé. I'd lost count of the number of times Darryl had been pressured to sell the bar, some forceful, but he'd held his ground, unmoved by money or the threat of progress or bodily harm.

A splashy mural featuring a variety of sweets and spirits blanketed the outside walls. The sign, white, with prismatic lettering, hung outward, so folks could see it coming down the street from either direction. A bird had done its business right on the sign again, blotting out a part of the word LEMON. Darryl was convinced that some unnatural force had set the birds onto him. He'd asked me if I could help, which had earned him a raised eyebrow. Vodou didn't work that way, and he knew it.

I opened the door and stepped inside. Air, trying hard to be frigid but settling for tepid, washed over me, cooling the sweat trickling down my back. The springtime weather changes had a tendency to bring on a cold. I'd take a viral defense tincture when I got home: a pinch of vervain, fresh sage, and a sprinkle of chamomile leaves, a whispered healing incantation. My clients couldn't get enough of them.

After the brightness of the afternoon sun, the Lemon Drop was dark as a bear's den. The mirror behind the bar, spanning nearly the entire length of the wall, caught a wedge of sunlight and tossed it into the spotless room, illuminating shadowy corners without so much as one dust bunny. The picture of my littered dining table came to mind.

Customers were strewn around a dizzying array of two- and four-seater tables. More than I expected for an early Friday evening. A few glanced up from their glasses and gave customary nods as I walked in. The back stage was empty at this time of day. But come nine o'clock, local musicians were allowed to play for free as long as they bought liquor and food.

The telltale floor stickiness of other Tremé haunts was absent. It was as if Darryl's place were more a hipster coffee shop than a hundred-year-old bar. Here, an errant chicken bone was swept up faster than one could order a Sazerac. Tributes to New Orleans jazz greats past and present—Dizzy, Scott, Marsalis, Dr. John, and everyone in between—danced across the walls, their gleaming portraits encased in elegantly gilded frames Darryl took down and cleaned once a week.

"Sweet Belly's in the back." Jimmy was the latest and best in a lengthy string of bartenders my friend Darryl had employed over the years. He had been busy taking up space and fiddling with his phone but grinned when he saw me. "Want me to go get him for you?"

"I'll wait, Jimmy. No rush." I maneuvered around empty tables and ducked beneath the too-low ceiling fan, despite the fact that even with the extra height gifted me by my padded sneakers, I was still just shy of five foot three inches. "Helps keep my customers cooler if the fan is closer to their heads," Darryl liked to joke.

I sat near the big picture window that looked out onto Saint Louis Street. Darryl was a notorious tightwad, his electric bill a frequent source of consternation, and that meant no lights on during the day. He'd nearly taken my head off when I'd suggested he look into solar panels. They *had* become more affordable.

But he'd loosened the purse strings on the picture window and the other smaller ones spaced evenly near the ceiling. Ample light on a sunny day. Darryl mumbled obscenities if anyone dared complain on one of New Orleans's frequent rainy days. "Light a damn candle or something," he'd grumble. Of course, soon after, crystal candleholders and the requisite tea-light candles had appeared on each table.

"Tea, then?" Jimmy asked with my mug already in his hand. I smiled, clasped my hands together in a prayerful plea. Darryl kept a box of jasmine green tea next to the vodka behind the counter just for me.

Unlike the floor, the table was sticky with barbecue sauce and spilled liquor. Poor Jimmy would get an earful about this. I caught his attention and pointed down at the table. He dutifully grabbed the spray bottle with Darryl's secret cleaning concoction and a clean cloth from a bin and scrambled over.

Darryl's clientele was mostly local; only the occasional lost drunk wandered in too far from the French Quarter. An old-fashioned jukebox stood in the corner for show, while satellite music strummed from speakers mounted near the ceiling. Trombone Shorty's "Hurricane Season" filled every corner of the room, and I found myself bobbing my head along with the beat. This song embodied New Orleans; if you didn't get that, you did not, absolutely could not, fathom this city.

In the past few years, many of New Orleans's children—musicians and artists, cooks and entrepreneurs—had returned home, and the neighborhoods from Lower Nine to Gentilly were the better for it. All except Lafitte, where Darryl still lived in a small apartment that he said was just fine for him, thank you very much for your unneeded concern. He'd been closemouthed and sullen when I'd brought up the last burglary. I'd draped his home with a protection spell, but they didn't last all that long, and there were limits to the powers the lwa granted me.

"Rain." Darryl's husky baritone yanked me out of my reverie. He had that New Orleans twang only natives fully mastered. My friend was the epitome of old school. White T-shirt and jeans held up by a belt tucked somewhere beneath his paunch. Black orthopedic shoes. Salt-and-pepper afro lined with a razor. A simple silver cross dangling from a length of leather twine, not a gold chain. He worked his way over to me, swishing an old-fashioned mop around in a bucket of soapy water. I may have been mistaken, but it seemed like he was favoring that left knee. "What'chu doing in here? Don't you got some charms to sell or something, girl?"

"My mistress said you needed me, Darryl, and here I am." Darryl's big grin faltered. Even after all these years, the man had an unhealthy fear of the spirits and of my patron, Erzulie, in particular. I suspected it was because the larger-than-life Mr. Darryl "Sweet Belly" Boudreaux had been so unlucky with women.

He recovered quickly, replacing that startled look with his carefully cultivated see-everything-at-once swivel. It took only a moment for him to surmise, likely from the stern set of my mouth, that this visit was not a social one.

CHAPTER FIVE

I removed a tiny gold-striped box from my purse, set it down, and slid it across the table with my index finger. Darryl glanced at the offering and peered at me from the corner of his eye. He picked up the box, sniffed, and tugged at the green ribbon. He affected a mask of indifference. I'd seen that look many times, but it didn't fool me. I knew that inside, his anticipation was that of a child the night before a Mardi Gras parade.

With the box in the palm of his hand, he removed the small lid. His eyes positively danced over the contents. He sniffed, nodded his approval, and instantly popped one of the buttercream-filled chocolates into his mouth. The sounds of the bar—glasses clanking, murmurs and shouts, back slaps—all ceased. All except for the five interminable ticks of my mental clock before my best friend's face split into his gap-toothed grin.

If you counted yourself among the exclusive group of people Darryl chose to share in his network of secrets, this was the cost. His friendship and loyalty, reserved for an even more select group—those were free.

Once, I'd heard one of Darryl's patrons, upon having the abomination of a fresh-from-the-factory bag of treats outright rejected, exclaim, "Chocolate is pretty much chocolate, ain't it?" That had earned the poor man an hour-long lecture that disabused him of that kind of foolishness. Yes, Darryl "Sweet Belly" Boudreaux knew his chocolate—pretty much all candy.

He nodded his acceptance. "Guess this ain't about the jambalaya recipe you messed up, huh?"

I winced but let the barb go. "My guess is, like always, you know exactly why I'm here. They claim I'm the one with the magic, but you must have a djinn or fairy creature locked up out back that whispers things in your ear too."

Sweet Belly bristled at the reference to the fairy, as he did anything that had to do with magic. The man had seen more trouble than the bottom of Lake Pontchartrain, but hint at the mythical or unexplained, and he was reduced to a quivering five-year-old boy.

"May or may not," he said after he'd recovered.

It was no secret that Darryl loved his role as the center of the trade in sometimes useless, more often useful, information almost as much as he loved candy. "This thing over in the Quarter, with the Voodoo Real owner, Salimah. You heard anything?"

"How'd you hear?" I suspected Darryl didn't appreciate someone stealing his thunder by telling me the news before he could.

"Ms. Lucy stopped me on the way home, but she didn't know much. Of course, that didn't stop her from demanding I do something about it."

Jimmy came by the table then to drop off my tea.

Just then, another customer came through the door. It was the hunched, slue-footed form of Chicken, Darryl's *other* best friend. We both waved to Chicken as he took up his habitual spot at the bar—the stool closest to the door.

"Busybody," Darryl said, and I was sure the irony in the statement was lost on him. "Yeah, I heard a thing or two. Look here," he said, turning serious. "This ain't no joke—they got her up on a murder charge."

"Murder?" Obstruction. Disorderly conduct. I'd even entertained the tried-and-true assaulting-a-police-officer possibility. But murder? No, not for a minute.

"Say she used some of that hoodoo—"

"Vo-dou," I corrected for the millionth time, emphasizing each syllable with a smack on the table.

"Like I said," Darryl continued, unbothered. "Cops say she used some of that stuff to kill this young fella that lived upstairs from the shop. Say they found all kinda evidence up there to point to what she did. And you know who was probably first one on the damn scene. Walking around with his Creole nose all pointed up in the air like the rest of us smell bad."

That would be one Detective Roman Frost. I'd wanted Darryl and the man whom I'd thought I'd marry to be cordial. All right, I'd hoped they could also be friends, but while, for my sake, they were never openly hostile to one another, they often managed to find themselves at odds over the smallest things.

He leaned back in his chair then and rapped his knuckles on the table. Feigning nonchalance, looking out the big picture window at those strolling by. A cue that he had more to say and was waiting for me to ask the right question.

"I wonder what they found up there that pointed to Salimah. Besides a body, I mean." I sipped my jasmine tea and found it had just the right amount of honey, two generous squeezes. Jimmy had been trained well.

As expected, Darryl perked up. He looked both ways, as if expecting the lead detective to pop out from under the next table. "Wasn't just a body," he said and then sucked his teeth. "Pieces of a body, more like."

"What?" I nearly lost my grip on the teacup, spilling a drop on the table. In an instant, my hyperhygienic friend snatched a towel from his back pocket and wiped it up.

He shook his head and continued. "The boy's head was in a pot on the stove. Vegetables and potatoes up on the counter right next to it, like, like somebody was cooking a Sunday dinner."

"You've got to be—"

He held up a hand. "Ain't finished. Rest of him was inside the damn stove. They found an altar and some magic shit right by the window. That's how they figured that mambo did it. Can't find hide nor hair of the girlfriend. Ain't no way she coulda done that mess by herself anyway. Way the cops see it, either Salimah was mad about rent or some such bullshit or she helped the girlfriend, mad over another woman or whatever else it is women always mad about."

There had been robberies and murders in the French Quarter for as long as I could remember, but this was something altogether new. "Somebody cut up the body and had it in the stove?" Darryl's infamous sources must have had it wrong. Despite the hot tea, I shivered.

"Bad business." Darryl gazed out at a gray-haired couple walking by arm in arm. "Folks have gone damn-fool crazy."

"Do you trust me?"

"Go on 'head and ask the real question you want to ask. That one's just the primer."

Guess he didn't need his glasses to see straight through me. "Who told you this?"

"How'd you come by a Haitian spirit that lives in your head and lets you do things nobody else can?"

Touché. We sat there, annoyed with each other, until Darryl pointed at my teacup. "Jimmy, come heat up Rain's tea."

Jimmy did so and returned moments later. My hurt feelings mended.

"Salimah didn't do this." Even the increasingly corrupt houngan Lucien Alexander wouldn't do this. But the police would use it to make us all look bad if they could.

"Hell naw, she didn't do it. We know that." Darryl leaned back again and crossed his ankle over his knee. "Cops probably do too. But that don't mean they won't try to make it stick. Think about it. They need some easy wins—mayor been all over their asses about crime in the Quarter. They could have the paperwork finished in an hour and file this one in the closed-cases column. Unless—"

"Unless somebody doesn't let them get away with it," I said, finishing his thought. Only I wanted no part of it. The whole thing creeped me out.

"Way I see it, you got two choices: go on down to that jail and see if you can get in to see that lady, or you can call that detective of yours and see if he willing to talk."

He wasn't mine, not any longer. And I had no desire to see the inside of the jail again. My skin crawled with the thought. The panic that even setting foot inside the place would give them some excuse to keep me. I shuddered, thinking of Salimah sitting in a disgusting jail cell. "Or option three," I said, draining my teacup.

～

In some cities, spring might ease itself into position without much fanfare, winter gathering her frosts and trailing away like the last few precious notes of a song. But in New Orleans, the first hint of warmth was like two off-key musicians warring for control.

I'd left my car at home and walked. For the exercise and for the chance to think. I regretted that decision. A damp, smothering heat had battled back the morning cool. It was working its way up to one of those sweltering evenings that slicked the skin with sweat and frizzed even newly relaxed hair. On these nights, front porches would be full, bottles passed. Music would spill from every window.

Heedless of the fact that my clothes might be soaked through by the time I got home, I channeled a smidgen more water from my pores.

The cooling effect was immediate, and so was the patch of wetness at my back.

As I walked, I tried to imagine the crime scene Darryl had described, and I shivered despite the heat.

There was something the police were overlooking. And that was where I had to start. Sophie and Virgil hadn't been there when I'd introduced myself to the new mambo, so they had to have moved in sometime after that. Darryl had told me the boyfriend had worked as a cook at Deanie's Restaurant. Aside from the fact that we shared an alma mater, an afternoon with Sophie hadn't yielded anything significant about her life.

My client's timely visit had either saved her from suffering Virgil's fate or had provided a passable alibi. Her disappearance fueled several unpleasant possibilities: she had information she was intent on not sharing, she'd committed the crime and was on the run, or the real murderer had taken her along to finish the job elsewhere.

And if what Darryl said was right, a fellow priestess had been wrongly accused. Unacceptable. Sophie Thibault was likely the only person who could tell the police what really happened. But she was missing.

The Lemon Drop was a fountain of knowledge—for some. There, for the price of a sweet treat, you could drink deeply of the latest parish news and political intrigue. But there was another person, a pricklier sort, who should've been called upon in the delicate case of locating someone who didn't want to be found: one Tyka "Grip" Guibert.

She'd earned the nickname back in high school as a wrestler. Legend had it that if she got a grip on you—on the wrestling mat or in the occasional street brawl—you were down for the count.

I tried her number and was unsurprised to find it disconnected. The girl's phone was in a constant state of flux, off one month, on the next. She'd eventually get it turned back on or purchase another burner.

In the meantime, I had no choice but to start with her last known residence and keep circling in hopes of spotting her. Tyka and her father were always in need of a home-cooked meal, the perfect peace offering. The last time I'd spoken to her, pressing again about college—a future that, unlike her current dubious path, would see her live to welcome her twenty-fifth birthday—I'd been told, no, warned, in no uncertain terms, to back off.

Who was I to give out unwanted and unsolicited advice? The gift of motherhood had not been granted to me. It wasn't the first time Tyka had reminded me of that fact in the decade that I'd known her. My brain, my heart, refused to acknowledge it. Where Tyka was concerned, I never would. Erzulie wouldn't allow it, even if I'd wanted to. Being a deity of water and love, she held a special place in her heart for children.

I got home and set to work in the kitchen. It was time to try Darryl's jambalaya recipe again.

Before I began, I clasped my hands together and closed my eyes. Thoughts of all I'd lost greeted me like old friends. My lips mouthed the prayer that had thus far remained unanswered. I wished again for a child of my own.

CHAPTER SIX

I was walking around to the passenger door to get the pot of gumbo when the sounds snared me. I spun around, looking in all directions; the shouts were coming from behind Tyka's house.

Drawing in what moisture I could from the air, heart pounding, I raced toward the sound. My hands pulsed, ready to unleash.

And my breath caught.

A loose crowd of nine or ten onlookers stood waving money, shouting, and high-fiving. At the center of it all was my young friend Tyka. Her dust-coated face was alight with joy. There on the ground, firmly in her grasp, was a man caught in such a hold that sweat trailed down his grimacing face.

Her left arm was wrapped beneath the man's chin, her hand secured at her own right shoulder. Her other arm somehow wrapped around him and clutched her left.

The poor man struggled and spit, clawed and huffed, but couldn't free himself.

"I got five on 'im!" one spectator shouted. "I think he gon' pull out of it."

I doubted that, and likely so did the other man who took his money.

I wanted to intervene. Part of me feared Tyka would kill this poor fool. But just as I was taking a step forward, he reached out and tapped the ground a few times. My friend released her captive. Cheers and groans erupted, money passed hands. Tyka shot up like a bullet, arms thrust in the air, relishing in the hugs and slaps on the back.

She turned and offered a hand to the man she'd had in the choke hold. He shook hands with her like a good sport, then pushed past me, eyes downcast, rubbing his neck.

"Mambo," Tyka said, stuffing money in her jeans pocket. "All right, y'all," she said, turning to her friends. "Got some business to take care of."

With that, the crowd drifted out front, granting me distance and respectful nods.

"There are easier ways to make money," I said to Tyka as she patted dust off her clothes.

"You call sitting in some cramped-up office with some self-import-ant asshole breathing down my neck for some dumbass report easy?"

She had a point.

"Help me get something out of the car," I said as we headed back out front. I opened the passenger door and took out the gumbo.

The way Tyka managed to greedily take in the pot balanced on my hip while affecting an air of indifference was an impressive exercise in facial calisthenics. Her hunger shy as her unspoken gratitude, tangible as the lovely mole beneath her left eye.

Aside from what Darryl and I forced on her, it was unclear how the girl managed to feed herself some days. She'd let slip that her father received a small military pension, but I suspected the neighborhood bars saw more of it than his daughter did. Darryl had chased him out of the Lemon Drop so many times that he'd had the good sense to choose other haunts.

"Brought something for your father." Yes, using him was under-handed. Likely didn't fool her, but if that made it easier for her to accept a decent meal, I'd live with it.

Tyka regarded me with that look on her face, the one that said she wasn't buying the lie for a second and was trying to decide whether to call me on it. Depending on her mood, or more likely, the depths of her hunger, she might send me packing with whatever offering I had still in my hands. This time, though, Tyka came over and took the lid off the pot while I still held it.

"You let Sweet Belly help you with the roux this time?" She replaced the lid and took it from me.

"I can follow a recipe as well as the next person."

She raised an eyebrow, smirked. I leaned against my car and watched Tyka's retreating form go put the food away. I grinned at my friend's sure swagger.

On our first meeting, I'd found her in an alley, scrounging around in a dumpster. Erzulie's surge of affection for the child was like the feel of a million watery kisses against my bones. Those doe eyes regarded me with a determination to defend herself that had no place on a preteen's heart-shaped face.

With the lwas' help, I'd coaxed her away from the dumpster, persuaded her to drop the shard of glass she'd been clutching, and given her a bed and a plate of food. When I awoke the next morning, she was gone. I searched all over for her. When she was ready, a full month later, she found me again.

I hadn't lost sight of her for more than a week since.

While I waited by the car for Tyka to return, dusk crept in like a river of shadows. Leaves whispered on a breeze absent the day's heat. A Vodou priestess wasn't afraid of the dark but had sense enough to be wary of her secrets all the same.

A common misconception was that Erzulie's touch safeguarded me, that all vodouisants were protected from harm. I had a cut on my finger from a vegetable-chopping mishap, along with a dozen other scars and blemishes, that said otherwise.

Defenses, though, I possessed in good measure. Erzulie's wrath, that tempest in my bones, was always there at the edge of my consciousness. But the spirits were not pets to be called upon at one's whim. Her aid was a trump card you didn't play until the game was on the line.

I replayed everything I knew so far from the day's events. The little that Ms. Lucy had told me and the bits and pieces Darryl had filled in. My past experience with Roman. If I could find Sophie and get her to go in on her own, I'd be able to avoid stepping anywhere near that jail. Roman had not-so-subtly hinted that if he saw me down there again, he'd make up whatever charge he needed to, just to make sure I never left. An extreme threat to be sure.

But in some things, I could take a hint.

My young charge had been inside a few minutes now, which meant that she was either sampling or arguing with her father. If the shabby lean-to they'd called home these last couple of months had not already been condemned by the city, it should have been at the top of someone's list. I'd never been invited in and knew that invitation might never come. Among the myriad places they'd squatted, there were some that she wouldn't even let me get a glimpse of.

By the time Tyka reemerged, night had leeched away the last glimmers of light. She'd applied a dark, berry-colored lipstick. She wore her long hair in a ponytail without adornment. She favored jeans or sweats and was partial to New Orleans sweatshirts of any kind. She didn't walk but stalked the streets both day and night like a cat. She sidled up to the car and, for a blissful instant, leaned her head against my shoulder in one of her rare shows of affection.

It stirred in me again that familiar ache. The want of a child to cuddle, to cradle a perfectly shaped, unsteady head. To—

"So, what up, Mambo?" Tyka said and then bit at her nubby nails. A whiff of air, thick with spices, flowed out with her words. She'd tasted the gumbo, and I smiled inwardly.

"I told you not to call me that."

"That's what you are, ain't you? I'm just being respectful, like my daddy taught me." A chuckle. She was actually very pretty when she allowed a smile to erase her customary scowl.

"Looking for a girl . . . ," I started.

Tyka cocked her head at me. "I didn't know you rolled like that, Mambo—uh, *Reina*—but ask and you shall receive."

She took in my outraged look and laughed even more. Finally, she composed herself. "Okay, okay. I'm just messing with you. Tell me about this girl. What did she do? I'll check her out."

I knew that "check her out" was slang for something I didn't want at all. "You know Voodoo Real? The apartment upstairs from the shop? I'm looking for the girl that lived there."

"What you want with her?" Tyka stood to her full stature, alert like a soldier who had just received a new mission.

"I just need to talk to her and convince her to do the right thing. I don't want her hurt or anything."

"What if she ain't in a listening-and-cooperating mood?" Tyka looked away, peered at me from the corner of her eye, and kicked at a piece of trash in the street.

I hesitated. I didn't need two people down in jail. "Don't approach her. Just find out where she's holed up and call me."

Tyka looked up then, and I couldn't tell if her expression was one of wounded pride or disappointment. "See what I can do," she answered, then turned her back and walked toward the little home she'd made for her father and herself. I climbed into the car and watched until she shut the door. The intoxicating warmth drained from my body, and I pulled on a sweater from the back seat.

I didn't need to ask about a new phone number or inquire as to where I could find my friend; when the time came, like always, she'd find me.

Tomorrow I'd go and visit the only person I knew who might in fact have some sway with the NOPD: Lucien Alexander, fellow vodouisant ("Houngan to the Stars" would be a fairer descriptor), self-professed master of the game, and first-class asshat.

CHAPTER SEVEN

Lucien had been planning the public ceremony for months. In this, one of our most sacred rituals, we paid homage to *egun*—our ancestors. The event was being held at Congo Square in Louis Armstrong Park. It was fitting that we honored them at the place where so many freed and enslaved had gathered every Sunday. I'd enjoy the ritual and then talk to the houngan afterward.

If what Rashad said was true and Salimah had already spoken to Lucien, there was a chance that he'd called in some favors for her. Maybe the same contacts who had made it possible for us to have the ceremony in the park. All I had to do was confirm that hypothesis and plant my nose back in the untended garden that was my own business.

I hovered near the edge of the gathering and acknowledged the centuries-old souls that called the park home. The spirits were harmless—to a point. But they wouldn't or couldn't leave this place. I wasn't sure which.

I nodded at the earless ghost of Louis Congo. In Haiti the spiritual was pervasive, but since my initiation, some places, like the cemetery or this park, brought the spirits even more to the forefront. The wraith floated among the parishioners, his back bent, sadness tugging at his diaphanous eyes. He raised a hand. A slow flutter of fingertips, like encumbered wings.

Sometime in the early 1700s, Louis had been given an impossible choice: remain enslaved or serve as public executioner. He'd chosen the latter, and was given his wife's freedom from hard labor, a plot of land, and enough wine to help him drown the memory of his deeds. He carried out whippings and hangings and, in a particularly nasty bent, oversaw the practice of breaking on the wheel, where the poor accused were strapped to wagon wheels to have their bones broken one by one with a cudgel and left to die. I don't know if it's true, but it was said that sometime during his twelve years on the post, he'd cut off his own ears in an attempt to silence the screams of his subjects.

Louis watched me for a while as if wondering whether I, too, judged him harshly for his choices. I wished I could tell him that I did not. Almost as if he understood, he lowered his hand and floated off through a little boy before disappearing into the crowd.

Lucien's voice drew me back to the podium where he held court, Louis Armstrong's eleven-foot-tall bronze sculpture behind him. New Orleans's most renowned houngan. His shoulders wide and set but not rigid with nerves. His voice rose and fell like a symphony, conducting people into a fog of hero worship. The man was a gifted orator in a way I didn't bother to dream about. And only a tiny morsel of his spectacle was just about showing off.

No, Mr. Self-Important had flip-flopped on any number of issues concerning the direction of our Vodou in New Orleans, but he'd never wavered on two things: his love for our tradition and his place at the head of it.

Lucien's gaze brushed the edges of the gathering. There was barely space for a mosquito to buzz around, but Lucien wouldn't be happy unless a line was winding all the way to the Quarter just waiting to get a glimpse of his majesty.

After an alarming downturn in the 1940s, New Orleans and much of the African diaspora had flowed back to their natural religion like a ship righting its course. And with it came more mambos and houngans—many of them fraudulent zealots—but that didn't matter to the average tourist. Salimah, though, she was one of the good ones.

During one vodouisant meeting, Lucien had railed, threatening to bring more of the masses back from the other religions by force. *Make them shake off the countenance of the enslaved and serve the lwa as they should.* And maybe that was what troubled me about seeing our practice as a religion. Religion had long been twisted and manipulated to suit whoever was in charge at the moment. Forbidden from practicing their own religion, like the uncanny survivors they were, our ancestors had improvised: they'd adopted all that Catholic imagery so slavers couldn't tell they were still praying to our African gods. Some things stuck. Religion or sacred tradition, the practice of Vodou was uniquely ours—an amalgam of a thing handed down to us by our enslaved ancestors—and we would spend our lives honoring it.

In the end, fortune favored us through methods all her own. One celebrity, then two, and then a flood converted, and, like good sheep, the people followed.

I wove through the mass and tangle of sweaty bodies, intoxicated as they were in hero worship, acknowledging a spattering of other vodouisants with nods and smiles. I stopped where I had a clear view of the dais, the raised platform featuring all the tributes for Lucien's patron, Agassou. Red candles and offerings arrayed on a white tablecloth. A statue of Saint Anthony of Padua with a red ribbon tied around its body—a product of Lucien's more Catholic-leaning religious affiliation.

Let him tell it, and our two practices were different. Please! His insistence on this always tried my nerves. Our tradition sprang from the same well, the source, Ginen. And aside from an infusion of New Orleans Creole and English, and a more prevalent use of Catholic imagery, our traditions were the same.

The podium was sheathed in a leopard-skin cloth in another tribute to the priest king, Agassou. Lucien wore a simple high-necked black robe, a slice of white peeking through the tip of his collar. His wife stood to his left wearing a regal Ankara-style dress and matching *gele*. His daughter stood off to the side, a bored expression on her face. And there, behind her, stood Kiah. I frowned. Lucien called him a devout follower. I called him a goon.

I scanned the rest of the crowd for kicks, but I knew I'd more likely see his son on Mars than anywhere near one of his father's ceremonies. Lucien probably stood atop a crate or a stack of books because he looked closer to Kiah's height than his true five-foot-nineish frame. It was a reasonable height, but Lucien must not have thought so. I'd bet in his private prayers, he begged for a few extra inches.

"You cannot know," Lucien began and then paused. His eyebrows knit together, the only sign of his annoyance. It didn't take long before the offending chatter died down. Some of these folks newer to the religion needed a lesson in respect. He squared his shoulders and scanned the crowd. His eyes settled on me, and he gave a chilly head incline, which I returned.

Then he continued in that voice that still commanded all who were listening to take note. "You cannot know who you truly are if you cannot call the names of your ancestors going back seven generations. But for many in the Americas, that is an impossibility. What we have left, then, is reverence. Reverence for our ancestors. For those who endured, who died, who suffered. For those canonized in the Congo Square sculpture. Whatever feelings you have about how our ancestors went about their business and what you may or may not have done differently are idiotic. You have no idea what you would have done and will never, God willing, have the chance to find out."

Rumor and the two grown children put Lucien at about fifty years old, but if he told you he was thirty-five, you wouldn't have cause to question him. You'd just assume that the few spirals of gray hair sprinkled in that sea of black were there prematurely.

Lucien's eyes narrowed. I followed his icy glare to a man in the first row of parishioners, wearing a pair of reflective sunglasses. I shook my head. Probably a tourist. No true follower would leave his eyes covered during a ritual. The houngan turned ever so slightly and gestured for Kiah to come over from where he stood with his hands clasped in front of him, looking every bit the angelic soldier. He covered the microphone and whispered a few words. Moments later, the offender was discreetly removed. I had little doubt that Kiah would teach the man some manners on his way out.

Lucien turned his attention back to the proceedings.

> *Iba se Egun.*
> I pay homage to the spirit of the ancestors.
> *Emi Lucien Alexander, Omo* . . .
> I am Lucien Alexander, child of . . .

He went on to recite the names of his ancestors seven generations back and three more thrown in because that was just the way Lucien rolled.

Earlier that month, I'd sold him some spirit water: a base of herbal tea made with water from the Mississippi, anisette, and a drop of my sangswe wine. Now he poured the liquid into a bronze chalice and turned the empty metal container toward the crowd. They murmured their approval.

He handed the container off to one of his assistants and, taking the chalice in both hands, descended from the dais. Heads bowed in respect as he passed, and I could almost see his chest swelling with pride at their approval.

He took his time. I didn't think he'd do so, but it would have been disastrous to spill even a drop. I hadn't made such a mistake since I was a young initiate and didn't plan to do so ever again.

Lucien practically glided to the manicured patch of land set up to receive the spirit offerings. He raised the chalice, uttered a silent prayer, and set it atop a miniature altar. Next, children came forward bearing sticks of wood, leaves, and baskets of fruit. He accepted the gifts from each and carefully arranged them around the chalice. As a hand fell upon a shoulder or a freshly coiffed hairdo, the children beamed.

Finally, he motioned forward an assistant. She took a small shovel and cleared away a clump of earth in front of the chalice, careful not to disturb the other placements. When she was done, she handed him the candle, tall and encased in glass. He took it with his left hand, turned from the crowd, and lit it with a chant. Now that was a showy, unnecessary piece of magic if I'd ever seen one. That, too, joined the offering.

To finish the altar, he called upon volunteers from the crowd. They lifted specially selected rocks from the pile off to the side of the dais and marked off the altar. When they were done, he stepped back to admire his work and nodded in satisfaction.

He ended with a prayer that bade the ancestors goodbye. The ghosts of Congo Square drifted away. And then he moved to the small table that had been set up to act as a place for the receiving line. It held one of his infamously ornate donation lockboxes.

As he positioned himself at the opposite end of the table to receive his followers, his customary smile gave way to a grimace. I turned and spotted the object of his ire, momentarily relieved that it wasn't me. The police were a fixture at public ceremonies—really anyplace where Black folks were out in numbers greater than two—but detectives, particularly Roman and Darby, were not.

―

The detectives hovered at the already-fraying edges of the crowd like buzzards scanning the scraps of a relinquished feast. Aside from the instant when Lucien's gaze shot over to his donation box, he was an oak, his expression softened to something just shy of a smile.

They didn't suspect me or Lucien of anything. But Roman relished the opportunity to assert his perceived authority wherever he could.

Right or wrong didn't have anything to do with it. I went to stand beside Lucien.

"Houngan," I said to him, trying to ignore Kiah, who had sidled up behind us. Pretending he wasn't there wasn't an easy task when I could feel him glaring at the back of my head.

"Mambo Dumond," Lucien answered as he shook a last hand. "Good of you to come out to the ritual. And I see you've brought some friends."

"No friends of mine," I said, glancing over at him. A man practiced in the art of fluidity: alternately poised and menacing.

The situation reminded me of the first time I'd seen the houngan. An abandoned warehouse in New Orleans East. I'd witnessed him transform into the leopard king and turn that fiery ire on me where I perched on a crate, peeking in through a broken, pigeon shit–encrusted window.

For nearly a year after that, dusk was a willowy prelude to a recurring nightmare.

I had been fresh out of high school, seventeen years old to his thirty. The vodouisant community at the time was a field of wildflowers, while I was the lone daffodil subsisting on the other side of the fence, hungry roots straining to cross over and join the party. But Lucien's connection to Agassou had already turned him into a demigod. *He's gonna be the most powerful houngan in the city—hell, probably the country,* the whispers declared.

He had called the first-ever congregation of the city's Vodou priests and priestesses.

All except me.

I'd prized the secret location from a priestess who took pity on me but warned me to stay away. Of course I didn't listen. Who would? What with all the talk, I imagined the man to be eight feet tall, shrouded in mist, and walking on water. I *had* to see for myself.

That day had dawned like all others until then, plump with youthful curiosity, nurtured by a steady diet of boredom-fueled recklessness.

The sky was the color of cooled ashes. I'd left my car two blocks over and cut through a warren of backyards, where I came face-to-face with a German shepherd, impervious to every charm I threw at it. I waited the dog out on a tree branch that strained under my weight.

There were no lights on inside the warehouse save for the watery glow cast by innumerable candles. A rectangular table covered in white dominated a stage at the front of the large room. Where my own altar to Erzulie was (and remained) haphazardly arranged, it was as if the houngan's altar to the priest king followed an invisible grid.

A beautifully beaded *ason* reigned at the center of a labyrinth of tall, slender candles. A life-size Agassou vèvè hung from a rafter overhead. The priest king's symbol woven with sequins and jewels: a triangle at the base, curlicues sprouting from the edges, a regal serpent wrapped around the line sprouting from the tip.

Lucien knelt atop a silken cushion, eyes closed, hands clasped in prayer. Time and again, he stopped and started a barely audible chant, banging his fist on the table more than once. Sweat streamed down his body, bare to the waist.

But soon he gained a rhythm. His voice swelled. And the warehouse heaved as if infused with a heartbeat.

The chant spilled from Lucien's lips in a tangle of foreign vowels, urging forth a pellucid feline paw that oozed from the center of Agassou's vèvè. When the paw reached Lucien, claws sprang out and sliced his chest.

When the lwa rode someone, the person could, in their own way, mimic the spirit. But mimicry was far too pedestrian for Lucien. I watched in horror as the ruptured skin on his chest peeled back. The grisly flaying continued until a loose pile of skin had amassed at his feet, then knit itself back over his body, transforming him into his lwa's leopard form. The houngan hadn't cried out once.

The Lucien-leopard swung his feline head toward the window, where I stood wide eyed and frozen. His eyes flashed golden, then back to black. A seed of sound reverberated against my eardrums—a purr. But when that curious, contented tremor cranked up to a roar, a sound like a saw cleaving wood, I screamed bloody murder and hightailed it out of there.

I didn't attend that gathering of priests and priestesses that day, but I would meet the houngan not much later. I was leaving the Business Administration building at Southern, and there he stood, looking every bit the part of a priest king, even simply attired in slacks and a jacket. I walked up to his car without a word, and we got in and laid our mutually unique relationships with our lwa on the table.

We'd go on to develop a rapport of sorts in the intervening years.

Roman and Darby snapped me out of the memory. They had taken their time getting to us, pausing to hassle a parishioner or two.

"I don't know how a bunch of heathens got the city to agree to this spectacle, but if it was up to me . . ." Detective Roman Frost paused and whistled. "I'd shut you all down—for good. We already have one of you locked up for using your shit to kill an innocent man. It was only a matter of time."

Lucien stood with his hands clasped behind his back, the picture of serenity, while in my mind's eye, rage was painted all over my face. I straightened and tried to imitate Lucien's resplendent calm. I had opened my mouth to speak, but as usual, he beat me to it. Worse, he actually held up a hand, as if commanding me to be silent. If I hadn't been afraid of being taken to jail, I would have bitten his finger right then and there.

"Detective Frost," Lucien said, and I was surprised he knew him by name. I'd never formally introduced them. Even if he'd heard the name, how would he know the face? And Roman had never mentioned knowing the houngan either. "So good of you to come out to the ritual to pay homage to our ancestors." He nodded at Detective Darby. "No offense, Detective. But the ancestors I refer to are ours alone."

"None taken," Detective Darby said. His scar-pink skin flushed with the midday heat. His collar was already opened. Unlike Roman, he always hated ties.

"Can we help you with something, Detectives?" I wasn't going to let Lucien do all the talking. I felt him stiffen beside me. Roman leveled those sultry, round eyes on me. In that unblinking gaze of his swirled a feeling like a song stuck on replay in my head, a song I hated but couldn't shake.

"I think that both of you . . ." He paused to cast a glance at the mambos and houngans who still lingered, most within earshot. I beamed at the support. "All of you are connected with what happened at the voodoo shop in the Quarter. I can probably tie you to half a dozen crimes around the city right now. It's only a matter of time before we put it all together. And when we do?" He mimed handcuffing his wrists.

I hated Roman Frost. I still loved and craved Roman Frost. No, I hated Alton Darby for standing there letting him put on this ridiculous show. To his credit, he had the decency to look down.

"Detectives Darby, Frost." By putting Darby's name first, Lucien meant to put Roman in his place. Nice underhanded touch. "Ours is an ancient, noble religion. We don't use it for harm. Never have—"

"And never will," I added, like a fool.

"Mr. Mason Ely," Roman countered. It was a story I'd heard before. "New Orleans Parish. September 1985. Assault and disfigurement, laid at the hands of a French Quarter voodoo priest. One who fled to Nigeria. Ring a bell?"

I knew the details of the case by heart. In our time together, Roman had hurled them at me like a battering ram, determined to shake my faith. I'd returned the volley, laying out all the wars, skirmishes, and street fights waged under the banner of every religion known to humanity. All the destruction wrought in the names of gods, dating back thousands of years. For all the good it had done.

Lucien bristled, took a step forward. "I think after your investigation, which I know will be as thorough as it is complete, you'll find that Mambo Grenade had nothing to do with whatever you're accusing her of. That simply isn't the nature of our practice. I don't know how to convince you of that, even with all the good we've done for the city. I've broken no laws. Neither have my followers. Now do you have a question for me, Detective, or you planning on inflicting us with more of your impassioned but painfully flawed rhetoric?"

Roman glowered but said nothing, his flame doused. Darby smothered the lingering embers. "That's it for now, *Mr.* Alexander, but if you've got any travel plans, cancel 'em."

Dropping the "houngan" honorific was petty, even juvenile. Roman going over and grabbing Lucien's donation box behind that icy smile of his was the work of someone approaching expert status in ax grinding.

Kiah's hand slid behind him, likely going for the weapon I'd heard about but never seen. He'd taken a step forward when Lucien's right hand shot out to stop him.

As Roman and Darby turned to go, I felt a surge of energy electrifying the air around Lucien. The man loved money almost as much as he did his family. He was calling on the lwa, and I didn't know if it was for comfort or combat. He muttered a prayer, a chant I couldn't make out. If he was going to do something silly, I'd have to stop him. A handful of vodouisants stood, watching, waiting.

"Lucien," I whispered and then almost choked on the invisible waves of malice that flooded the square. Even the ghosts reappeared in anticipation of a spiritual brawl.

"Lucien!" My voice rose to the octave between alarm and panic. I began pulling what moisture I could from the air and earth. The other practitioners took cautionary steps back.

As Beninites, our magic called to us in a distinct patois, undecipherable by the other. But just as I sensed his, Lucien would no doubt be aware of me calling to the vapor crooning on the breeze and plucking at the strumming moisture buried in the soil. Erzulie and I, we ruled the currents and wielded them when we needed to. I didn't want to use my power against Lucien, but to save him from himself—save us both—I would. I grabbed his arm.

He drew down on the energy. The detectives were now safe from whatever lesson he'd wanted to teach them. But then Lucien turned on me.

"I'm going to hope that what I felt was not you thinking to raise a hand against me." Lucien and I stood shoulder to shoulder, watching the detectives' retreating backs. He even managed a small wave when Roman turned to glower at us before he got in the car.

"I hope," I said, turning to him after the car screeched off, "that what I felt was not the great Houngan Alexander acting like he was going to go after two police detectives because they stole his collection box."

Lucien painted on a hyena's smile and shrugged. "Flexing and stretching," he said. "I was up there a long time. Just releasing some pent-up energy."

"I wouldn't expect anything different."

Lucien waved away Kiah, and he fell back like a rose lamenting the loss of the sun's rays. "I'm glad you came out. The show of support from you and the rest of the community is noted and appreciated." Lucien coughed. I was sure it was, because his throat was unaccustomed to saying anything remotely kind to me.

"All in service to the lwa," I agreed, and then turned the conversation to more pressing matters. "What about Mambo Grenade?"

"Let the justice system work. If she's clean, it'll come out."

"That's it? You host politicians for dinner more than your own relatives. At the very least, you should be able to get in to see her. Ask her about what happened."

"I've many accomplishments, many honors, but I don't count passing the bar exam as one of them."

"What about the show of support you were just talking about?"

"Go home, Reina. Take care of your own business. By the way, I referred a client to you. Someone better suited to your skill and, shall we say, payment terms."

With a flick of Lucien's head, Kiah appeared at his elbow, and off they went toward the latest in a long line of luxury cars, while I stood there nursing my affront and giddiness at the prospect of a new paying client.

The pompous bastard hadn't agreed to do a thing to help Salimah. And he hadn't even offered me a ride home.

CHAPTER EIGHT

A habit had crept up on me with the subtle insistence of drowsiness in the middle of a bad movie. In the span of years between adolescent rebellion and adulthood assent, I'd begun to measure the men in my life on a sliding scale, with my father at the center. Too powerful, too self-assured like him was a no, but showing yourself as his complete opposite didn't earn you any brownie points either.

Lucien was a lot like him. Formidable in their bond to the lwa, opinionated and obstinate. And back in Haiti, Papa had rivaled Lucien in political clout. But they wore their power differently. Lucien's was a switchblade, concealed but no less dangerous, while Papa's authority was more like a bejeweled dagger worn at the hip. Formal, admirable, but approachable.

At least it was before he fled Papa Doc's henchmen and landed in New Orleans.

So I knew that, on the matter of Salimah's predicament, they would be united in their stubborn agreement that I remember my place: a healer, no more, no less. Of course I'd ask him anyway.

I grabbed my tablet and a sweater and went outside to sit on the yellow bench in the backyard, where I could wrap myself in memories of home. The lush greens, the insistent warmth, the scents of blooming and birthing. Legs tucked beneath me, I inhaled and tasted the air. The humidity was blessedly north of 70 percent.

I urged the microscopic pores along the length of my body to swell. When Erzulie felt the balance shift a hair too much, she contracted them. What I did was dangerously addictive. And water intoxication, even for me, could prove fatal.

Satisfied with what she'd allowed me, I feasted. I could pull in only a tiny amount, not enough to change the weather. There, for those blissful seconds, I let the moisture travel through me. I shuddered, suffused with a warmth that had nothing to do with heat.

When the feeling passed, I opened my eyes, contracted my pores, and settled in to call Papa.

"You there?" He tapped on the screen and drew it inches from his nose, closed one eye, and peered right into the camera.

"Back up, Papa." He looked like one of those exaggerated cartoon drawings. "I can see you; just put the phone on the stand I gave you." A moment later, the phone was properly positioned, and my father smiled the smile of someone continuously amazed at the little twenty-first-century gifts I gave him.

Over the last year, his hairline had receded enough that a ridge of wiry gray now began closer to his crown than his forehead. His skin, though, was still smooth and taut, a feat that he attributed to never leaving a warm clime. Having the lwa Atisou—the master of healing—on speed dial didn't hurt either.

Papa had left the home he shared with my mother and moved to the Manchac swamplands a year before the storm. She'd been resistant to leaving the city, and though Manman had visited him, she'd refused to give up my childhood home. She'd increasingly spent most of her time there. Now that house was gone and Manman with it, and Papa and his swampland perch were all the home I had left.

Papa and I covered what little neighborhood gossip there was and then moved on to complaining about Haiti's new president; then Papa tried to tell me about some lady Manman had known for a hot minute when I was a kid.

"They were best friends one week, hated each other the next. You remember, don't you?"

Only I had no idea what he was talking about. And the curly hairs that never grew past a quarter of an inch at the back of my neck stiffened. After one too many conversations where my slack-jawed silence consumed the space between one of his recollections about Manman, Papa had uncovered my memory loss.

"When you fell out of the tree, she brought you home," Papa said, looking annoyed. He was a man used to having people listen and understand what he said. And even if they didn't, they should just nod as a show of respect and let him keep on talking. "That scar you got right there at your hairline. How is it I know more about your own bumps and bruises than you do?"

Instinctively, my hand shot up to the spot above my right eye, now covered by one of my many scarves. I shook my head, incapable of verbal confirmation of what I knew to be true. I tried like I had as a kid to mask the worry that wanted to take over my face.

"Ain't the first memory you lost," Papa said, leaning too close to the camera again. "You used the bowl to try to find that woman again, didn't you?"

"Papa," I said, trying to stem the flow of complaints and rants I knew he was about to rattle off. A litany that would require me to sit still and uh-huh and nod through his nonsense for the next hour. I'd tried before to mutter something about a bad connection, but I didn't think that would work this time.

"Told you there'd be a price to pay for what your mother did—probably why she ran." He was convinced that Manman hadn't disappeared along with all the others during the hurricane, but had taken the opportunity to escape from us for good. Guess it was easier than admitting to himself that it was him that she may have run from.

Papa had been training me in the craft ever since I could remember. Funny how none of those memories were gone. I had watched many possessions from the sidelines with a longing that other kids probably reserved for toys or sweets. Contrary to what those looking in from the outside might have thought, possessions weren't anything to be afraid of. Just the opposite: to be chosen to commune with Bondye's messengers was the greatest honor.

I learned the rituals and healing practices, and I could recite the names and roles of all lwa the same way other kids knew the Jackson 5 family tree. Papa would hit me with verbal quizzes at the oddest times, irritating me to no end. But in this way, I came to love, understand, and respect our tradition.

I was seven years old when Erzulie finally chose me. Some considered that too young, but I wasn't one of them. Seven is a special number too. About fifty folks had gathered for the ceremony to honor Erzulie. Drums could be heard for miles, dancers stepping in time. One person after another was mounted by the lwa and ridden to a point of exhausted ecstasy. I merely danced along at the edge of the crowd, watching with as much pride as my little heart could muster about how Papa commanded the space.

Then I heard the first burble, a seed of sound not in my ears, but from within. It was the call of fresh water, murmurs of Erzulie's watery riches. Goose bumps erupted on my arms, though I felt like I stood at the center of a flame. I stood stock still, eyes wide with anticipation. More surprised than scared. Papa had been chosen by Atisou in his late twenties, and there I was, still struggling to learn long division.

Soon Erzulie had control of my body, and everything turned golden and sweet. When my pores swelled and took in that first embryonic stream of Haitian moisture, it was if I were drowning and learning to truly breathe at the same time. From outside myself, I watched as people cleared the way for my shambling dance.

As others swayed on their feet and passed out panting, I strutted around, full as an overflowing river, for more than an hour. Papa stood by. I watched him from above, and the expression on his face scared me somewhere deep beneath that golden glow. But I wasn't too bothered. I knew Erzulie had me because she wanted me, and when she was done, she'd let everybody know.

But when my mother peeked out the back window and caught sight of her baby girl jerking around like a rag doll, she charged outside. She grabbed me by the shoulders, then yanked her hands away, screeching. She dropped to her knees as Papa raced up, and I passed out. Erzulie wrenched away from me before she was finished. And while other lwa often left their worshippers at the end of a ritual, she left a little part of herself with me. I was so happy that I cried myself to sleep.

Papa wouldn't admit it, but he never really forgave Manman; nor did Erzulie. And now, because of my mother's mistake, whenever I dared call on the lwa, used the tiniest bit of magic in an effort to find her, I lost another precious memory.

"You listening to me?" Papa's complaints had lulled me into the past, and his gruff voice brought me back.

"I am now."

"You watch your tongue."

"I didn't call to talk about Manman."

Papa seethed but didn't hang up on me for a change. I parroted back the scant details I had about the French Quarter murder and settled in to wait as he leaned back in his chair, large hands clasped over the soft roundness of his belly, gaze skyward. Most people would find our silences awkward, but Papa had taught me that in much idle chatter, deep thought is mangled into something akin to pulp.

I was eyeing the wedding band still on his left hand when he said, "I know what you're planning." He sat up, poked out his lips, and shook his head vigorously. *"Okipe zafè w."*

I'd lost much of the linguistic crystals of Haitian Creole long ago, but I'd know the words "Mind your own business" anywhere. Once he'd made such a pronouncement, the discussion was over. At least it was for him.

"I think we—I mean, I think the vodouisant community here— should do something to help her."

"Should, yes. But you can't."

"Tell me why not?"

"What did Houngan Alexander say?"

"What does it matter? I'm asking you."

"So he agrees with me. You can't do anything about the police up there. Only thing you can do is take up a collection and get that lady a good lawyer."

I pouted.

"Don't give me that look." Papa's eye was on the camera again.

"I'll talk to you later, Papa."

"And stay away from that bowl."

"I love you too."

Night had descended. I got up and stretched my cramping legs. That was new. Maybe Darryl and Tyka had teased me about acting like an old lady so much that my body had taken notice. As much as I hated to admit it, my twenties were in the rearview mirror, and forty was bearing down on me like an angry bull.

Back in the kitchen, I took out the small container of gumbo I'd set aside from the pot I'd made Tyka. I thought microwaves were evil, but I'd done little to convince anybody besides Papa of that fact. I'd warm it properly on the stove, but best to let it get to room temperature first. So I grabbed a glass of fresh, sweet water, left it on the counter, and went to my altar.

I lit each candle from right to left. A gold chain hung around my newest—a gift from a client who couldn't pay. The rest of the mantel was decorated with beads, trinkets of gold. The jar of candies needed replenishing. I'd do that later.

In my prayers to my mistress, I asked that she spare my memories, but I knew she would exact whatever price for what she wanted. Salimah, Tyka, Papa, Manman, Darryl, and New Orleans rounded out my well-wishes.

I spared no prayers for Lucien Alexander.

CHAPTER NINE

The knock at the door didn't annoy me so much as the fact that it was eight o'clock in the morning. An unannounced visitor was bad, but one who came before noon was just rude. I had a client scheduled for later in the afternoon, and that was at *his* house. I wondered if it was Ms. Lucy coming to see about that cough. I'd forgotten to take her the tincture.

But when I peeked out the window, it wasn't Ms. Lucy standing there at all. I would have almost welcomed one of her smooth-as-barbwire put-downs. No, Detective Roman Frost stood there looking fresh as the morning dew, and I hadn't so much as run a toothbrush over my teeth yet.

I yanked the curtain closed. *God dammit! Gadon w kaka!*

I cursed him in English *and* the broken Haitian Creole I remembered.

"What are you doing here?" I had barely cracked the door; I bet he could see only my left eye.

"Could have used my key." Roman smiled at me then, and resolve, my faithful resistance, began to pack its bags.

"Could have," I said, and almost of its own volition, the door edged open. "But I changed the locks."

He managed to look impressed. "Unlike my comrades on the force, I never could stomach a dumb woman."

I opened the door another inch.

"Look, Reina, I need to talk to you. You wanna do this out on the porch or inside, where I can get a glass of water? It's already heating up out here."

I stood aside to let him in and noticed Ms. Lucy standing on her front porch across the street. Unlike most people, she didn't look away when I met her gaze. She acted surprised when I called to her, made a show of eyeing Roman's car, double-parked out front, and then strode up to the door. I went to grab the vial I'd left on my altar: beef tongue and honey boiled for the base, cedar and hematite for overall good health, a pinch of mustard seed, topped off with barbiton moss. Van Van oil and the water from my veins sealed and boosted the spell. This would help her cough. Following directions, though, was not my nosy neighbor's strong suit.

"You have to do as I say for this to work," I told her. "Nine drops. Three times a day. Nine days." I repeated the instructions for good measure. "And stay out of that bar—the smoke is no good for you."

"Don't tell me what to do." She snatched the vial. "Everything all right in here?"

She curled her lip at Roman, who hovered at my shoulder. He winked at her.

"I'm fine. Just do as I say."

She narrowed her eyes at me, nodded, and then walked off without a backward glance or a thank-you.

In the moment it took me to lock the door, Roman had tossed his jacket on the sofa and was heading back to the kitchen. The gesture was so familiar, felt so right, that I forgot this man was no longer mine. I did a passable job at shaking off that feeling and followed him in.

He took out a small tumbler from the cabinet near the window and filled it right from the tap. He knew better. Before he could raise that mess to those exquisite lips, I took it from his hand, emptied it in the sink, and got him some decent filtered water, with a hint of mint from my garden, and handed that to him as he took a seat at the table—this, too, without asking.

I felt his eyes on me and wished I'd at least grabbed a robe. My nightshirt felt woefully short. And my bare feet were badly in need of lotion. I hurried over and settled in the chair across from him. He sipped and raised his eyebrows.

"What was that all about? Showing up at Congo Square? And why did you take Lucien's donation box?"

"That man doesn't know his place. We reminded him," Roman said. "I'm surprised you care—you don't even like him."

He had a point, but that didn't mean we should be harassed.

"How you been?" he asked. He'd set the glass down and was looking into it as he twirled it around between his hands. When he glanced up at me, furtive and quick, I wanted to touch his hand.

"Fine." I kept my hands to myself. "And you?"

"Getting by."

We sat there in silence for a while, him twirling and me holding back. This man, the shy, thoughtful one, was the man I loved. The detective, the one who pranced around like a rapper on a stage—that one I couldn't stand.

I had to do something, so I got up to make myself a cup of tea and immediately regretted giving him the opportunity to watch me. And he did so without shame. My hands shook so bad that I decided to forgo the loose tea and just grabbed a generic store-bought bag and set my kettle on to boil.

I heard Roman's chair scoot backward, then his footsteps coming up behind me. I waited and sighed at the familiar feel of his arms circling around my waist from behind. His body pressed against mine. I leaned my head back into his chest and placed my hands over his.

We stood that way for a moment, and his body responded, as did mine. He released me, and I turned to face him. He took my hands and kissed them both, but when his mouth moved toward mine, I turned and offered him my cheek.

"Me and my toothbrush haven't quite had a chance to connect this morning."

He laughed. "Wouldn't be the first time."

I allowed him to hold me, allowed myself to enjoy the cocoon of his arms. We had taken a few steps toward my bedroom before I stopped him.

"Roman, what are we doing?"

"Do I need to spell it out for you?" The sarcasm in his voice, that grating, irritating superiority. I pulled away.

"Why did you come here?" I moved around him and went back to get the teakettle, which was whistling away on the stove. I poured my cup and sank down at the table, trying to mask my disappointment. With a loud exhale, he followed. I couldn't meet his eyes.

"This murder over in the Quarter," he began, and his voice was all business again. "Let us do our jobs. If that broad didn't do it, it'll come out."

"Broad?" I said. "If she was a member of your father's church, would you call her a broad?"

"She ain't a member of my daddy's church, now, is she?"

"I don't want to have this argument with you again. I'm not going to."

"I didn't come here to argue with you either. I'm trying to do your ass a favor, but you never could listen to what I had to say."

"I haven't even done anything," I said.

"Good," Roman said. "And don't. I'm telling you, Rain, stay away from this mess. It don't have nothing to do with you. Let that woman's lawyer do his job. You stick to doing"—he paused to wave his hand around—"yours, whatever it is."

"Why? I mean, you don't have to believe in what I do, but you know a mambo would never use Vodoun the religion to kill somebody. Especially not in her own place of business. Even you should see that doesn't make any sense."

"Miles Jones, Baton Rouge, 2007," Roman quoted and then leaned back in his chair. I'd heard this story too. Unlike the other case, it was bogus. "Admitted that he tried to use black magic to kill his wife. He walked us through everything he did and even signed a confession, and you sit here telling me it could never happen."

"He tried," I admitted. "But he didn't go through with it. That's enough for you to condemn the whole practice?" He'd done it, drawn me into defending myself like a child caught with candy under her pillow. It hadn't gotten me anywhere the first one hundred times, and I was sure it wouldn't this time either. I should've just shut my mouth. I didn't. "Name me one other case."

"Do we need to get your father on the phone and talk about why Papa Doc sent the Tonton after the houngans? You wanna go there?"

Ouch. Pause. No, hard stop. I was tired of replaying this same old argument.

"I don't want any of this to land at your doorstep," Roman started, and when I went to open my mouth, he held up both his hands in a gesture of pleading. "I know what I said at Congo Square, but that was for Lucien's sake. I'm not saying *you* were involved; I'm just saying I don't want you to be."

Lucien again. I wanted to ask how he knew the houngan, but it could wait. "Fine," I said and then sipped some tea, burning my mouth. I sputtered.

Roman slid his water glass over, and I regretfully took a sip. He giggled and so did I.

He took my hand, and I didn't pull away. "Sure you don't want to?" he said, tossing his head back toward the bedroom.

I did, very much, want to. "No," I said. "Thanks for coming, but I—"

"Wish I had." Roman stood to leave, and I didn't follow him. I heard his footsteps retreat, then him sliding his jacket off the sofa and leaving. This time, there was no overnight bag. He'd taken all the things he'd left at my house the previous year.

Roman and I hadn't lasted as long as I'd hoped. The wedding, the children I'd already named, weren't to be. He was a decent man, for a cop. Had a good sense of right and wrong, though it was off sometimes. He was neat, mostly respectful, and had wanted a family. I didn't care how far medicine had come; I had no desire to be somebody's new mother when I turned fifty. Forty was as far as I was willing to take it. If my body, my unique physiology, cooperated.

But my chances had just walked out the door. His absence unlocked the cellar where I stored the longing for a baby of my own. Even if we could have moved on from all our other issues, we never could have moved on from our religious differences.

He was a devout Christian who never went to church but had no problem telling you what he thought was morally right or wrong. Breaking these rules himself somehow didn't apply. In the end, a Haitian American vodouisant and a Christian boy from Houston could never quite come to terms. Who cared if our gods had different names? If his relied on angels and mine on spirits? Magic that turned water to wine or another kind that infused drums with a powerful hidden language. *What did it matter?* We'd had the same fight so many times, but in the end, he dismissed my gods as heretical, and I dismissed his as bigoted. And that, as they say, was that.

I set the whole matter aside. It was time to get a few things prepared to go see the client Lucien had gifted me.

CHAPTER TEN

Taking client castoffs from Lucien Alexander was thorny. Picture a swanky Canal Street hotel. Penthouse suite. Shed the soft-as-a-summer-breeze cashmere robe. Your entire soul intent on luxuriating in the cultured marble bathtub. You grab a bar of French-milled soap that cost more than every bar you've bought in the last year. You open it up and come face-to-face with a springy, dried pubic hair. That's what Lucien's referrals were like: they looked good at first, but they always came with an ugly surprise.

Sad as it was, it was true. Even half of Lucien's hourly rate was to me a windfall. And my gratitude for his charity was so vast, so unsettling, you would have thought he'd handed me a blank check from a fat offshore bank account.

My new client, Nathaniel Surtain, lived in a brick ranch home on the outskirts of the Plum Orchard section of New Orleans East. Bounded by the Industrial Canal, the Intracoastal Waterway, and Lake Pontchartrain, it was in a part of the city that tourists avoided and the media maligned. Locals knew differently, though. The East was like any neighborhood in any other part of the country: some good, some bad, and everything in between.

And it was where my mother had chosen to call home. I veered onto her old street, not far from the I-10 interchange. I rolled to a stop, cut the engine at the curb of the empty lot, and refused to look at the spot where my parents' little house used to sit. Memories nudged, bade my gaze to settle on the barren land.

Weeds battled bits of detritus for control of her formerly lovingly tended flower beds. A row of pipes poked out of the ground where the kitchen used to sit.

In the blurred weeks after the hurricane, I defied orders to stay away and searched in vain first for any sign of Manman, then for anything I could salvage. Tears wouldn't come. Maybe Erzulie had held them back; after all, she'd never forgiven my mother. When the bitter memories coalesced like a rock in my chest, I left.

With a few minutes to spare, I arrived at my appointment. Nathaniel Surtain answered the door with a slippery smile to match his silk bathrobe and slippers. He led me through a living room draped with abstract art and stuffed with tasteful if oversize furniture.

The table overwhelmed the small dining room, such that when he pulled out the chair at the head of the table for himself, he had to slide in to sit down. I chose a seat on the outside, where there was a little more room.

Over the phone he'd requested a negativity-cleansing ritual, and I'd told him the things he'd need to have ready when I arrived: a brown paper bag, a small glass, his favored whiskey. The dining room table, though, was empty save four yellow place mats and a bowl of tacky yet dust-free wax fruit.

That wasn't necessarily a bad thing. Doctors will tell you how their patients will schedule appointments for anything other than what really ails them. Fear? Shame? Who knew the reason? My clients were no different. All needed some kind of healing, physical or mental. But you often wouldn't know the truth until you met them face-to-face.

I watched Mr. Surtain. He'd turned the chair to the side and crossed his legs. A forearm rested on the table—and didn't fiddle. He had no trouble meeting my eyes. Everything about him oozed comfort, confidence. So why the games? I needed the cash more than my annoyance needed assuaging, so I dispensed with the small talk.

"It appears you want something other than what you mentioned on the phone," I said. "Why don't you tell me why I'm here, Mr. Surtain."

At this point, a new client would typically respond, "Oh no. Please call me Nathaniel." Mr. Silk Robe did not.

He stroked the goatee that ended in a point at his Adam's apple. He sucked his teeth—a grating gesture if I ever heard one—and smirked. "You can read minds, too, huh?"

I had to blink hard to keep from rolling my eyes. "Predict the weather. Reveal tomorrow's winning lottery numbers."

He laughed.

"And tell you the exact day of your death."

He stopped laughing. "Okay, okay. I see you just messing with me. But, you right. I need something else."

"I'm listening."

"Kiah said you don't have kids. That right?"

None of your damn business. "Why do you ask?"

"See, what I really need has to do with my wife. My lady. I mean, I'm gonna marry her next year. I don't want no kids. I got my career to think of, and so does she. She's smart, you know? Anyway. A hysterectomy costs too much, and I heard it takes a long time to heal up. She wants me to get a vasectomy. I told her I would, but I ain't having nobody cut on my—"

I raised an eyebrow.

"What I want is a spell, a work, to make it so she can't get pregnant instead."

The image of me throwing a chair at this idiot flittered beneath my closed eyelids. A spell to make his girlfriend barren? My mistress was the goddess and protector of children, among other things. My veins ran ice cold. I clamped my mouth shut to keep my teeth from chattering till the feeling passed.

71

"I don't know who told you I would, but to do that to her without her knowledge—that isn't how I work. It isn't how any of us works." I grabbed my purse.

"But I know a mambo that did it before."

I scooted my chair back. "Then I suggest you go talk to her."

"Can't. I had an appointment all set up, but when I went by the shop, it was all closed up with police tape and shit."

I froze. My purse suddenly felt like it weighed a ton. I was about to hit Nathaniel with a barrage of questions, but that wouldn't work on his type. A gentler approach was called for. "Truth is, under certain circumstances, exceptions can be made. Tell me about what this mambo did."

As expected, he brightened at the prospect of educating me. "This dude I knew back home had a voodoo priestess take care of something like that with his girl. She straight up trapped him. Told him she was on the pill. It was because she lied that the mambo agreed to it. Her brother set it up."

Couldn't be, could it? "You said, back home?"

Nathaniel beamed. "Houston, born and raised."

The lwa didn't believe in coincidences, and neither did I. That meant it was possible that Salimah was willing to bend the rules if it suited her. But dismemberment? That was still a leap. I was about to leave when I remembered that if I wanted to light my home with something other than candles, I needed the cash.

"I won't do what you asked, but what I can do for you is something that will suppress your, uh, virility."

He looked doubtful.

"No snips or cuts involved." Erzulie would probably be happy a man like this wouldn't have access to any children.

It was likely that others, perhaps even the girlfriend in question, had withered under the flat stare Nathaniel leveled at me. I yawned.

He threw up his hands. "Let's do this."

I excused myself to go out to the car and get my bag from the trunk. Other, more fitting spells sprang to mind: the break-up-a-couple *wanga*, a bon voyage spell that would send Mr. Surtain to be a blight on another city. And there were spells of the darker variety that, while tempting, were not part of my practice.

Nathaniel watched me from the door, as if afraid I was going to leave. I'd do the reverse of a fertility spell. I thumbed through packets and vials. I didn't have any vetiver, but I'd substitute in dried patchouli. I'd ground a fresh batch of the bushy herb last week, taking care to include the pink-white flowers.

With my client banished to the far-eastern corner of his home with directions to kneel and recite ten rosaries (five more than was strictly called for, but I didn't like him and I could be petty), I got to work. The powder was a simple enough mixture. I pulled out one of my small metal bowls. For all but the most complicated works with my father, my days of using measuring cups and utensils were long past. I dumped a bit of the patchouli into my hand and rubbed my palms together to further reduce the powder. Then exactly three pinches of sage, two rose petals. Instead of the cinnamon that the fertility spell called for, I opted for the bitter herb common wormwood. This last piece doused male potency.

I dropped in a bit of Florida water. That bound the ingredients and turned the consistency to a muddy texture that swirled and bubbled. The chaos continued until the bowl had settled and dried into a mixture that looked like a seasoning packet. I poured the contents into a free glass vial.

When Nathaniel returned, I was standing. I didn't want to be in his presence any longer than necessary.

"Sprinkle this on yourself before any intimacy—only a pinch. Let it fall away naturally."

"That's it?" he asked. Skepticism creased his face again.

"Store in a cool, dry place." I took out my tablet and slid it across the table to him. "Enter your contact information and payment details."

"Yeah, about that." He didn't touch the tablet. "I don't have a credit card, and I'm actually running a little low on cash till payday."

There were spells of a certain variety that I'd heard Papa and other vodouisants whisper about. All right, I'd read about some of these spells. It was my job, after all. Revenge spells. The coffin spell, the bad-works number. Spells that in the wrong hands could turn healing to harm. There were also more pedestrian options like a kick to the groin.

But I didn't. Instead, I accepted his bullshit apology, his even more bullshit promise to mail me a check next week. But I didn't leave empty handed. I had Nathaniel's sweaty, crumpled twenty-dollar bill in my pocket and a packet of boudin in a plastic bag.

The sounds of Lucien's and Kiah's laughter dogged me as I drove away.

Instead of going home, I took the twenty-minute drive over to Lake Pontchartrain and settled onto a bench looking out over the estuary that many mistook for a lake. I needed to think without someone showing up at my door and interrupting me.

Gentle waves crashed against the embankment. Water the color of a darkly brewed tea smelled faintly of trash. An ant trail of joggers and a few slower strollers made laps along the concrete path at my back. The melody of a child's laughter drew my gaze.

A woman sat on a blanket with two children. One, no more than a toddler, ignored the shiny LEGOs before him in favor of a napkin he was ripping to shreds. A look of sheer delight on his face. The woman managed to keep an eye on him while cooing to the infant in her arms at the same time. She'd been blessed with *two* children.

Why not me? It was a question with no answer. I'd always imagined myself as a mother. Just *knew* I'd have a baby, maybe two by now, but the lwa seemed to have other plans for me.

As if sensing my despair, the water called to me then in a lullaby of ambient whispers. Spray planted light kisses against my skin. Its life-giving sustenance sank in, attempting to buoy my spirits and fill the hollowed space in my heart that only a baby could fill.

With effort I centered my thoughts on what my new, poorly paying client had let on about Salimah. This was certainly an interesting tidbit about her character that shed a different light on what she was capable of. But a questionable spell was still a long way away from a gruesome murder.

Both Lucien and Papa had taken the same stance, unsurprisingly. In that, they were, for once, united with Roman. Of them all, I understood my father's reluctance to get involved the most.

It was the reason we'd fled home. Haiti's supposedly progressive new president, François "Papa Doc" Duvalier, had successfully stamped out a coup attempt. Things went downhill quickly. The same had happened in other countries since the beginning of time. Opposition was silenced. Dissenters beaten or worse. At first, he revered the country's Vodou community, turning to them for healing and other traditional works.

But as he fought for more control, his fear, his paranoia, raged. He became convinced that the vodouisants were against him. Truth? He thought everyone was against him. One by one, priests disappeared. Papa tried to ignore it, thinking the cases were isolated. That soon things would settle down. Mostly the trouble was contained to the capital, but soon the police force moved up into the countryside. Toward us.

Others had begged Papa to get involved. They looked to the most powerful houngan to step in. To use his political influence on their behalf. But he was worried for my mother and me. Families weren't immune to retribution. So he stayed away.

And then they came for his best friend, a fellow practitioner, not more than a few miles from our home. Papa sprang into action.

He handed out powerful talismans to protect the people and the community. Worked spells that he wouldn't even let me see. Secreted himself away with the remaining priests and priestesses to try to defend us all.

But then the Tonton Macoute picked off one, then another. When it was clear that they were going to silence everyone, we threw everything we had into a few suitcases and were spirited away to the airport by a sympathetic member of the force.

Papa was going to stay behind, but my mother begged and pleaded, and at the last minute he came with us and brought along all the guilt he carried for what he perceived as starting a war and then abandoning his soldiers. Stories of the demise of much of the vodouisant community followed us, told by my grandfather.

I figured the guilt and my grandfather's rebuke dogged Papa and eventually sent him out into the swamplands. A place where he found what little peace he could. He talked of going home, but even now, when he knew he could, he refused. I always thought he stayed for me.

Backlash.

When you made the decision to get involved, to make a stand, this was one of many possible outcomes. Papa was worried about me one day having to make my own hasty getaway.

That Salimah Grenade was a human being meant that we should all care if she'd been wrongly accused. That's what kept the rest of us human. And when what you believed in most, your religion, was called into question, that just added fuel to the fire. Sometimes caring put you in harm's way. It could mean your life would be upended, like ours had.

It could cost you your family, your respect, even your life. That was no small matter, and I had to admit it gave me pause.

But how much worse would I feel for not trying?

CHAPTER ELEVEN

When the phone rang, I gratefully logged out of my banking website and closed the lid on my aging laptop. Staring at the numbers any longer wouldn't change the piteous state of my financial affairs.

A perceptive person might have pointed out the fact that there were spells, powerful magic, designed to address such monetary challenges. I'd done them myself, more times than I could remember. But unless that perceptive person was a duly initiated mambo or houngan, they wouldn't know that to practice this type of magic on oneself was forbidden. We served the lwa, not the other way around.

After Roman's visit, I couldn't say I didn't hope, for a moment, that it was him calling, but caller ID revealed it was Tyka.

"What's up, Grip?" The nickname was well earned but reserved for her *other* set of friends. She hated it when I used it.

"That don't even sound right coming outta your mouth," she said without a hint of laughter in her tone. The child needed to work on her sense of humor. "Maybe you should come up with a French name for me—something foreign sounding is what I need. Use that Haitian accent you try so hard to cover up too."

Trying to cover up? Was I . . . no, I wasn't trying to cover up anything. That dig didn't justify a response. I supposed next time I'd just call her Tyka. "What can I do for you, Ms. Guibert?"

"What I can do for you, more like," Tyka responded with a chuckle. "I found the girl you was looking for."

"Sophie? You mean you found Sophie Thibault?" I'd had to stop myself from blowing up Tyka's phone to check on her progress. But now that she'd actually found Sophie, doubts began to creep in.

"That's who you asked me to look for, didn't you?" Tyka's hint of impatience was hard to miss.

"Look, I'm not sure I should get mixed up in this. Let me think on it a little more." My father's words played across my mind. "In fact, forget I asked. If the cops want to talk to her, they'll find her."

"Aw, man, Rain. I done lost skin on knuckles over this one."

I remained silent as, not for the first time, I was unsettled by Tyka's choice of words.

"Her friend wasn't, you know, forthcoming with the information. And before you jump all over my back, I did ask nice first."

She didn't sound upset about it, really. And I knew that despite our many talks about violence, when I called on Tyka for help, she'd use whatever means she had to. Guilt that I might one day get this child in trouble gnawed at me. And it also made me feel like I at least had to meet with Sophie, if Tyka had gone through the trouble of smacking someone around on my behalf. I only hoped nobody'd been hurt too badly.

My good sense receded right along with the warning from my ex-beau, Detective Frost. I used his last name when I needed to put some distance between us. I was already moving toward the bedroom, where I could change my clothes. The bedroom where Roman and I had almost ended up again. "Where is she?"

"She holed up at some friend's house over in Gentilly. This time of day, figure we can get there in 'bout an hour."

"We"? Did she just say "we"? I was pulling my skirt up and stopped midthigh. Bringing Tyka along, things could go badly, but then if they did, it sure would be nice to have her by my side. I wouldn't need to call up any nefarious magic; she was quick with her hands and feet.

"I'll come pick you up."

—

I hadn't asked if Tyka and Eddie had moved from the place they were squatting, and since she hadn't told me any differently, I pulled up outside, and just as I was parking, she appeared out of nowhere, from behind a tree, a car . . . a shadow?

She slid into the passenger seat. I waited for the telltale click. When none came, I leveled my gaze on her until she huffed and finally buckled her seat belt.

"You need a new car." She made a show of inspecting the interior upholstery. "I know somebody that could hook you up with this sweet-ass whip."

There was little doubt that some law skirting would be involved in such a dubious procurement. "I don't need a new whip or anything else. This car is paid for and runs just fine."

"At least let me have somebody upgrade your audio. You need Bluetooth."

I promised to allow her to do so at some undetermined future date.

"Where's our little fugitive holed up?"

"Selma Street. Off Elysian Fields. You went to school out that way. You know it?"

I chewed my lip. "Not really. Southern U is farther north."

"Head out toward Dillard, then, and I'll show you from there."

Tyka pulled out her phone, and with a few swipes and taps, Lauryn Hill's voice flowed from the tiny speaker. It was a song I didn't recognize, but that woman could sing her ABC's and sound good doing so. Tyka plopped the phone in my cup holder and tapped her hand on the armrest in time.

My mind was on overdrive. Lucien, Papa, Roman. They'd all told me plainly to stick to what I did best. Though it grated to have all three of them trying to tell me what to do, it was sound advice.

But I was positively *itching* to talk to Sophie Thibault. The possibility that she'd used me to cover for her, or someone else, irritated me to no end. And if she knew something that could get Mambo Grenade out of jail, I'd try to convince her to speak up. Plus, I could finally return her thumb ring.

Gentilly was a nice middle-class neighborhood. Home to Southern (my alma mater), Dillard University, and a smattering of other institutions of higher learning. My young friend would bristle, but I'd raise the thorny topic of college again. "You give any more thought to the Southern University pamphlet I gave you?"

I had only a vague idea of the things Tyka did to support herself and her father. Darryl said that she'd honed her street craft like she was grinding a knife on stone. It was a miracle she'd never been arrested. But underneath all that was a smart, sensitive girl. Still young enough to have a shot at a good life. If I could just convince her father to let her go. The man was like a boat anchor chaining her to a puddle of muck.

"I lost it when we moved." Her tone was flat, final. But all I heard was an invitation.

"I'll get you another one," I countered. "Better yet, why don't you just come with me? We can go over there and talk to a counselor. I know we can find something you're interested in. You have to start thinking about your future." God, I sounded like my mother.

"Rain," Tyka said, turning to me. "I know what you trying to do, but I ain't ready for no college. Ain't got no way to pay for it anyhow. I just . . ."

She trailed off, her gaze swiveling toward something outside my window. "Stop!" she barked. "Pull over there."

We were near the Free People of Color Museum on Esplanade. At the urgent sound in her voice, I swerved over and parked. Before I could turn off the car, Tyka had darted across the street.

Whatever scent she'd caught might cause us to miss Sophie. I followed anyway.

Tyka shot me a look that begged me to get my slow, flowy-skirted behind back in the car, but I held my ground. She huffed and then moved on. I couldn't tell who she was following, but I ripped out a satchel of confusion powder from the spot sewn into my hem just in case.

Tyka sluiced through the darkness like a water moccasin slithering through muddy water.

"What are we doing?" I hissed.

Tyka inclined her head and pointed. The ponytail gave Eddie away.

He stopped at a ramshackle shotgun around the corner from the museum. He had even paused to smooth back his hair before knocking on the door.

Tyka and I crouched in the shadows as I pictured Sophie Thibault slipping away under the cover of night.

"What are we waiting for?" I whispered. My skirt was gathered in a very unladylike bunch between my calves, and my knees were beginning to buckle under the strain.

"Shh," Tyka chided without peeling her eyes away from the heavily gated front door.

I glanced at my watch, wondering how long we had before I lost Sophie forever. I could've asked Tyka for the address and left her to deal with her family issues herself, but I tossed out that thought as soon as it had come into my head. The girl had never not answered my calls for help—well, on occasion she had. Anyway, I wouldn't abandon her.

When Eddie finally came out this time, my legs had cramped and Tyka's scowl had deepened. He tottered out of the house on unsteady legs, grinning from ear to ear. The scantily clad woman at the door gave him her cheek, and he straightened enough to plant a kiss there; then he slapped some bills in her hand, turned, and stumbled down the stairs.

When he got to the end of the walkway, Tyka sprang up in front of him. "Goddamn you, Daddy." She whipped out the baton so fast I wondered if she'd used some of my own confusion powder on me. I grabbed at her raised arm but came up with air as the baton thudded against Eddie's temple. She hefted the man over her left shoulder. He hadn't had time to do anything more than stare slack jawed at his pending doom.

I could only follow on her heels as Tyka schlepped him back to my car, where she brusquely tossed him onto my back seat. She wasn't even breathing hard.

When she asked me to drive them home, I gave up any possibility of making it out to Gentilly, and maybe that was for the best.

Back at their place, I helped Tyka haul her father out of the back seat. This time, I held his feet, and she grabbed him under the arms as we maneuvered him to the front door. We propped him against the wall while Tyka fished in her pocket for the key. She opened the door and hit a light switch. She dragged him inside herself.

I hesitated before entering. She hadn't invited me, but she hadn't asked me to stay in the car either.

A single light bulb hanging from the ceiling flickered to life, illuminating the studio-size space.

I could tell she'd tried to clean the place, but there was only so much that Pine-Sol and a good scrubbing could do. Holes in the wall were covered over by cardboard, with mismatched furniture crammed into every corner. The bed was tidily made with a duvet so faded as to make its original color a mystery.

A sprinter could leap the distance to the tiny kitchenette to my left in one bound. The space held a scarred white refrigerator, a countertop covered in neatly trimmed cardboard. A hot plate sat next to a sink too small to wash a proper pot. At least it smelled of jambalaya.

"Mambo Dumond," Eddie said when he noticed me, and he tried to straighten himself up. When that failed, he giggled like a schoolboy and slumped back down.

Tyka switched on the television and headed to the bathroom.

"Now, you know I can't sleep with the TV on," Eddie mumbled, with his eyes already closing and his head leaning back.

"I don't give a damn what you do," Tyka spat.

Eddie sat up, strangely lucid. "I never wanted this job, and I did the best I could before your mother up and died. I don't work steady, but you old enough to take care of yourself now."

"Like I was when I was twelve?"

I wished I could disappear, but even to leave now would draw too much notice.

A cloud fell back over Eddie's face. "You watch how you talk to your old man, now. I ain't past taking a belt to your grown-ass behind."

"I wish you would." Tyka stood, a towering bundle of menace. Eddie had already leaned back and now started snoring. I saw Tyka's eyes drift to the pillow beside her father and wondered whether she thought to prop his head up or put the man out of his misery.

A flutter in my chest warned me just before the lights cut off.

From the fading sunlight coming through the window, I saw Tyka tense and stand stock still.

There was little moisture in the air, but already, I gathered in what I could. I heard Tyka moving in the darkness, the flick of her baton. I found her near me, peering out the front window. She'd barely made a sound. I wondered idly if this had anything to do with the meeting we were obviously very late for.

Without moving the curtain, Tyka crouched down and looked in the space between the ragged edges and the windowsill. Her gaze scanned back and forth. The vigil continued for several minutes more before she tiptoed over to the front door. I followed before she hissed at me. *Me.* A duly initiated Vodou priestess. "Stay here."

I followed her outside anyway, and Tyka motioned with her hand to an electrical line it looked like she'd rigged from the house next door. As I looked along the length of the line to where it ended at the shack, I could see clearly where it had been cut.

The only question was by whom.

"Guess that got your attention," a husky voice said from the dark. Tyka turned and narrowed her eyes. The voice had come from somewhere behind the tree line on the side of the house.

"Best you go on and drop that baton if you don't want it to come down against the side of your head."

"Come take it from me," Tyka said and then took a sure step forward in the direction of the voice.

A rough chuckle came from the other direction. Were there two of them? Already, water swirled around inside me, ready for release.

"She ain't no joke, just like you said," another distinct voice said.

"Yeah, but she's still a girl. I'll drop her ass with one punch."

Sweat beaded my brow. There were three of them.

The broken streetlamp near the car flickered on, a small blessing from the lwa. Tyka feinted right and then sprinted for the safety of the light.

Footsteps, too many, sounded behind her. I waited and followed behind them. She hit the outer edge of the light, turned, and with a wide, high arc, brought the baton down on the head of the man who was right behind her. He cried out and crumpled to the ground.

I didn't have enough water to conjure anything more potent than a rain slick, but I'd drain every bit of moisture from my body to protect her. As my pores swelled, Tyka pulled a knife out from somewhere behind her, prepared to hurl it into the eye of the next attacker, probably so she could have the last one all to herself. Her hand was on the hilt, coming forward, when a voice stopped us both.

"Tyka, wait." The figure darted behind a parked car. "Wait, girl. Don't go and kill nobody—we just testing your reflexes."

"Bounce?" she said as I moved up beside her.

"In the flesh."

The man emerged from behind a car, his gold front tooth glinting in the light. I recognized him as one of the onlookers betting on the wrestling match the other day. He spared his friend one glance and grinned at Tyka in open admiration. I was surprised when she returned the look.

CHAPTER TWELVE

I hadn't released the moisture I'd gathered into my body as I probably should have. The imbalance gave me the sensation of being slightly tipsy. This was the reason I didn't drink. With effort, I leaned away from the driver's seat and released a bit of water, enough to make it safe to drive again.

I'd left Tyka to speak with her companions and waited impatiently, trying to settle my racing heartbeat. They'd conversed for all of five minutes before I blew the horn to break up their little coven.

"I guess calling and asking you whatever he wanted would have been too easy," I said to Tyka. We were back on the road finally. I had slim hopes that Sophie Thibault would still be in Gentilly by the time we got there. Tyka's little search-and-rescue mission and the subsequent recruitment to criminal activity, whose particulars I'd rather remain ignorant of, had cost us over an hour.

"Men never grow up," Tyka said dismissively. "They like to play their little games."

"What did they want?" I asked, despite myself. I really shouldn't have been so wishy-washy.

"You don't want to know."

"If it involves you getting into trouble, I do."

"Well, if you're determined to be an accessory. Bounce said your boy Kiah approached him about some work."

"Kiah?" I said. "Does Kiah have work outside of what he does for Lucien?"

"Your guess is as good as mine," Tyka said. "Turn right here. It's the blue house about halfway down the block."

Sophie was holed up in what turned out to be a powder-blue shotgun so close to the street it may as well have been on the curb. White columns framed the narrow abode, elevated on a red brick base. The front facade sported one lonely white-trimmed window encased by black shutters so glossy they must have been freshly painted.

While lights shone in the windows of the other houses on the street, I couldn't see one ray of light from this one.

We walked up the concrete path set in the middle of a grassless patch of yard. Tyka vaulted the four steps to a porch barely wide enough for a slender bench. I followed at a pace and manner more befitting my age and lack of exercise.

The door was painted the same shiny black as the shutters, the two glass panels covered from the inside. I knocked a few times, to no avail. I was just about to chastise Tyka for the time wasted corralling Eddie when a noise came from inside, and someone moved the curtain aside and peeped out at us. The eyes went wide.

The door opened, and the girl behind it was tall and thin, blonde and brown eyed. She wore a pair of cutoff shorts, revealing bony legs. Her bare feet were long and narrow, toenails painted a neon pink.

She didn't introduce herself and looked around behind us as if inspecting the street for intruders, then stepped aside. "I'll get Sophie."

It didn't take long for me to connect the bruising on the side of her mouth with twin marks on Tyka's right hand. It would've been hypocritical to scold her. It was my fault, after all.

"You can wait here," the girl said to me, refusing to look at Tyka.

Boxes, paint cans, a lone painting on the wall. The recently done drywall was taped, one wall painted a maroon bordering on the color of blood. A little spooky for my taste.

Plastic garbage bags were stacked in a corner. A pile of shoes in disarray beside them.

This was a house in transition. Whether they were moving in or planning a hasty exit remained to be seen.

I sat on the sofa, and as expected, my ever-watchful friend eschewed the lone chair opposite me and took up a station against the wall, near the door. She even moved the curtain aside to peer out the window.

"Did you hurt that girl?" My tone was hushed. Murmurs continued in the other room.

Tyka studied her shoelaces. "She look all right to me. Ain't laid up in the bed or nothing. Got all her teeth as far as I can see."

"You could try reasoning with people sometimes." I couldn't help myself and started in on the lecture I'd given her too many times before. "You don't always have to—"

"Mambo Dumond?" Sophie Thibault emerged from the dark like a wraith. She was so pale I almost mistook her for one.

"Sophie," I said, rising. A quick scan didn't reveal any cuts or bruises, but that didn't mean she hadn't been involved in the murder somehow. There was a twitch in her left eye I hadn't noticed before. "I'm so glad you're okay."

Sophie fidgeted. She looked as if she hadn't slept. Or bathed. Smelled like it too. Perhaps the rehab on the house had yet to reach the bathroom. "What did you come all this way for?"

I went back to the sofa and grabbed my purse, then fished the thumb ring out of the side pocket. "I wanted to return this to you. And I wanted to ask you about what happened at Voodoo Real."

"I'm not talking to the cops." Sophie slid the ring back in its place. "They're just going to try to pin this on me, and I didn't do anything. I . . . I just found my Virgil like that when I got home." Sophie broke down in sobs. Her unnamed friend moved to her side, but I waved her off. I took Sophie by the shoulders and guided her over to the sofa. The friend handed her a tissue.

"Did you call the police?" I asked.

Sophie wrung the soiled tissue in her hands. I cringed. "She told me not to."

"Who?"

"Mambo Grenade. She heard me scream and came upstairs. She said she knew somebody that could help. While she called him, I got out of there. I couldn't stay. I mean, what if the killer had still been there, hiding in a closet or something?"

"I know you didn't do anything," I began, but I didn't *know* a darned thing, and that's why I was here. "But you know the police are holding your landlady. She's been charged with Virgil's murder. So, if there's anything you can do to help her, to clear this all up, I'm asking you to do it now."

Sophie straightened. Curiously, she didn't register a note of shock or concern for Salimah. "I can't do anything about that. I mean . . ." She sobbed again. "For all I know, she did do it. I just know I didn't. But I watch all those crime shows, and the first thing those cops are going to do is point the finger at me."

"Tell me why you think Mambo Grenade could have done this."

Sophie dropped the soiled tissue on the floor and dabbed at her eyes with the hem of her New Orleans Saints jersey. On her slim frame, it was a nightgown. "Virgil couldn't hold down a job for very long. He always ended up getting into it with somebody for one reason or another. And then he'd be back at my apartment. Angry, sullen, often drunk." She stopped to look at Tyka, wrapped her arms around herself.

"Go on," I nudged.

"I was only waitressing. But I'm in nursing school at Tulane. I want to work with babies. Student loans help out some, but I don't earn all that much, and sometimes we're late with the rent. Virgil argues with

Salimah—uh, Mambo Grenade. They both made threats, you know, but Rashad was always there to calm them both down if I wasn't."

"I don't think late rent is enough to make her kill a man," I said, unconvinced.

Sophie looked up at me and blinked. "He shoved her, once. She was so mad she spoke in tongues. Virgil thought she'd cursed him and all because he couldn't even find a construction job after that."

I didn't talk to the new mambo enough to know anything about her business or her renters, but Lucien seemed to think she was doing well financially in the Quarter. I doubted she would have stood for some man touching her, though. She might indeed have cursed him.

"I mean, who else could cut him up that way?" Sophie screeched, and she curled into a ball on the couch. Her friend rushed into the room but took a step back just as Tyka took a step forward.

"Grown folks ain't finished talking yet."

The woman's gaze flickered over to Sophie, clearly torn, but she backed away, and Tyka resumed her perch near the entryway.

Sophie unfurled herself. "It's okay, Alicia," she said to the friend. She turned back to me. "Somebody with powers had to do that, and with all the tools of the trade around, I know it had to be Mambo Grenade. I just know it. I wanted him to stay with me. I didn't want him dead." Sophie dissolved again.

"If they come and find you, it'll be worse. You know that, right?"

Sophie blinked. "They've already got somebody locked up; they won't bother looking for me."

She was probably right. Unless, that was, I told them where to find her.

"Did Virgil have any other enemies?" Where had that question come from? Had I been watching too much TV, like Sophie?

"Virgil didn't have any friends or enemies that I knew of. Just that lady that had come slinking around. Heard her on the phone once, and Rashad told me that he'd left with this woman—this Black bi—uh, lady—that had started coming by to see him when I was gone. He carried around a lot of guilt about something, but I never could get him to tell me what."

If that word had slipped out of Sophie's mouth, I would have let Tyka slap her. She thought for a moment, then continued. "And the nightmares," she said, exhaling loudly. "He rarely slept through the night."

"Why did you come to me, when Salimah was right there and could have helped you just as easily?"

Sophie stiffened; that look in her eye, the one that had chilled me during our session, returned. I inhaled the moisture from her breath. She'd been drinking. "I didn't need her in my business. And Virgil was right there too. I don't know; maybe I just wanted to come to the best—aside from Houngan Alexander, that is. Even Rashad had some doubts about his cousin."

Aside from Lucien? Please. I decided to let that pass. "You said he had nightmares. Did he ever discuss them with you? What was bothering him?"

Sophie sighed. "He wouldn't tell me."

Either she was a convincing liar, or she was telling the truth—at least as far as she knew it.

"Don't you think it's a little convenient that you came to me instead of the mambo right where you lived, and when you get home, your boyfriend is dead?"

"I know how it looks. Mambo Grenade didn't like Virgil. She'd told me I could do better. Why would I ask her for help keeping a man she didn't like?"

Why indeed.

"Any trouble with anybody at work?"

Sophie shook her head and scrunched her eyes closed as if trying to force out a few more tears. A performance if ever I'd seen one.

"If Tyka was able to find you, that means the police can too. Probably already know where you are. If you leave now, you'll just raise suspicion."

A fleeting image of Detective Roman Frost passed behind my eyelids. I banished it. Sophie nodded between sniffs. "Stay put and out of sight," I said. "I'll get in touch with you if I learn something more about what happened to Virgil."

Tyka and I left after it became clear that I'd gotten everything I was going to get from Sophie. I thought of driving over to Southern to give her a tour of the campus, but that could wait; my mind was churning.

Sophie was holding back. The little she'd revealed had just left me with more questions. The more I heard about Mambo Grenade, the more I realized how little I really knew her. And a person with recurring nightmares was running from something. Virgil Dunn had likely earned those nightmares through actions of his own making. And if I could find out what those actions were, I might just be able to find out who'd killed him.

If Salimah was the hack I was beginning to suspect, I'd find out. The lwa demanded as much.

CHAPTER THIRTEEN

Last night's activities had convinced me of one thing: Sophie Thibault was a *mistè*. The confident young woman with the chilling smirk who had come to see me a few days ago may have been capable of murder. The one bawling her eyes out last night, unlikely.

That didn't rule out collusion.

To be fair, if she was in the clear, discovering one's boyfriend cut up into roast-size pieces in your home and having to flee the scene could really wreck a person.

One thing was certain, though: she had no intention of lifting a finger to help anyone other than herself. She was a consumer of my religion, a borderline believer. Someone able to benefit without conviction. Sophie was not invested in whether Vodou suffered malignment because of an untrue accusation. That responsibility was mine.

Wait a minute. Had I lost my mind? Somehow forgotten my chosen line of work? Mambo, vodouisant, servant to the lwa—these were proper titles. Police officer was nowhere on that list. I had been warned and scolded by people with more experience in these matters than me. I thought of an online course I'd bookmarked and forgotten. One that promised revelations on how to become a better listener. That was perhaps where I should direct my energy.

All I had were probabilities anyway. Mambo Grenade probably didn't murder Sophie's boyfriend, and Sophie probably didn't murder him either. Despite some unpleasant surprises I'd learned about Salimah, as a suspect, she didn't make any sense.

But the deep-seated emotions required for a person to commit murder, especially this kind of murder, rarely made any sense at all. About as much as finding a jelly doughnut on the menu at a beignet shop.

Anger, jealousy. Hell, having a bad day could be enough to send some folks down a path they couldn't turn away from. A few heated words and a weapon close within reach could be all it took for somebody to end up dead. So if you asked me if either of these women *could* have killed Virgil Dunn, then I'd have to say yes: anything was possible.

Besides Darryl's description of that poor man being chopped up that way, I didn't know much else about how Vodou had been implicated. The cops weren't likely to invite me into the crime scene for inspection, and Roman certainly wasn't going to be forthcoming with any more information. There was only one thing I could do.

I needed to see for myself.

I crossed the backyard, ignored the call to take up my perch on the little canary-yellow bench, and instead scooped up the terracotta jug that I kept tucked behind my potted plants. Though I had to lean my shoulder into it to close the door on my little shop, as soon as I did, I exhaled the tension that had bunched up in my chest.

At the altar, I found the lighter tucked on the nearby shelf and lit the candles. The room became a soothing backwater spa. Yes, this would do just fine.

At the rear of the room, I pushed the curtain aside and set the jug on the counter. With a spin of the lazy Susan beneath the sink, I spotted my lovingly and painstakingly curated but most pedestrian of silver bowls.

The art was thousands of years old. Some called it scrying; some called it hydromancy. Vodouisants, though, we called it water gazing. And like all magic, you had to treat it with the respect it was due or suffer unpredictable consequences. Some parents read their children fairy tales before bed. My father had recounted stories of Vodou magic gone wrong.

The water-gazing bowl, it no plaything, now. We knew Houngan Frantz was losing his eyesight 'fore he did. Old fool was always bumpin' into things. Had the bumps and bruises of a prizefighter past his prime to prove it. But he wouldn't hear nothing of it. The stubborn man took his gazing bowl outside and fouled it with well water he used to wipe him skinny behind. Next time he gazed, not only was his sight gone, so were his eyes.

And the stories got progressively worse from there. If Papa intended to scare me, it worked. No way this mambo would be making any of those kinds of mistakes.

Back to the bowl. It could be anything from glass to brass, but I'd chosen silver because it wouldn't break and I wasn't a fan of patina. Selecting the right bowl was much like buying your forever home. You went hunting for just the right look and feel, testing for imperfections. You might even buy a home or three before you settled on just the right one. But eventually, you'd find one where the fit, the feeling, was mutual.

The water was trickier.

A typical practitioner might use any number of water formulas. Creole water, for instance, was quite popular here in New Orleans. Florida water more in the Gulf states. But being a Haitian-born mambo bonded to the goddess of rivers made me anything but typical.

I started by splashing in two swigs of rainwater from the terracotta pot, which I'd set out every evening and then brought back inside in the morning. Doing this for one week charged the rainwater that I collected in a larger bin for such purposes.

The next part involved a sampling from the Mississippi River. But you couldn't just go traipsing down, dip a bucket in anyplace along its length, and go about your merry way.

Before emptying into the Gulf of Mexico, the great river became deepest right here in New Orleans. Algiers Point, to be exact. And that's where I went to collect. The water couldn't sit forever, either, so I got only as much as I thought I'd use in a month or two.

As soon as I lifted the pitcher holding the river water, I winced, remembering I had depleted my stores back home. When had I last replenished? Had to have been before Christmas, right? I pried off the lid and peered inside. It wasn't enough. Maybe it was enough. Okay, I'd have to make it work. Papa's warnings wormed in my gut, but I pretended it was gas.

In order to call on the spirits needed for this spell, six ounces of anise seeds went in next. All I needed for the last part was the water from my own body. How easy it would be to step outside and pull from the tantalizing breeze. My pores swelled as if in answer to the thought. But every time was a risk, another chance that my body would never stop, that I'd fill to the point of kidney failure. I downed a glass of water from the refrigerator, just to be safe.

Veins surfaced and split, tiny bubbles and rivulets of fluid crawled along the insides of my hands and dripped into the bowl. I knew blood plasma was about 90 percent water. When it joined the other ingredients, they set to a low simmer, as if sitting on a stove. The aroma of the anise filled my shop, and the steam emitted soothed the skin. On the rare occasions when I'd had to use the bowl, aside from one excruciating instance, it had never failed me.

While I waited for the contents to settle, I balanced the bowl in both hands and took it over to the table. A few deep breaths provided clarity of mind.

You had to have a sense of where you were looking. It couldn't just be someplace you'd never been.

First, I fixed the date in my mind. Next, I pictured Voodoo Real, crammed into its French Quarter storefront. The outside visage plus what I recalled from touring the place and the one subsequent visit. Then I went back to the day of the murder. Recalled the crime scene tape, the crowd gathered outside, the front door propped wide open. I gazed into the water and waited. There was no timetable on these things; they couldn't be rushed. The bowl would reveal what it wanted you to see if and when it was ready.

The shortest time was about two minutes, when I'd needed to discover where Ms. Lucy had misplaced her medicine after her hip surgery last summer. She knew it was in the house, so it had been easy to find.

My longest gazing was an off-and-on running total of ten years. In all that time, the bowl had not revealed my mother's location. My father claimed it was because she didn't want to be found. I thought it might've been because she was gone, though I wasn't ready to say such a thing out loud.

I realized my mind had wandered and tried to clear it again with a few more breaths. I refocused.

And when I opened my eyes, there it was. A mental projection of myself had been pulled into the bowl. A starkly gaunt, diaphanous version of me, anyway. Like an untethered balloon, I drifted in through the open front door.

An indeterminate amount of time later, bits and pieces of the shop—the counter and register, the walls, the floor—coalesced and solidified like a hearty stew.

Unlike other shops in the Quarter, Salimah's place hadn't been crammed floor to ceiling with gaudy trinkets and other Hollywood nonsense. It had a homey feel to it. But that was before.

I saw upended shelves that had been lined with gris-gris, dolls, and potions. Display cases smashed. More roots and herbs littered the floor than the dregs left in the few remaining mason jars. Scratches and dents marred what I recalled had been lovingly restored maple floors. The police had been thorough in their search for clues.

There was an entrance to the upstairs apartment outside in the alley, but also inside. I sailed through the long beads covering the narrow passage to the back room without disturbing them. Here she had a small buffet crammed into a corner. A college-size refrigerator with a microwave on top of it. A chair at the small kitchenette lay overturned. The lone cabinet door stood open, some of the contents on the floor. The door that led to the bathroom she never let customers use was closed. The other led to the upstairs apartment.

I'd seen it only once as a prospective renter. My memory was vague, but it proved to be enough.

I floated through the unopened door and ascended the narrow, dark hallway. Another thing that had warned me off this place was the steep staircase. At the landing, I entered and gasped. I sputtered between places, my shop and hers. Half-me, half-wraith. I steeled myself and went back.

I imagined officers moving around the space, working with their practiced detachment and trying to avoid looking at the same time.

Boxes of chicken stock lined the counter. Beside them, a cutting board with a handful of carrots and celery in various stages of decomposition—so far, the makings of a good étouffée. A hunk of flesh sat nearest the stove. Breezing over, I looked closer, then into a pot to find other pieces of what . . . dear God in heaven . . . were human. Virgil Dunn's remains. The opened oven revealed a roasting pan with human arms and hands. Hearing it was like the drone of a newscast playing in the background. Seeing it was envisioning the sawing, hearing the screams.

My stomach flipped, threatening to erupt, but I had to finish the vision. What struck me besides the gruesome nature of the scene was the iron-sharp precision with which the limbs had been cut. This was no hack job.

If that horror wasn't enough, in the corner of the room below a dust-coated window was what appeared to be a Vodou shrine.

A small table had been decorated with candles, incense, dolls, and gold coins. Pouches of herbs and other implements. I wished I could say that it had been done by inexpert hands, which would have cleared Salimah Grenade outright. But I couldn't say anything of the sort. It was well done.

Even though my body sat miles away, I felt the sweat trickling down my back, my erratic heartbeat. The revulsion that tensed my shoulders. I had to get away from here. I broke the vision just as, from the corner of my mind, I saw something odd.

I knew better than to pull out with such a jolt. I tried to stand but was dizzy and sank back down into my chair.

In that carefully crafted, macabre scene, two things didn't add up: the unexplained absence of blood, and the blond-haired, blue-eyed voodoo doll. It was like finding one of our unique aboveground cemetery tombs in Montana. That doll, the Hollywood voodoo addition, was a plant. Poppets weren't made to look like people, and they weren't used for malice. I had scarier dolls as a little girl. Was the plant a sloppy mistake or done with intention? A question in need of an answer if I ever saw one.

I had dated a detective long enough to know a few things about murders, particularly one as grisly as this. A wise woman would place her bets on the fact that this had been done by someone close to the victim. Someone angry. And who pissed you off more than the people closest to you? Still, without access to certain, uh, abilities, few people could accomplish such a feat.

And that begged the question of who Virgil Dunn really was. All I knew was that he'd had trouble holding down a job. Was he from New Orleans or a transplant, like so many of us? How had he spent his days if he wasn't working? And were all his nights spent with Sophie? She *had* just purchased a spell to try to keep him close.

I wondered if there was a time that life was different for Virgil. A time before the hurricane that had been washed away and lost, like so many lives. Like my mother.

The trick was to ask questions of the right people, to explore the recesses of the city that I didn't normally frequent. And to do that all without drawing the attention of Detective Roman Frost, the NOPD, or the killer. Because if I tripped up, then open practice could be stamped down, practitioners attacked, or worse. I could also find my own self locked up, and I wasn't about to let that happen again.

CHAPTER FOURTEEN

I'd overslept. I didn't use an alarm clock because I didn't keep regular hours, but I generally awoke with the sun. After I'd viewed Virgil Dunn's remains, sleep hadn't come easily, and when it did, it was less than restful.

Reading about such things had done nothing to prepare me for the sight of it. That something so gruesome could be tied to my faith? Repugnant.

From my experience, a problem was rarely solved by asking the same question over and over again. You had to approach it from a different angle. Until now, I'd been hell bent on figuring out *who* had killed Virgil. After last night, what I'd seen, I couldn't help asking myself *why*. What had he done to merit such a horrific ending?

Finding the pieces to that puzzle would have to wait. My other life, my real life, needed tending to.

After taking care of all the morning essentials and pulling on a pair of loose slacks and a blouse, I checked my calendar. A full docket, starting at noon, ending at six o'clock. Three return clients in need of various kinds of healing, one needing a Seven African Powers candle restocking, and one gris-gris bag pickup. By the end of the day, my finances would be off life support and well on the way to recovery. Ruminations on crime and punishment would have to wait.

It was closer to lunchtime than breakfast, so I settled for a cup of tea and a boiled egg while I prepared what would be my dinner. Cooking helped me think, and I needed all my wits about me.

Neither of my parents were what you'd call good cooks. Serviceable, yes. We'd subsisted on the most basic of meals and relished in the culinary delights that poured in from my father's customers. Ultimately our home-cooked meals were devoid of what Darryl "Sweet Belly" Boudreaux would call the secret ingredient, love.

Takeout.

I considered it for no more than a minute, but even so, I pictured Darryl shaking his head at me in disgust. I put down the phone. Tremé's most famous southern restaurant wouldn't be getting my precious few remaining coins today.

Aside from watching a smattering of culinary reality shows, I'd done little to practice the handful of dishes I was trying to master. I was a sucker for a good challenge, though. I plodded into the kitchen to check the cupboards. Canned vegetables, dried beans. Chicken broth.

Images of the macabre preparations laid out at the Voodoo Real crime scene struggled forth like a school of fish swimming against a current.

Chicken stock, green peppers, onion, shrimp, and those herbs on that kitchen counter turned murder scene. A hint that pointed to a dish I had yet to master: étouffée.

Darryl's first rule on the road to becoming a master cook was to never rely on your memory. That was for experts such as himself. So I dutifully riffled through the junk drawer next to the oven and pulled out his recipe. At the top, in his neat block print, it read SWEET BELLY BOUDREAUX'S GENUINE NEW ORLEANS ÉTOUFFÉE.

I didn't have any crawfish, which I preferred in the dish, so I'd have to make do with the boudin I'd gotten from Lucien's barely paying client referral, Nathaniel Surtain, and the shrimp I had in the freezer.

I pulled out the shrimp. Frozen solid. A bowl of hot water would take care of that while I whisked up the spices.

Had Virgil's murderer really intended to cook him up like a Sunday meal, or had it been staged just for show and shock? I suspected the latter. The whole thing, however grisly, seemed staged. The fact that it had obviously been set up by someone who knew what they were doing, but with that blond doll tossed in, gave it away. The intent, then? To frighten. And to disparage my religion in the process.

Mission accomplished.

Darryl would argue the point, but whatever Virgil's crimes in life, nobody deserved such an undignified death.

My stomach growled to remind me that at this point, it was running on fumes.

After I'd wolfed down my egg and tea, the shrimp still wasn't fully thawed. At first gently, then more insistently, I peeled apart the lump, ripping a few tails and meaty bits off in the process. They were pretty well mangled by the time I was done.

Whatever.

Once I'd drained and patted dry the shrimp, I sprinkled the dry seasoning mixture on top. Then, the skillet went on the burner with a drizzle of olive oil. In went the shrimp. The last of my tea called to me, and I sipped and let my gaze travel outside the window. My view was of my fence. At least it was painted.

As my seafood sizzled in the hot oil, another question surfaced. Though I'd seen the aftermath, I still didn't know *how* Virgil had been killed. A gunshot wound? Blunt force trauma to the back of the skull? Questions I might never have the answers to. And did it matter, really? Cutting up a human body that way required precision. Something strong and metal, something sharp like a surgeon's instruments and a surgeon's experience. Or assistance from—

My shrimp!

I yanked the skillet off the stove and took in the sorry, overcooked state of my shrimp. I sighed and dumped the wilted pieces into a bowl.

Time for the butter. Only I had none. I did, however, have a huge tub of butter substitute.

Close enough.

I spooned a bit into the skillet and mixed it in with the remaining spice blend. I also pulled out a package of frozen veggies that Ms. Lucy had gifted me and set that aside.

Hmm. Sophie had come to me to have a poppet made in order to keep her wandering boyfriend at home. She'd brought everything I needed. The very next day, or perhaps that same night, Virgil was dead. Did she find him first?

Dammit. The butter looked weird. I plowed on with a sprinkle or two of flour and whisked the ingredients together.

I did doubt Sophie's innocence. I knew angry lovers were capable of extremes. Women weren't exempt. And according to Sophie, she was so shaken that instead of calling the cops, she'd freaked out and bolted. If that was true, couldn't say I blamed her there. That would be the last phone call I'd want to make too.

In went the chicken stock, and I had what might, in certain light, pass for a gravy. A bit of Worcestershire sauce and a generous dash of hot sauce, and the shrimp went back in, along with the veggies.

With Sophie gone and Virgil still in that state right upstairs, Mambo Grenade, perhaps hearing Sophie's scream, finds the body, and unlike her tenant, she calls the police—after she calls Lucien. For her trouble, she's thrown in jail.

Lucien seemed strangely unconcerned, especially seeing as how particular he was about image and our craft.

And what about our victim?

I at least had some familiarity with everyone else, but I knew next to nothing about him.

The étouffée!

It burned. Okay, it scorched. Apparently, my idea of simmer and Darryl's were two totally different things. At that moment, I remembered the recipe, sitting right there on the table next to my empty cup of tea. I'd had to work out the details of my case, hadn't I?

One thing led to another, and time just got away from me. I could follow a recipe more or less as well as the next girl, but my problem was concentration. A ritual, a ceremony, most client consultations, I was there. But cooking seemed to float right out of my mind like a passing breeze.

A question lingered. Who was Virgil Dunn? And what had he done to make someone want to kill him?

The phone's ring interrupted my thoughts.

"Look here," Darryl said. "Chicken got some info to share with you. You need to hightail it on over tonight."

I was dumbfounded. In all the years I'd known him, I'd barely heard Chicken say more than a few words at a time. And now he had a story to tell? I didn't know how he and Darryl considered themselves best friends. Still, nine times out of ten, if I stopped in at the Lemon Drop, Chicken would be perched right there on the same stool, sipping at an unidentified drink.

"Chicken?" I finally muttered and realized I didn't even know this man's real name.

"You heard me," Darryl said. "Don't drag your behind, neither—he won't have all night. His wife's gon' be waitin' on 'im."

"Wife?" I said to the dial tone.

⌒

After I'd taken care of my clients, I made my way to the Lemon Drop empty handed. Darryl had called me, not the other way around, so a sweet treat wasn't expected. Those were the strictly enforced rules of the game. And because of my cooking mishap, there would be no new dish for my mentor to taste.

I found what for a select few vehicles could pass for a parking spot a few doors down and wedged my car in between a way oversize SUV and one of those new tiny rent-by-the-day subcompacts.

I slid my purse strap over my head, turning it into a cross-body-type affair, making me less a target for the run- or bike-by snatching that had become so popular. Roman had questioned why women even carried purses. Only a man who hadn't struggled daily with where to put his keys and wallet, phone, and notebook would ask something so ridiculous.

With the day edging toward early evening, the Lemon Drop was busier than I expected. A few women I hadn't seen before were seated at a table, and all the barstools were occupied.

And there, at my favorite table by the window, sat none other than Kiah. What was Lucien's muscle doing here? He looked up and leveled his flat stare on me like a heavy, wet blanket.

Our story had begun in grade school. Kiah and his sister were my neighbors, if not my friends. Hezekiah, as we knew him then, was a small boy for his age, nothing like the behemoth he'd grow into. The other boys bullied him. One day at the bus stop, when I'd grown tired of it, I stood up for him and his sister. Not with magic, but with a lead pipe I'd found nearby.

Only my little stand backfired. Instead of improving, Kiah was then further tormented for having a girl come to his rescue. His sister, from what I understood, grew up and moved to Paris, while Kiah and his smoldering anger remained here, just to spite me.

I returned the gesture and made my way to the bar, where I was unsurprised to see Chicken perched on the stool that may as well have had his name etched on it.

Darryl motioned me over and barked "Get up!" to the youngish man with the mohawk who occupied the stool next to Chicken. He turned the glare that he didn't dare level at Darryl on me, took his beer, and trudged away.

I climbed up on the stool, wishing that Darryl had instead cleared my favorite table. "What's Hezekiah doing here?"

"Far as I can tell, drinkin' and stewin'." Darryl cut his eyes over at the table. "Stewin' and drinkin'."

I didn't have to turn around to know Kiah's forever perturbed gaze was locked on my back. And there was no way he was just here to pass the afternoon with his nose buried in a glass. He didn't even drink.

"Chicken," I said to the wiry little man nursing a shot of brown liquid.

"Hey, baby." Chicken had an inexplicable accent. Cajun for sure, but there was a hint of something else. Evidence that maybe as a child, he'd spent his summers somewhere else, somewhere up north.

"You ain't brought nothin' else?" Darryl broke in. "Somethin' in the car?"

I winced. "Almost. I'm afraid my experiment met its end in the trash can."

Darryl threw his hands up in the air. "I will never understand why you can't follow a simple recipe that I done took the time to write out so darn simple, even that lil' old gal could do it."

Like me, Darryl had met Tyka when she was barely twelve years old, and he'd been calling her "that lil' old gal" ever since. And she'd hated it then too.

"Well, like I said on the phone, Chicken here got somethin' we thought you'd be interested in hearing 'bout that new client of yours."

Chicken sipped his drink and exhaled when he set it down. I took a good look at him like I hadn't in ages. And he *had* aged. Deep lines carved up the sides of his eyes and mouth. The hairs sprouting from his chin were mostly gray. And his skin a startled but subdued pink. He was so thin I wondered if he'd gotten the button-up shirt he wore from the boys' department. But there was still strength in the overlarge hands that cupped his shot glass.

Darryl leaned forward, elbows on the counter, and almost on cue, a couple of customers seated nearest to us at the bar got up and moved to a table farther away.

"That Sophie Thibault?" Darryl spoke instead of Chicken. Why was I even surprised? "Born and raised right where Chicken grew up, round New Iberia. Most of her peoples moved on, but he still knows a few. Decent folk mostly," he added, "but fell on hard times like all of us. Cause you to do some things you otherwise might not if you had another way. Know what I mean?"

I did and nodded my assent.

"That boy she got mixed up with? The one that met with the wrong end of a hatchet, hear tell? That boy used to be a cop."

Chicken's gaze shot up to his friend, his expression unreadable.

Roman hadn't mentioned that. And he hadn't made such a huge omission by chance either. Might've explained why he was so desperate for me to walk away.

"Whatever he'd gotten himself into tore him up so bad he left the force. Guess he had what you call a conscience. Couldn't hold a job any better than his liquor after that. No family to speak of."

"You sure he was a cop?" I was shocked. "Here in New Orleans Parish?"

Chicken looked over at me as if I'd asked him if he was certain the levees broke and washed away half the city with it.

Darryl huffed. "Yeah, he's sure."

"Did Virgil spend a lot of time with Sophie in Iberia? I mean, did they have friends? I can't find many folks here that know much about them."

"The only one willing to speak on it told Chicken what I told you. That's all he know. Anything else, probably ain't meant to come out. And this may not have anything to do with what they got your other mambo locked up on—just felt that you should know what you getting yourself into."

"Can I buy you another drink, Chicken?"

Chicken stood up and made a show of straightening the belt around his narrow waist. He turned the shot glass upside down. "Only one a day," he said. "I promised the missus."

He slapped palms with Darryl and, before he turned to leave, said, "First thang I'll tell you is that you shouldn't go messing around up in Cajun country. But let Sweet Belly tell it, you ain't one for listening to advice you don't care for. They ain't afraid to mix it up. That's all I'll say on the matter."

With that, Chicken inclined his head first to me, then to Darryl, and strode out of the Lemon Drop and into the setting sun.

A moment later, Kiah followed.

CHAPTER FIFTEEN

It was the kind of morning that begged for you to stay in bed. A light finger-thrumming of raindrops against the bedroom window. The air cool enough to warrant the light blanket I was snuggled in. The fragmented memories of a pleasant dream featuring my former love lingered just out of reach.

After the previous night's restlessness, I'd set an alarm. The earsplitting sound reminded me that if I wanted to learn anything more about the murder victim, I'd better get up.

It was still dark out. Chicken had said that what remained of Sophie's family had moved from New Iberia to Lafayette, where an uncle managed the family restaurant on Johnson Street. That was where I'd start. The trip to Cajun country would take at least a couple of hours, and I needed to arrive before the restaurant got too busy preparing for a possible lunch rush.

Instead of having a nice long soak in the tub, I quickly showered, dressed, and swallowed a piece of toast and two cups of tea, barely tasting them.

Though I would have been glad for the company, and the backup, taking Tyka along was a wild card I didn't want to play. Trouble followed that girl like a temperamental second shadow. I hesitated in the car, pondering Chicken's warning . . . and Roman's. Talking to Sophie was one thing—I had the excuse of concern for a client, for returning her thumb ring. But poking around with her family was wading into choppy waters.

I'd navigated those kinds of waters before. So I found myself driving down 90 West solo, a tangled web of thoughts making laps around my head.

I sped through a series of small towns, marveled at rice fields and crawfish ponds and tucked-away beaches. Places that only those who knew where to look ventured to find.

By the time I made it to Lafayette, the morning commuter traffic had thinned. The restaurant was as easy to find as the parking spot two doors down. I got out and stretched out the kinks in my back and neck. There was a lone man sweeping up the parking lot. More an ineffectual back-and-forth with a push broom that yielded nothing that I could determine in the way of trash.

He bent over and picked up a coin on the ground. He gave me a two-finger salute and a smile, which I returned.

The door was open, so I walked in and was immediately met with an outstretched hand. "Sorry, ma'am, we don't open till eleven." The pronouncement, delivered in a friendly tone, came from a woman I judged to be in her middle years with a name tag that read Ruby. She wore black jeans and a black T-shirt, marking her as part of the waitstaff. Her bronze-colored hair was definitely from a box, not a salon. Her forehead . . . well, she could have used bangs.

"I'm not here to eat," I said, plastering on a good-girl smile. "I was hoping to talk to Mr. Thibault."

Ruby's gaze lingered on me for a moment before she quickly glanced over her shoulder. She leaned in and whispered, "You from the health department?"

"Hardly," I chuckled. "I'm—"

"Can I help you?" Mr. Thibault had the same small mouth and pointed chin as his niece, Sophie. His tone was that of someone who was worried. Whether it was the health department, making this week's payroll, or a troublesome niece in New Orleans remained to be seen.

I stuck out my hand. "I'm Reina Dumond, a priestess from New Orleans Parish."

"Get back to work!" the uncle barked at the waitress. She flinched and rolled her eyes but dutifully complied. Sophie's uncle shook my hand, giving me the over-the-top man squeeze. The one that was supposed to convey confidence but only made you look weaker.

"Albert Thibault. You one'a them conjure women, huh?"

"Do you have a few minutes to talk, Mr. Thibault?" I felt him weighing his answer and decided to try to tip the scales in my favor. "It's a family matter."

Ruby was making a show of reorganizing the condiments on a table nearby, watching us from the corner of her eye. Mr. Thibault asked me to follow him. I inclined my head to the waitress, and she quickly looked away.

We maneuvered through the dim interior, overcrowded with tables so close together you were bound to hear your neighbors' conversations, whether you wanted to or not. The fluorescent lights overhead were coated with dust and grime.

At the back of the restaurant, we pushed through a set of swinging doors that led to the kitchen. Here things were only marginally better. An entire crew was hard at work preparing for a long day of serving customers their special brand of Cajun classics. Some cooks chopped vegetables, while others half-heartedly cleaned as they went. Large pots simmered with surprisingly delicious-smelling dishes.

Beside a large industrial sink filled with an assortment of pots and pans was the office. The smell of cigarettes hit me at the door, well before my eyes landed on a desk with not one, but two overflowing ashtrays. Mr. Thibault took a seat and, thankfully, didn't light up.

He didn't suggest I join him, either, so I cleared some junk off the chair closest to the door and dumped it into the other. Unidentifiable stains warned me off sitting. I wanted to perch myself right on the edge of the seat, but that would have made me look anxious, and I needed to appear in control, despite the uncle's bad manners.

"So, what's this all about?" Mr. Thibault asked. He leaned back in his chair, clasped his hands behind his head, and regarded me with colorless eyes, tinged red at the corners. He'd been drinking last night, a little too much but not so much he couldn't get up to run the restaurant today.

"Do you know a young lady by the name of Sophie?" I'd start with something simple and see if he'd lie about the small things. Only a knock at the door interrupted us.

"Everything okay, Albert?" Where Mr. Thibault—Albert—made you think of Sophie, the man who filled the doorway with his bulk may as well have been her twin, other than being twice her size. The hairs on the back of my neck stood up, and I felt my magic stir.

He wore the garb of head chef. Didn't bother hiding the malice in his eyes. And I wondered at where it came from. Did a woman from New Orleans really elicit this type of wariness?

Albert waved the man—Sophie's twin—away. "I'm just having a chat with this lady from the big city. Was about to find out what brought her all the way out here 'fore you knocked."

The head chef spared me one more scowl before he left. Perhaps I should have brought Tyka, after all. Chicken's warning surfaced in my mind.

"I was asking about Sophie," I said after the door had closed.

"What about her?"

"Sophie's got herself into a bit of trouble, and I'm trying to help her out. I just need some information about her boyfriend."

"You know Chicken?"

I winced. "Who?"

"Look, she barely even comes up here anymore." That was a lie. Chicken had told me Sophie and Virgil spent a fair amount of time up here.

"How's she related to you?" I just wanted to get the man talking on something innocent enough that maybe his tongue would loosen up on other stuff.

"Didn't say she was." And the door that had been cracked open a centimeter slammed shut. Albert stood up. "Got a lunch crowd about to flood this place in less than an hour."

I rose with him. "Thank you for your time, Mr. Thibault." On my way out, I saw the waitress, Ruby, watching me. I was hustled through the double doors and past the checkerboard-clothed tables.

"Mind if I use your ladies' room before I go?" Ruby had something to tell me but wasn't going to do so out in the open. I had to give her time. Mr. Thibault looked stumped. His southern hospitality wouldn't let them refuse a lady a visit to the restroom.

"That way." Albert Thibault tossed his hand in the direction of the back of the restaurant, down a side hallway. "See yourself out when you're done. Don't come back and see us now." He stalked off.

The bathroom smelled of fish and human excrement. I gagged and was about to turn around when I realized I needed to give Ruby a moment to get here if she was going to do it. I held my breath and played at my hair in the mirror. Sure enough, the door swung open— much, much too long later.

She went into the stall, and my heart dropped. Maybe I'd been mistaken. A moment later, though, the bathroom door opened again and another similarly dressed waitress popped her head in. She looked around, scrunched up her nose, and went back out. I was certain she was going to stand by the door to listen.

The toilet flushed in the stall, even though I'd heard nothing that warranted a flush. Ruby emerged, washed her hands, and turned to leave, but not before sticking a piece of paper in my hand. An address, hastily scrawled. She hadn't even met my eyes.

~

I knew she was Sophie Thibault's mother as soon as she opened the door. The only difference besides the telltale signs of age was the profound defeat written into the lines and hollows on her face and the hunched shoulders. I considered the fact that either of Sophie's relatives may have called ahead and warned her mom. One way to find out.

She sized me up, then glanced around as if expecting an ambush. Instead of hello, she said, "What?"

I hadn't expected a warm welcome, but this was downright rude. In my experience, the thing that Black people had to contend with, often in a split second, was whether the person you were dealing with was giving you attitude because they were a racist or because they were just an asshole. The jury was still out on Sophie's mom.

"Good morning, ma'am." I forced a smile to lift the tense corners of my mouth and proceeded with the cover story I'd cooked up on the drive over. The direct approach hadn't worked with her uncle. "My name is Nicole Hubbard, and I'm a parole officer from New Orleans."

There was a sudden stiffening of her shoulders. I charged ahead before she could slam the door in my face.

"I was hoping—"

"What's Sophie done?" She'd crossed her arms and hissed the words.

I wanted to play along; the fact that she assumed I was here about her daughter was intriguing. I'd tease that information out of her, but I had to win her over first.

"Actually, I'm looking for a friend of your daughter Sophie's. Alicia." I didn't know the girl's last name. "Your daughter is quite a lovely young woman, by the way, but her friend . . ." I affected a look of concerned consternation. Whether this woman shared that opinion didn't matter. If she did, confirmation bias guaranteed a loosening of the lips. If she didn't, then she'd consider it her duty to convince me of just how wrong I was.

"Connelly?" she asked. "Alicia Connelly. I told Sophie that girl was trouble. Wouldn't show her face back here after that first time. All my son did was ask her out. Proper-like, you know? And she acted like he'd asked her to do something unnatural. Got a mouth like a rattlesnake and the good nature of a cottonmouth. Oh, excuse my manners—you better come on in."

Maybe Sophie's mom wasn't a racist, but it remained to be seen whether she was an asshole. The house wasn't quite the abode of a full-fledged hoarder, but I could tell that unchecked, she'd be there in less than five years. Boxes large and small were stacked in a couple of corners. Nascent piles of other junk here and there.

Instead of a decorative log or candles, the fireplace was neatly filled with old newspapers. The settee and chair were neat and clean, though, and Sophie's mother asked me to have a seat. I could see into a dining room and sliver of kitchen, where things were only marginally better.

"I ain't surprised she's gotten on the wrong side of the law. That girl thinks she's a man," Sophie's mother said. She still hadn't introduced herself.

"Who?" I was genuinely confused. The woman eyed me suspiciously.

"Didn't you say you was here about Alicia?"

"Oh, of course," I said, cursing my stupidity. "So it sounds like you haven't seen her either?"

When the woman shook her head, I realized two things: she was waiting for a story, and if I hoped to get her talking about my real target, Virgil Dunn, I'd have to spin one for her. "Alicia was a no-show for her last appointment. She has your daughter listed as her only emergency contact. Your Sophie is a good friend, a loyal friend." I was almost embarrassing myself. "Only she isn't going to tell me anything to put her friend in harm's way."

That last bit seemed to smooth away a few of the wrinkles from the old woman's face.

"If I knew something, I'd sure as hell tell ya," she said with the certainty of a mother who hated her child's choice of friends. "Our family's got some ears, some influence, though. If I knew a bit about what she's done, I might be able to get my boys to figure out who she'd be running with."

Sophie had at least one other brother besides the one I'd seen at the restaurant, and apparently they were used to jumping at the matriarch's command.

"I shouldn't say, but I can tell you it's a matter of assault, involving another young woman." That wasn't technically a lie, only Tyka had been the one committing the assault.

"What'd I tell ya?" The woman slapped her hand on her bony thigh. "She tried that mess with Thomas. I don't even know where Sophie met that kind of girl. Then took her in like a stray dog or some such. I don't think Virgil likes her either. But my Sophie is headstrong if anything. That little incident with the cheerleader. Well, them cuts on her face healed up just fine. Nothing more than scratches. Come to find out the boy she was fighting over never did go pro."

I blinked. Sophie had sliced up someone's face? And Mrs. Thibault had spoken of Virgil in the present tense. The conversation was going exactly where I wanted it to go, but this was an unexpected development. I had to tread carefully. "Virgil?" I offered. "Is he a friend of Sophie's?"

Mrs. Thibault pursed her lips. "For the moment, he's my little girl's boyfriend."

"I know that look." Time to see just how much Mrs. Thibault was willing to share. "My mother doesn't like my boyfriend either."

"It ain't that I don't like him; it's just that he's a little old for her, you ask me." She hesitated, as if wondering why she was talking so much before continuing: "And that landlord of theirs slipped up and told

Sophie there was some woman sniffing up around Virgil. Wouldn't give her name or nothin'. I think the poor man is losing his way."

Before she could tell me anything else, the front door opened. "Ma?"

I locked eyes with another of Sophie's brothers. He didn't share the family resemblance, perhaps taking after the father. He wore overalls with no shirt and a pair of boots that were more befitting a lumberjack. His hands, balled at his sides, were the size of bear claws. His glare shifted between me and his mother.

"Who is she?" I watched as his mother shifted uncomfortably with the realization that she may have said too much to someone she'd never even asked for identification.

"This here's Ms. Hubbard, a parole officer from the city." She spoke as if she were testing the words in her mouth, considering them herself for the first time.

"What do you want?"

The son didn't introduce himself. The mother stood and went to his side. I shouldered my purse and stood as well. They were unfortunately between me and the door.

"Just looking for a friend of Sophie's, but after talking to your mother here, I realize that this might be the last place that she would come. So I thank you for your time, ma'am. I'll be going now." I took a step forward. Neither member of the Thibault clan moved.

"What would this friend be doing here?" the lumberjack asked.

"Just checking everywhere I can." I could see Chicken sitting on his stool in the Lemon Drop, just shaking his head at my ignorance.

Sophie's mother returned to her earlier demeanor under the reproachful gaze of her man-child. "Come to think on it, she got to asking all about Virgil too."

At that moment, I heard a sound that let me know I was in trouble. It was the creak and slam of a back door and the sound of another man calling out: "Ma, whose car is that out front?"

I recognized the voice. The restaurant, Sophie's twin, the redwood. I tried to sidestep the first brother's attempt to grab me, but then his forearm was around my neck. I strained to reach down, going for the gris-gris pouch sewn into my skirt's waistband.

I struggled as I watched the other brother heading straight for us. I did the only thing I could. I bit down as hard as I could on his arm. When he yelped and released me, I snatched the gris-gris bag and ripped it open.

Snake sheds, powdered blue glass, golden lodestone, and one surprise ingredient. *A fear spell.*

The shimmery concoction didn't fall to the ground. No, it hovered there, undulating before me, awaiting my command. I drew my palms together around it. The Thibault clan's movements slowed to a crawl.

The granules danced around my fingers, and I loosed a trickle of sangswe wine from my pores. When the mixture was just right, I swung my palms outward. The powder split in three and spiraled out toward its targets.

My eyes closed as I felt that little slice of myself work its way inside mother and sons. The fear spell's goal: go deep, deep. Find the target's innermost fear and work its magic.

It came as no surprise that the family matriarch feared God above all. Inside my head, a chuckle. Whether mine or the spell's was unclear. For her eyes and those of her creator, the magic laid bare her numerous, troublesome sins. Mrs. Thibault buckled under the weight of her creator's condemnation. She collapsed to the floor in a fit of sobs.

The younger brother, behind me, was next. The spell betrayed his fear of strength, primarily that of his older brother. For him, my spell cast him back years prior, the much smaller, sickly younger brother. With mother away and baby sister crying in her crib, he was pummeled by the redwood and beaten to a bloody pulp. When older brother was done, he dragged him outside by the scruff of his collar and allowed other boys to join in.

I saved the redwood, Mr. Head Chef, for last. Like the others, soon his deepest fear was revealed. It was so unexpected that I almost laughed. Born and raised in a virtual swampland, the eldest son of the Thibault family feared water. No, not just water, drowning. With all the mirth it could muster, the spell invoked a raging flood. Sophie's brother thrashed and kicked, swam with such determination to survive that one could almost admire it. But the water surged, and his strength waned . . .

All this happened in the time it took for me to cross the room, turn to look back at the family caught in the throes of their individual terrors, and then leave. There was a final ingredient to the gris-gris, the evil eye. It lay there on the floor at Mrs. Thibault's feet. Those in the know would recognize the warning. I wouldn't have to worry about them coming after me.

Their suffering would end within the hour, and I'd be halfway home. I was glad that I'd handled the situation myself without calling on Erzulie for help.

CHAPTER SIXTEEN

Regret at what I'd done to Sophie's relatives was a throb at the base of my skull. Guilt, its faithful companion, was a tightening in my shoulders. The kicker? The absence of any rebuke, any sanction from Erzulie.

In the manner in which all things were about as clear as the bottom of the ocean, the lwas' rules were sometimes ambiguous. The first one, though, was plain as day: do not use your gift to bring harm to another person unless you are certain you are in mortal danger.

Certain.

The first time I'd run afoul of this rule was not long after we'd come to America. I must have been eight or nine. An angry mob could wreak havoc; hardened criminals could and did inflict harm. These things were expected. But what we didn't talk about, what flew under the bad-behavior radar, was the fact that there was nothing more spiteful than a young girl with an ax to grind.

Had it been my accent? Rich brown skin that failed the paper-bag test? Maybe it was just the fact that I was different, my patron lwa setting me apart, even then.

Whatever it was, when the bullies came for me, I reacted. Badly. I lashed out, siphoned water from their bodies (another no-no). I took too much. Brought it into myself and rode the giddy euphoria. The first girl complained of a dry mouth; another fell to the grass screaming about a cramp in her thigh; judging by the way she clamped her little hands around her head, the third got a headache.

I kept pulling until Erzulie intervened. She cut off the flow and settled a chill on my bones that set my teeth to a weeklong chatter. My parents thought I was sick, and Papa plied me with all manner of cures that did nothing until I'd relayed the playground story. He showed me how to make amends. The chill abated, but the lesson remained.

Yet here I was again. I was certain Sophie's family had intended to harm me first. Okay, at least I thought they had. Fine, I guess I hadn't waited around to see what was going to happen. Had I overreacted? Should I have tried to talk my way out first?

A frigid jolt through my body. Guess in the lwas' infinite wisdom, the answer was yes. In keeping with the rules, I would ask for forgiveness. That meant I must begin with a spiritual cleaning of my home and everything in it, including me.

I went out back and snipped a few fresh flowers. Everything else I needed was in the kitchen. The prayer was already in my head. I laid the ingredients on the table: salt, my homemade perfume, and pennies from the coin jar that had saved me from starvation more than once. The last thing was rum. I opened the cabinet where I kept a bottle for my guests and frowned.

I held the bottle up to the window over the sink. No matter how I tilted and shook, there was no getting around it: barely more than a drop remained. It would have to do.

I tapped out a bit of salt into my palm and went to the parlor. I sprinkled a pinch into each of the room's four corners. Working from the front to the back of the house, I did the same in each room until I ended up in the kitchen again.

Next, the rum, or what remained of it. I got out the broom I used specifically for this purpose and watched as the woefully inadequate drop of liquor fell onto the bristles. I swept down one wall in each room, speaking the whole time about the kind of vodouisant I wanted to be: kind, an expert healer, giving, a proper servant.

With that part done, it was time to take up the salt. In a modern twist, I got out my hand vacuum, taking care to make sure it was empty and clean. I sucked up the granules and flushed them down the toilet.

Back in the parlor, I lit a blue Peace candle and placed the fresh-cut flowers around the altar. I asked for forgiveness and then repeated each of the lwas' names in succession.

By the time I'd whispered the last name, instead of a clean slate, mine felt muddied. A sliver of the guilt was wedged painfully in my throat. I should have brought more rum.

A cup of tea was in order. I riffled through the assorted bags I'd accumulated, some gifts from customers, and settled on a green pomegranate. While the kettle heated, I recounted what I'd learned.

Sophie, like most people, was not what she seemed. She'd sliced the face of another girl in high school, a cheerleader intent on stealing her boyfriend.

I thought back to that chilling smile she'd given me when we first met and realized the signs were there. That innocent act was a shield. And Sophie had beef with Virgil. But I doubted she had the knowledge to set up the altar that way. Perhaps the former high school slasher was trying to change, however ironic her choice to become a nurse.

My parents had always told me how smart I was. And I believed them. So I had no explanation for why, for the second time in as many days, I was about to do something stupid.

I'd barely escaped Cajun country—a fact I was prepared to keep from Darryl and Chicken. But I'd learned some things that had made me even more curious about this case. I was willing to admit it now. I was intent on seeing this through. Even if, at this point, the clues to who had killed Virgil Dunn were all leading in different directions.

There was another person I hadn't spoken to, and honestly I hadn't entertained the possibility of her guilt. That person was Mambo Salimah

Grenade. Unfortunately, she was still sitting in a jail cell with a murder rap on her back.

That meant a trip to the precinct. Exactly the place that one Mr. Roman Frost had told me to stay away from.

From the beginning, Roman had hated having the altar in the house, calling my practice, my life, un-Christian. Based on some of the things I'd heard him tell me about his fellow officers, all practicing Christians, it seemed that being un-Christian was the best decision I'd ever made.

I knew it was just as wrong to put down someone else's religion as it was for them to do the same to mine. Sometimes, we were all hypocrites. What I wouldn't stand for was a religion that tried to put itself above all others. Everybody had their gods or goddesses; we may have called them different names, but underneath, they all served the same causes. Meaning, love, redemption. And I, for one, didn't think that one group had any leg up on another. My practice was mine and always would be, but if praying to a merman from the lost city of Atlantis gets you through the day without the need to hurt or demean or rule over someone else, then I'd say go for it.

I added a Seven African Powers candle to the others on the altar beside the fireplace and lit them. My mood brightened with each little flame. I closed my eyes and let the subtle glow wash over me for a few precious quiet moments.

I removed the gold bangle from my arm and draped it, along with the gold beads I'd snagged from the last Mardi Gras parade, in between the candles. I lowered myself onto the cushion, closed my eyes, and recited the prayer.

Oh, Seven African Powers, who are so close to our Divine Savior, with great humility I kneel before you and implore your help before the Great Spirit. I ask for your continued protection. I ask for your mercy. I ask that you spare my memories when it serves you, for I still hope to one day find my earth mother and to recognize her and remember her. I promise to honor your names. To give you credit for the miracles you grant me. I promise to help others with the gifts you have bestowed. Amen.

I finished my devotion and sat still for another half hour in perfect, silent bliss. There, by myself, in that cocoon of the spirits, my home, my life slipped away. My soul drifted upward, toward the day's thick cloud cover. I hovered, by the slimmest of threads, just beneath it. Yet I was able to see both above and below. Guilt dissipated in a fine mist. Existing in both places, I could see clearly.

There was another trail, as yet unexplored. Bright as the sunrise. It led to the woman at the center of things.

It was in this way that I realized what I must do. I had to find a way to get in to see New Orleans's newest and most controversial mambo.

~

The last thing any intelligent, sensible Black person wanted to do was to voluntarily go to a police station. Only under two circumstances were we normally forced to circumvent this reality: if we were arrested, justly or unjustly so, or if we were lucky enough to be picking up released friends or family. I take that back: some voluntarily decided to work there. Go figure.

Mambo Grenade fell under the first category. But she was a member of the vodouisant family, and for that, Mr. Lucien Alexander and I had an obligation to support her in any legal way we could.

Lucien had floated the idea of a Vodou council of sorts the last time he'd gathered all the local mambos and houngans together. This was right after Mardi Gras last year, once the scandal about the home invasions had blown over. A fake mambo and two goons had robbed several homes under the guise of providing in-home Vodou services and consultations.

The police blowback had been swift and hard; we were all under suspicion. All harassed at home and office. That, surprisingly, was how

Detective Roman Frost had barged into my life, waving his badge and his Christian sensibilities.

Lucien had of course assumed he'd be the de facto leader of our little band. When I challenged that assumption, he'd reacted childishly and called off the other meetings that had been scheduled. The divine mating of a princess and a leopard, his lwa, Agassou, was formidable. A Beninite like me, Lucien carried a bit of the priest king and his gifts with him. Nobody had been willing to side with me and move forward. Cowardly, but who had time for grudges?

Still, rumblings about the council had begun anew, and Lucien was at the helm. If he wanted to lead us, then it was time for him to lead.

I didn't have any concrete numbers, but judging by Lucien's Garden District home address and the sheer amount of clothing his wife, who didn't work, seemed to own, Lucien's practice was a successful one. Curiously, although he counted some of the city's richest among his impressive clientele, he still kept his business in the Lower Nine. A wife, a fat bank account, and two children to my none. Admiration and envy never failed to trip me up whenever I was in the man's presence. Not today.

Coming to this part of town consumed me with other emotions, the bottomless feeling of loss chief among them. My mother's best and only friend, the one who had filled her head with the idea of escaping to New Orleans, was buried in Lafayette Cemetery No. 1. Manman had visited frequently, bringing flowers, trinkets, whatever offerings she could muster.

It was where she'd wanted to be buried when the time came. But that time wasn't now. With a wordless sob, I avoided driving down Washington Avenue, like I'd done so many times before, hoping against hope that I'd spot her, weaving among the raised tombs, and chased the memories away.

I pulled up in front of the converted two-story structure where Lucien conducted his practice. I grimaced at the cars crammed into the impressive parking lot beside the building, no doubt a gift from one of his political cronies, and parked out front instead. Land was expensive in the city after the storm, and Lucien had rebuilt without batting an eye.

The houngan had employed Priest King Agassou's colors tastefully. White house, tan and yellow trim. Juliet balconies attached to floor-to-ceiling windows off the top and lower levels. A gabled roof. The lawn had no right to be so green at this time of year either.

I passed through the gate and approached the building, positioned about twenty feet away from the curb. I opened the expertly carved wooden door, shoulders already tensed and ready for a fight. The man behind the counter to my right gave me a grim nod. "Mambo Dumond," he said. He gestured toward the waiting room, already packed with customers. "The houngan has a full schedule this morning, but I'll let him know you're here."

As he disappeared down the hall to Lucien's office, my eyes landed upon a stack of the houngan's business cards. I snagged one and dropped it into my purse. If things went the way I suspected, I'd have an insurance policy that might earn me sway at the next stop I was bound to make.

Then I turned, taking in the packed waiting room, and smiled involuntarily at Lucien's musical selection. Ballaké Sissoko, the Malian kora player's sound unmistakable. Despite myself, my shoulders relaxed.

Until I heard Kiah's voice.

"Don't see your name here," Kiah said. He closed the door behind him and made a show of coming over and checking the appointment book, which I knew was mostly there for aesthetics. Lucien's setup was all tech. The man guarded his employer's time with the grit and determination of a jealous girlfriend.

"It just kills you, doesn't it?" I said with a toothy smile. "To know that despite your astute recognition of that fact, Lucien will still see me."

"The houngan has always been big on charity work."

"Why were you at the Lemon Drop?"

"Why are you here?"

"If it isn't the great priestess Dumond." Lucien came out of his office, trailed by a client, patted the man on the back, and turned to me. He wore a suit as usual, dark blue. White shirt and red tie. His hair recently cut, and that line was done with a razor, not clippers.

"Lucien." He shook my hand, and his felt like a cat's tongue. I hated this part of his sometimey greetings. But I wouldn't be the first to pull away.

"What brings you by this neck of the woods?" He thankfully released my hand. "I'd think you'd be busy with your own clientele. Hope things worked out with Mr. Surtain." To punctuate this jab, the African-drum doorbell sounded again as a stream of three customers came through the door. On a good day, I saw five or six clients. Judging by his waiting room, Lucien must have done that in a half an hour.

Lucien greeted the new customers, and I waited till they were out of earshot before I whispered, "We need to talk about Mambo Grenade."

Lucien's eyes showed something that on anyone else I would have sworn was fear. The man's mask never faltered. He turned and walked down the hallway without a word, and I took that as an invitation to follow. And so did Kiah. It was as if I could feel his hot breath on the back of my neck.

Luckily Lucien turned and caught sight of him. "It's okay, Kiah. Go ahead and handle that business we talked about."

Kiah slunk back to whatever lair he'd emerged from.

My eyes couldn't help roaming over all the shelves and cabinets. Barely an inch of dark-brown wall space wasn't covered by some manner of artifact. Nothing was dust covered, either, a suggestion that either he hired a housekeeper or, more likely, he had high turnover, his goods sold and replenished on a regular basis. I stifled the envy and marched behind Lucien's quick steps.

Some people never surprised, as predictable as the rivalry between Baton Rouge and New Orleans sports fans. Whereas my place was meant to feel cozy, warm, inviting to my customers and myself, Lucien's office was meant to convey the more prevalent aspect of his personality: ostentatiousness, extravagance, and a rather desperate need to impress.

The first time I'd seen the place, I'd been awed by the expansiveness. The entire back wall had been blown out and replaced by a massive window—stained glass at the top and paned slats at the bottom. The garden that it looked out onto had to have been maintained by professionals.

The walls were a muted tan. An oversize sofa sat a few feet from the back wall; the center of the room held a coffee table that looked like one long drum, framed by two love seats in the same black leather as the couch. Rugs covered the wood floors and blunted out the sound of his hard-bottomed shoes as they strode past the more comfortable love seat setting and to the too-large leather chair behind the too-large cherrywood desk.

I took one of the two smaller leather chairs in front of the desk. Point made: Lucien didn't consider this, or any of my other previous visits, of the social kind. I'd never be a friend of his and wasn't bothered by the fact. Even with all he had, the man still managed to hold some strange jealousy toward me.

Lucien sat behind the desk and, in a needless show of his power, blended so seamlessly with his chair and the wall behind him that he was momentarily invisible. As I was about to conjure a show of my own, he leaned forward, visible again, steepling his manicured fingers, and before I could utter a word, he said, "No."

"I haven't even said anything."

Lucien's mischievous smile revealed teeth as crisply white as his shirt. "Your father called. He told you, I told you the same, but you've never been one for listening to any of my advice. So, when you make a special trip down here and the first words out your mouth are about that mambo over in the Quarter, don't take much to figure out the nature of this here visit."

"But you act like you want to lead. You can't just be a leader when everything is going right."

"A leader knows when a cause is a lost one. And when getting involved in that cause will drag down everybody associated with it."

"You're just afraid of the cops."

"After last time, you should be too." Lucien leaned back, knowing he'd scored a point with that one.

"They weren't even vodouisants," I countered. "The police finally figured that out."

Lucien growled low in his throat. "They didn't figure out a damn thing. We did. And after all that, you took up with that detective—"

"Roman and I aren't together anymore."

"Whatever. Your detective was right out there at my public ceremony causing trouble. I don't want any part of it."

"You'd rather let Salimah go to jail for something she didn't do?"

"On a first-name basis." Lucien smirked. "I didn't think you even knew the woman."

"Can you answer the question?"

"You know, everybody else around here loves me. They respect what I'm trying to do for this city. But all you ever have is suspicion and disrespect."

"Is that a no? You aren't going to answer the question?" I uncrossed my legs, leaned forward, and gripped the arms on the chair. A look that did little to convey my air of control.

"It's the house's rat that eats the house's straw," Lucien said finally. "Know what I mean?"

I did a double take at the words I'd heard my mother speak so many times; I automatically pursed my lips, just as I'd done with her. In Haitian Creole, *"Se rat kay k ap manje pay kay"* more or less meant that the most obvious culprit was usually the one closest to the trouble.

Lucien was the only American I'd ever heard say it. Curiosity gave way to the matter at hand. "She's one of us, Lucien. If people think you'll pass judgment on them without even trying, they won't follow you over to the Quarter, let alone anywhere else. You at least owe it to her to hear her out."

"She can't tell me anything if she's locked up," Lucien countered.

"Which is why we need to go visit her and talk to her ourselves."

"The hell we do."

"Why not?" I sounded like a ten-year-old.

"After they dragged all of us down there like cattle for that mess with the break-ins, I promised myself I'd never see the inside of a jail again. And you think I'm going to go down there voluntarily?"

"And when you were down there, being interrogated for something you didn't do, wouldn't you have appreciated it if someone had come to try to help you?"

"Nobody did. If those fools hadn't slipped up and got caught red-handed, they would have forced our hand. Caused us to show them what we can do, and that would have cost us both."

He was right. One of the handful of times we'd ever agreed on anything. We weren't going to prison. But using our special brand of magic came with a cost.

"You're saying you just won't go visit Mambo Grenade with me?"

Lucien sighed with effect like he was trying to explain the simplest concepts to a gnat. "You haven't heard a word I've said. Me not going is a given—what I'm saying is that you damn sure shouldn't go either."

"Aside from that time last year," I said, "how do you know Roman Frost?"

Lucien's slippery grin held. "I don't."

CHAPTER SEVENTEEN

"Can I help you?" The officer's dispassionate gaze landed on me from where he sat on an elevated platform. He didn't appear angry or even suspicious, but mostly just tired. During our time together, Roman hadn't socialized, and he was so ashamed of my practice and how we'd met that I didn't think our relationship was a frequent topic of conversation. Besides his partner, Darby, whom I assumed would be with him, I wasn't the least bit worried about anyone recognizing me.

"Mambo—" I stopped myself from using the honorific, which would only agitate. "Salimah Grenade."

He tapped a few keys on his keyboard, somehow keeping one eye on the screen and the other on me.

He peered down at me, took in my skirt, blouse, and sandals. "Judging from the looks of you, you aren't her lawyer." He tapped the screen again. "And you don't look much like a Rashad Grenade to me."

"I'm her sister," I lied easily. "From Houston. I moved after the storm." He could try to look that up, but I could tell he didn't feel like it.

"Sister, huh? That's original." He picked up the phone, barked a few words into the receiver, and then nodded a few times before he set it back down. "Look, whoever you are, you may as well head back out that door."

I pulled out the business card I'd swiped from Lucien's place and handed it to him.

He raised an eyebrow, and this time, when he glanced back up at me, his expression wasn't one of respect but of resignation.

"Park it over there." He thumbed at a bench in the corner beside the entrance. "I gotta make a call."

I thanked him and turned to look at the only seat in the area. I wondered at the bodily fluids that may have been deposited on that bench. The fat wad of gum plastered to the armrest. I imagined the seat sticky with other waste. I was wearing sensibly heeled sandals; I'd stand.

And stand I did, for about an hour. I watched people come and go. Some cuffed and cursing, others desperate and fearful, asking after friends or loved ones. The longer I stood, the more chance I had of running into somebody I didn't want to see. I knew the cops were just messing with me. I could either leave or wait.

I'd just decided to leave when a voice snared me midturn.

"I knew it. God dammit, I knew it!" I turned to see Detective Alton Darby hovering a few feet away. I would've bet on the fact that Roman's schedule was still what I remembered. That he'd be out in the field at this time of day. This was why I never played the lottery—I was no good at gambling.

"Let me guess," I said. "Your schedule changed? Yours and Roman's?"

Darby ran a hand over his head, rolled his eyes skyward, and sighed. He was conflicted, and I wondered why. "The crime scene, Congo Square, and even in your own kitchen, Frost tells you to keep your nose where it belongs. Either you don't hear too good or this is your way of getting your boyfriend's attention."

"I know Roman's address as well as you do. I think you know this has nothing to do with him or you."

"Whose case do you think this is? Oh, that's right, for reasons that escape me, you think it's yours."

"Miss—"

My escort had arrived, but at that moment, a scuffle broke out as a loan officer struggled to bring in a short, compact, but incredibly muscular man. Even with his hands cuffed behind him, he'd torn away from the cop and sprinted for the door, giving me a view of a nasty cut down the center of his neck. Darby launched himself on the man. I was momentarily forgotten.

"Looks like they got that covered." My escort had appeared at my elbow. "You here for Grenade, right? This way."

He led me to a bare, dark room that smelled of piss. One dented metal table, two chairs, and an overhead light that painted the room a sickly gray.

The state of things hadn't changed a bit since my last visit. Shock first, then my heart wilted; finally, anger flared when I saw them bring Salimah in. Her hair was a mess. Bits of hair yanked out of the braids. An orange jumpsuit draped her body. She wore one flip-flop. Even worse was her face: her eye held a bruise, as did the corner of her mouth.

"Mambo Dumond?" she said as she was placed in the metal chair. I noted the question in her voice. "You should have called first. Would have given me time to fix myself up a bit."

How she managed to have a sense of humor about her predicament, I'd never know. "If it makes you feel any better, my skin's a mess beneath this makeup."

Salimah chuckled but winced, and I wondered if she had other bruises that I couldn't see.

"I don't have the tools of the trade to protect me in here. Still got these, though." She held up her shackled wrists, and I saw the bruises on her knuckles. "What are you doing here? Did something happen to Rashad? Did they hurt him? I don't think I could bear any more bad news, but go ahead and tell me—I gotta know."

I hadn't seen Rashad since the police had taken him away. Roman hadn't mentioned anything about him, and it was wholly possible that he was also being held. "I haven't seen him, but I promise you I'll look into it."

The look of concern on the mambo's face slowly transformed to something else. "Have you been by my shop?" she asked. "Is it open?"

I hadn't been by and told her so, but I promised I'd do so after I left, assuming they didn't barge in and throw me in the cell next to her. I may have been curious about Salimah's cousin, but I didn't know how much time I had and I needed to turn the conversation in another direction.

Not an easy way to say what I had to say next, so I just spit it out. "Did you kill Virgil Dunn?"

Salimah jerked. "I barely know you. You show up here uninvited and have the nerve to ask me that?"

In her place, I would have said the same thing. "Nothing else matters if the answer to that question is yes."

"No," she said, banging her manacled hands on the steel table for effect. "I did not kill Virgil. And even if I wanted to kill him, which I didn't, would have been easier to slit his damn throat than cut him up like that."

I noted the heavy rise and fall of her chest. The conviction written plainly on her face, and I thought she was telling the truth. But that didn't mean she didn't somehow have a hand in it. "Do you have any idea who did?" I paused, thinking of how to better frame the question. "Did he have a lot of visitors? Any trouble with anybody that you can remember?"

A painful expression rearranged her features. "It was Sophie's place, you know. Yeah, he was there all the time; he was her man. But I didn't like his ass either." Salimah hesitated, and I'd learned a long time ago that silence was the best encouragement some folks needed to continue talking. There was something Salimah didn't want to say.

"He and Sophie argued," she continued finally. "More over the last couple months, I guess. Just seemed like regular couple troubles to me.

I've never done anything to bring shame to the practice." That twitch in her left eye said differently. "I don't have anything to hide, but unlike me, there's more to that girl than meets the eye, though."

My client's words about what Salimah had done in Houston didn't match up to the innocent image she was trying to paint of herself. I'd press her a bit and see which version of the mambo would respond.

"That altar was put together by someone who knew what they were doing." I left out the doll clue. "That certainly isn't Sophie. And frankly, I don't know if I see a girl like her committing this kind of crime."

"Who do you think you are?" Salimah's nostrils flared along with her temper. "You and that uptown asshole think you're better than the rest of us, but you ain't. *Beninites*. I don't even believe you can do half of what you claim."

Anger, check. Jealousy, double check. Time to switch gears. "What does your attorney say?"

Salimah sucked her teeth, deflated. "I spent all my money moving here and opening the new shop. Can't afford a real lawyer, and the public defender they gave me doesn't seem too optimistic."

I hoped she wasn't expecting me to offer what I didn't have. She must have figured that out on her own because in the next breath, she said, "What about Houngan Alexander? Is he going to do something to help me or not?"

I didn't get the chance to answer.

━

The door banged open and crashed against the back wall. The sweet musk of his cologne hit me next. Roman strutted in, with two other officers at his heels.

They may as well have been bookends, so similar in appearance were they. Fresh faces that suggested they'd just graduated the academy.

The pair wore their bravado in the creases of their pants and the grimaces on their faces.

They yanked me up by the pits of my arms and dragged me, a duly initiated mambo, out of there like a sack of potatoes. I yanked away, an ineffectual gesture given where I was. We followed Roman down a hall where all eyes followed us, and I tried to struggle with my waning dignity. It felt like they'd already slapped cuffs on me.

"Have it your way," came one officer's voice from behind me. "Can't say we don't appreciate the view from back here."

Roman froze, then turned. "It ain't going to be about all that," he said. The cop held up his hand in mock surrender, and the other one smirked.

And Erzulie wasn't having it. She bubbled to life in my body, and I heated up like an overdone king cake. I relished the feel of her heat coursing through my veins and swore at the fact that I couldn't raise a hand to protect myself. Doing so would only further convince them of Salimah's guilt.

"In there." Roman pointed at an open office without looking at me. I was shoved into the room. He strode in after me and slammed himself into a nice leather chair behind a neat desk.

The two officers still stood near the open door, but when Roman glared at them, they left, closing the door behind them. We watched each other, both breathing hard with indignation. He waved a manicured hand at a chair. "Sit down, Reina."

"If I'm not under arrest, I'll stand."

"Sit your ass down, Reina," he said.

I didn't like his tone but figured if I put my ego aside, maybe I'd spend the night at home instead of in a cell. With as much attitude as I could muster, I sat in one of the two chairs in front of his desk. I took the one that let me see the door from the corner of my eye.

"Using Lucien as a calling card? Nice touch. Already had your mind made up, didn't you? Didn't matter what I said, never did," Roman said. He'd called Lucien by his first name. Curious.

I let my eyes roll up under the guise of really contemplating this ridiculous question. I would give him a ridiculous answer in return. "You got thoughts on so many things, Roman. It's so hard to remember what you're talking about."

That little split between Roman's eyes became even more pronounced, as it always did when I made him really angry. He thinned his lips and grabbed a pen. He did that thing where he tapped the end on the desk, flipped it over, tapped the other end, and repeated until I couldn't see straight. Irked me beyond reason, and he knew it.

"You don't even know her, do you?"

Roman never asked the questions I was expecting him to ask, and he always caught me off guard. "I've met her . . . twice."

"This is some solidarity thing?" He threw the pen down; apparently even he had grown annoyed. "Is that what this is?"

"Kind of." Short answers really got him riled up, and I had plenty more where that came from. I thought the vein at the side of his temple was going to burst and spray me with his blood.

His eyes bored into me, and he shook his head. "You do realize we're talking about murder here, right? A man was killed, and that woman back there in the cell is the one who did it. What don't you get about obstruction?"

"She didn't do it."

"The evidence says she did. And last I checked, the detective was sitting on this side of the desk."

"The evidence doesn't say any such thing." A couple of words too many. I should have shortened that a bit; the vein was subsiding.

"Obstruction. Assaulting a police officer. Accessory." He counted off each make-believe charge.

Who was I kidding? If they wanted to, they could certainly make the first one stick. "What aren't you telling me?"

Roman's mouth, a treasure for which I'd relinquished the key, opened and closed. His eyes went to the door, as if measuring whether the officers outside could hear. He turned back to me and leaned forward. "Drop it, Reina. This is the last time I'm going to tell you. You never could take the helping hand I tried to offer you."

"There is no way a vodouisant would be so stupid as to use Vodou to kill someone, especially not like that. And in her own shop? Come on, Roman. Set aside whatever issue you have with my religion and think." It was time to try for basic logic.

He stood, and I couldn't help noticing the way the perfectly ironed shirt fell across his shoulders. My traitorous heart skipped a beat. "Get out."

"Has Rashad Grenade been arrested?" I asked, and I couldn't tell whether Roman's expression was one of surprise or annoyance.

"Get the hell out." This time, he spelled it out.

I stood and turned to walk to the door, conscious of the fact that his eyes were on me.

"And the next time you want to see me"—his tone had lightened—"you know where I live. You're always welcome."

I put my hand on the doorknob with effort. Love could be an ugly thing, showing up when it was least wanted and abandoning you when it grew tired. Love could kiss my ass. I left Roman's office without a backward glance and more relief than I thought possible. I felt bad for Salimah, though; the police had a suspect and looked like they were ready to wrap this up, evidence or not.

She needed my help, only I felt wholly inadequate to step up to the task. She required better than me, but my mother would say that didn't matter. If the universe had seen fit to drop this task in my lap, then I'd have to wrestle with it as best I could. Next thing I had to do was figure out what they'd done with Rashad.

In real life, family resembled nothing of the sappy movies or dripping pictures poised on so many desks across the country. Family was messy, ugly, complicated. And sometimes brutal. There were a few reasons Salimah's cousin Rashad hadn't shown up to see her. First, it was wholly possible that he simply wasn't fond of his cousin. Family didn't always mean friend. The more likely reason, though? He, like the rest of the community, could've been scared witless.

My job was to find out which it was.

CHAPTER EIGHTEEN

I'd love to say that my brush at the police station the previous day didn't rattle me. But Roman's warning, as well as his cologne, still prickled like a thorny rosebush.

Sneaking in to see Salimah had been risky, but how could I, in good conscience, continue investigating if I sensed her guilt?

Truth be told, I was only slightly more convinced that she didn't at least know more than she was letting on. She ran hot and cold, that one. But one thing was certain, and that was the genuine concern she had for the whereabouts of her cousin.

Another job for Tyka.

But first, I pulled on my robe and sat down to check the day's appointments. A vodouisant's work must always be her primary concern. Only, I made the mistake of checking my email before my calendar. It was some nonsense update about my house, more specifically, the lease-to-own terms. I filed that in my "to read" folder and was pleasantly surprised to see an email form notification about an appointment for a general *wanga*.

The new client—Terence Burns—was pretty vague. The notes section of the form glaringly blank. Wangas were just spells to solve all kinds of problems and were one of my most commonly requested services. Love, money, people who didn't do what you wanted them to do—all were typical, but the more complicated, the more I charged. Mr. Burns was a paying client, and I needed the money. The case would have to wait.

Most of my practice centered on repeat customers. This was how a mambo or houngan earned and kept their hometown reputation. And even though New Orleans was a tourist town that dumped in new clients by the thousands, a practitioner couldn't survive without the steady income stream provided by what often amounted to lifelong, even generational, return clients. As soon as one problem was solved, life generally presented a new one.

I spritzed my hair with a homemade concoction of distilled water, jojoba, and a slew of essential oils, designed to refresh my dried tresses, and tied on my red satin scarf. I twirled and fluffed the ends that poked out beneath. I clipped on my large gold hoop earrings. White shirt, red flowing skirt. A slash of red-tinted lip gloss. Ankle socks and clean white sneakers.

Rumor was that the wait at Lucien's place could be hours. He was known to make phone calls, have leisurely talks with staff, even leave the premises between appointments. His shenanigans did little to hurt his clientele, though. They came, they waited, they paid his exorbitant prices and apologized for inconveniencing him. "Image," my dad had told me. "Lucien isn't any better than you at what he does, but he projects an image that makes people believe he is."

Barring the occasional emergency or overrun, I thought it was rude to make your paying customers wait. It was how my father had conducted his business and it was how I ran mine. With a half hour to spare, I made my way back to my Petit Temple Vodoun so I could get everything set up. When I opened the door, I was overwhelmed with thoughts of one of the last clients who'd passed through this door— Sophie Thibault. I wondered if, despite my urging, she'd hightailed it back home to her people or elsewhere.

Turning my mind back to the business at hand, I took the liberty of pulling out a box of multicolored candles.

Fifteen minutes till my appointment. I sat down at the table, gaze resting on Papa's machete. Salimah's denial had come with a certain conviction. She hadn't offered any other insight into who may have wanted to kill Virgil. Her focus, her fear, was for the cousin who had disappeared: on his own or by way of New Orleans PD, I didn't know.

Sophie's mother had confirmed her daughter's story about this other woman visiting Virgil. And Lucien, a whore for the spotlight and self-designated mouthpiece and religious evangelist, had gone mute.

And all this amounted to nothing but a bunch more questions I didn't have the answer to.

Three rapid clink-taps against the glass panes interrupted my thoughts. I hated when people did that. Why use a key when a knuckle did the job? Images of scratches aside, I opened the door, and in sauntered Terence Burns. He had the build of a lumberjack and the height of a preteen. His expression open, curious. Instead of marching over to the table like he owned the place, he quickly stepped aside while I closed the door and gestured for me to precede him. Either a gentleman or playing at one; time would tell which.

People were sometimes nervous being seen coming to a house of Vodou. Everybody needed us, but some would sooner admit to having a taste for raw meat than needing the services of a vodouisant. As long as they paid, that was fine with me.

"Have a seat." I folded my hands on the table in front of me. "What brings you here today?"

Terence leaned back and crossed his ankle over his knee. "I got what you call a people problem. I need to help someone see the error of their ways."

"You need a wanga," I suggested. "Perhaps you can tell me a bit more about the kind of trouble you're having with this person or people?"

Terence surveyed the room and scratched at the back of his neck. His eyes had lit up as I talked.

"This one neighbor," he said when he could meet my eyes again. "Caught them looking in my window. That ain't right, you know? Spying on people like that. Stirring up stuff you don't know nothing about."

I raised an eyebrow. A nosy neighbor. Ideas for spells were swirling around in my head. A few questions to narrow things down.

"Assuming, then, that you want a work to direct this person's attention back to their own home and away from yours?"

Mr. Burns shrugged. "Something like that."

Hmm. "Male or female?"

Mr. Burns eyed me strangely. "Does it matter?"

Looking at this man's build, I could only guess that he wasn't worried about one angle. "Are you interested in just having this person redirected or gone? Like to another city or part of town?"

The expression on his face wasn't one of outright malice. There was amusement, somehow more disconcerting.

"There's a spell I'm thinking of," I continued. "It helps you deal with a troublesome neighbor." I rose and retrieved a black candle and dressed it with castor oil. I grabbed a pen and paper and came back to the table. "Write the word 'goodbye' on the paper."

Terence did as instructed and slid the paper back over to me. I lit the candle and set it on top of the paper. Then I took out a piece of paper with the requisite line from Psalm 109, the Judas Psalm.

"Repeat this."

Terence looked at the paper and set it down. "I prefer Proverbs 26:17: 'Interfering in someone else's argument is as foolish as yanking a dog's ears.'"

Hmm. "Why don't you tell me what it is you really want?"

"Ain't me you got to worry about," Mr. Burns said. "See, you a lot like that neighbor. Don't know where to keep your nose pointed. But I can fix all that."

He shot out of his chair and shoved my table aside. It crashed against the wall as I stumbled out of my chair. No potions in hand. But there was no mistaking his intent.

His hand swept behind his back, and I heard the unmistakable sound of a switchblade flicking open a moment before he waved it in front of my face. A million options flashed through my mind. I backed toward the rear of the room, where all my powders and herbs sat. But I dared not turn my back. No time for a spell.

With no time to siphon water from him, I darted back to get the blurring powder.

I'd just laid a hand on the vial when, in what I could only call a playful gesture, he slashed at my back.

I screamed out, more from anger than pain. Though my sangswe wine swirled, I swung around and tried to deliver a groin kick, but he easily dodged it. That gave me time to grab the blurring powder. I blew at him, and he momentarily stumbled.

I charged him this time. I clamped my hands down around his wrists and opened my pores. Then I did something I'd never done before. *The evolution magic realm.* I channeled the sangswe wine from my pores into another human being. I had no idea how it would affect him.

My attacker wrenched away from me, blinking, his eyes reddened. He grimaced and began scratching at the back of his neck. He turned and bolted for the door. I glanced at the glass-encased machete on the wall, but there was no time. I pursued.

I found Terence facedown, halfway up the little stone path leading to the curb. I touched the side of his neck and found a pulse. Then I noticed the thick, ropy scar on the back of his neck. Something about that scar scratched at my memory's surface. Two blinks later, the wound changed. It hissed and bubbled. The festering mess spread in a widening arc.

I fought the sickness gathering in my belly and nudged him with my foot. Nothing. I ran back inside, locked the door. I hesitated. There was something familiar about that man, but I couldn't pin it down. It was time to call a certain detective who I knew would be pissed to hear from me again so soon.

~

In a few places, even mistakenly, people expected to feel safe: neighborhood barber or beauty salon, church, and home. From my experience, this expectation was not based on the fact that bad things never happened in these places; of course they did. But in most people's minds, they shouldn't have.

The man knocked out on the pathway leading back to my place of business apparently did not subscribe to the same beliefs as the rest of us.

"And you've never seen this man before?" Roman looked tired, more so than usual. Maybe it was me. Maybe the job had begun to take its toll on him. I'd told him it would.

"No." This was the second time he'd asked. And what surprised me was that he was genuine. I hadn't bothered to flip the man over, but when they had, his reaction had been the same. He didn't recognize him, but I had. He was the same man the police had been scuffling with when I'd snuck in to see Salimah. I was already feeling the fatigue from the dehydration. I'd released too much water. I braced myself for the next question.

"The paramedics say that wound on his neck . . ." Roman paused, looking upward at the night sky, which didn't hold so much as a cirrus cloud. He took me by the elbow, guided me away a few steps, and whispered, "His blood pressure is low, too low. And that wound on his neck. It looks like he's got some sort of infection, but that don't explain why he's out cold. Did you do a little something extra to him?"

I had indeed. The element of water magic evolution, in its physical form, can manipulate time, in a sense. Just as I could ripen a piece of fruit with a smidgen of sangswe wine, I could, apparently in this case, speed up the festering of a wound.

I didn't mention any of that to Roman.

I held up the stun gun that I'd bought to make him happy back when we were still a couple. "This." I lied well when I needed to. "This is the only thing I used. I don't know what else to tell you."

Roman arched an eyebrow at me, and I held the practiced blank expression on my face like a mask. I blinked once or twice to help pull it off. Darby hadn't made the trip out with him, so it was another officer who came up and tore his attention away from me. I watched as the intruder was loaded onto a gurney.

"Detective Frost." The policeman was a tall, thin man, pale skinned in a way that made me question his ethnicity. His eyes flicked over to me and back to Roman, probably trying to figure out why a detective had been called. "Couldn't get anything out of him. Okay to release the paramedics? They want to head over to the hospital."

"Yeah," Roman said. "We'll get someone over there later."

"Looks like another robbery attempt." The cop flipped his notebook closed and strode off toward his squad car.

Roman shook his head. "You sure you all right? Do you need to go get checked out?"

An unexpected turn. Despite himself, despite myself. There was still something—

"Reina?" He laid a hand on my arm. "You're freezing." He turned and waved over one of the paramedics.

"I'm fine." I'd held myself up longer than my body would allow. The dizziness took me at the same time as a muscle cramped in my thigh, and I stumbled into Roman. My protest went unheard. I was dragged over to the ambulance and parked right behind my attacker.

They listened to my heart, checked my temperature, and slapped what probably amounted to a Band-Aid on the scratch on my back. Then, thankfully, they handed me a bottle of water. With each gulp, the effects of the dehydration abated and I felt more like myself. It helped enough for me to shake them off. It wouldn't do to go to the hospital.

Nothing went unnoticed in New Orleans. The people who lived here knew it, and the outsiders who had decided to move here after Katrina had learned it. If the lights from the squad cars and ambulance hadn't drawn them, the noise and commotion would have. My neighbors stood, staring openly.

Ms. Lucy stood at the edge of the crowd and made a move to come forward. I shook my head lightly, and she remained in place. The old lady annoyed me to no end, but she'd jump on Roman's back in a heartbeat if she thought he was going to harm me. She knew him, never approved of our relationship, but she also knew he was a cop, and trust for his kind was pretty thin.

Roman took a moment to stare down each and every pair of eyes that watched him, some poised to do harm if they felt they could get away with it. They didn't know it, but I wouldn't allow that either. Folks began to disperse after that.

"You want to do the statement now, here, or tomorrow at the station?"

In response, I turned to walk into the house, and I heard Roman's light and springy footsteps behind me. I cursed myself for being glad of the fact.

CHAPTER NINETEEN

"How's your back?" Roman kicked off his shoes beside mine and followed me to the kitchen.

"It's a scratch," I said, and I wondered at why. My assailant had had a clear view of my back. Why not sink the knife in and be done with it? Why bother with a scrape at all? "Tea?"

"Sit," Roman said, then added after a minute, "please."

Though it sounded like a command, there was no edge to it. I filled a glass of water from the refrigerator and did just that. We sat across from each other, and I watched him watching me. I didn't flinch this time. Didn't turn away from that twinkling of concern. What, under more favorable circumstances, could've passed as love. I gulped the water down and then went for another glass.

"Tell me everything." I tensed at the lack of vitriol in Roman's voice. The sarcasm and barbs gone. If anything, he sounded tired. I let myself relax.

I stitched together the unlikely pieces of the story in my head and relayed them in one seamless stream. The new-client appointment that I'd been so excited about this morning. Exactly when I knew the ruse was up. I even did a passable job of choreographing the attack—minus the whole watery release.

"Why did he run?"

"Huh?"

"He had you cornered, alone. He'd already drawn blood. Did he take anything?"

He hadn't. I kept my mouth shut.

"Then, after drawing blood, nothing between you but a few potions and powders and those dolls you keep up on the wall." Roman was all business now. "What did you do to scare him off?"

These were all questions I had asked myself. Maybe I was becoming more of a detective than I thought.

"Maybe it was the stun gun," I said. "I don't know. Investigate. Find out who he is and then *you* tell me. And it wouldn't hurt to do the same for Salimah."

"This again?"

"Hear me out." I leaned in. "Salimah was probably at home asleep when Virgil was murdered. She showed up to work as normal and went on about her business until she heard a scream. Sophie Thibault's scream. Salimah goes upstairs and the door was already open and we know what she found. *She* called the police. And that altar y'all found? It was staged. There was a doll there with blond hair and blue eyes. That's not the way this works, and whether you want to admit it or not, you know that. That's the work of somebody that's seen too many movies. An amateur."

Roman didn't speak, but he leaned back, fist beneath his chin, and tapped his cheek with his thumb. I nearly leaped out of my chair. He was thinking. He was actually considering the facts as I'd laid them out. I could've kissed him. I *wanted* to kiss him. It was hard to miss how well he filled out his clothing. Not overly muscular, but toned and fit, just the way he'd always been.

He looked down, drummed his fingers on the table. "How'd you know about what was at the crime scene?"

At that moment, he lifted his gaze to mine, hoping to see me falter. Apparently, I was the amateur. I hid my nervousness behind another sip of water and fumbled through my two choices in the time it took to set the glass back down. "Before you arrived, Rashad told me."

This time, I watched Roman for any telltale signs that mentioning the poor boy's name would startle him in any way. It didn't, but that didn't mean anything.

"Your evidence is shoddy," Roman said. "Your clues amount to nothing. Every murderer that's ever murdered somebody was sound asleep at home. That's the oldest alibi in the book."

Each word was like a slap. I railed, "How can you say that?"

"The fact that somebody would even set up something to look like voodoo says a lot about your religion."

"Tradition." I slapped my palm on the table. "It's a sacred tradition. And how many people have been killed in the name of Christianity? A cool billion or two? Don't make me laugh. You call what you're doing an investigation. A street kid could do better. Is it time to fill another arrest quota? You made a shitty choice becoming a police officer." I stood up.

And Roman scrambled to his feet, came around the table, and kissed me. My arms lay at my sides at first, but as his lips traced a path down my neck, I embraced him. He held me, and we stood that way together for so long that the voice in my head that said this was a mistake was reduced to nothing. The anger, the case, everything gone except this moment and the memories of what it was like to belong to someone.

As Roman led me back to my bedroom, I resolved to allow myself this small pleasure. A glimpse of the life we could have had. The spare bedroom that could have become the nursery for the plump, gurgling baby we'd have by now. A future.

⁓

I watched Roman from the front porch, grateful that nobody else was up yet to witness him leaving. In the moment that I'd had to search his eyes before he leaned down and kissed me on the cheek, I couldn't discern whether the look of contentment on his face was merely an ecstasy-induced afterglow or the rekindling of something else.

He hadn't promised to call. No plans had been made. He hadn't really said a proper goodbye.

Roman glanced back at me after he opened his car door, his face full of something unreadable. I recognized the conflict, which sat like weeks-old collard greens in the pit of my stomach. He held my gaze for a breath that seemed like forever, then winked at me. I closed the door to the wrenching sound of his car easing away from the curb.

To me, anger was like a dragon. It sat alongside the good and moral part of you. It was the balance, you see. You wouldn't want to kill the dragon. You'd want to tame it. The fire could be useful in certain situations. When you needed to stand up for yourself. When you needed to stand up for someone else. And right now, that person was Mambo Salimah Grenade.

But first, I needed to start the seven-day cleansing process that would rid my space of all the previous day's negativity. My faith taught us to bless nature and support cosmic harmony for the purposes of mastering divine magnetism.

I dressed, then headed outside. My stomach made noises about breakfast, but I'd settle for a cup of tea when I was done. My energy and the energy in my home were off.

I avoided looking at the pathway as I padded across the grass; even the little canary bench couldn't sway my mood. I paused. Someone had invaded my sanctuary with what I now knew was intent to scare, not really harm. After a few deep breaths, I went inside, set my table right, and gathered up supplies in a small basket.

Murmuring prayers, I called to the lwa. Soon, my skin tingled with their presence. Soothing fingers caressed my skin with a touch even the most skilled masseuse couldn't match. Their healing breaths filled my nostrils with a scent like wildflowers. Grass swayed and bent as if under the forces of a cleansing brush.

It was as if the spirits carried me over to the spot where, the night before, my attacker had lain, handily subdued. I took out the talc powder and short-handled broom. After coating the area with the powder, I knelt and brushed it in with the broom.

Once that was properly worked in, it was time for the next part. Walking in a circle, I dropped a pinch of snakeroot every few inches. The whole area churned. Good.

Finally, in the center of the space, I measured out five drops of Van Van oil mixed with a little lemongrass. This mixture would eliminate any remaining negativity and ward off my assailant's evil spirit.

It was done, and the lwa, satisfied, returned to their realm. I mourned their absence each time.

With my house in order, I turned on the water for a bath and was going to grab the epsom salts when I saw the little box. My breath caught. Inside were the baby-size comb and brush set I'd bought in . . . hope? Anticipation? I shoved the box farther back on the shelf and grabbed the salts and oils. But the sight had forced the memory of the small pleasure I'd allowed myself to have with Roman and the emotions it had stirred up.

Among other lingering questions, he'd not given me an answer about Salimah's cousin. Whether he'd been arrested or the fright I'd seen on his face had driven him back to Houston, I wasn't sure. But I'd get Tyka to ask around.

When I was done, I eased out of the now-tepid water, oiled my body, and went to the kitchen. It'd been a few days, and I wanted to take Tyka and her father something decent to eat. I flipped through Darryl's list of what he called his "idiot-proof recipes" and settled on a dish.

It came as no surprise that I didn't have half the ingredients I needed. I knew just the little ragamuffin to make a quick grocery store run. I'd met Jason the previous year, standing outside the store hawking packs of M&M's. He was one of New Orleans's growing number of street children.

I hadn't seen him in a few weeks, which wasn't unusual: he was fiercely independent and had rebuffed all attempts to help him. But asking him to run an errand would give me a chance to lay eyes on him.

"Hello?" he said into the phone I'd given him.

"Jason, this is Reina. You have time to make a run for me?"

"Shut up!" Jason growled at someone in the background and then immediately code-switched, his voice again that of an eleven-year-old boy. "'Course I can, mistress."

How many times had I told him to call me Reina? I'd also told him he could sleep here if he needed to, and he'd never listened to that either.

"Can you come by here and get the money?" He roamed Tremé and likely robbed tourists in the Quarter. He was never too far away.

"Be there directly." The remnants of his late grandmother's Alabama dialect were all the boy had left of her. And it still sounded strange coming from his mouth.

My next call was to Salimah's public defender. I relayed all that I knew. I told him that he should put more pressure on the police to continue the investigation. He made little noises at the appropriate times—I might have even heard him scribble a note or two—but eventually, he huffed as if I'd dampened the better part of his day with my call and said, "Look, I have to be in court in fifteen minutes."

I resisted the urge to cast a nasty spell on the man but got him to agree to meet before I hung up.

I was sitting there staring with rage at the phone in my hand when I heard a knock at the door. There stood Jason. Aside from the smudge of dirt on his forehead, he and his clothes were surprisingly clean. I let him inside and handed him money from my wallet and the short list of things I'd need from the store.

"Where did you sleep last night?" I asked.

He looked up, as if searching for an answer that would satisfy me. "At my friend's house. From school—when I used to go."

I sighed. I didn't know which to be angrier about: the possibility that he was lying or the fact that he wasn't in school. I'd tried; the social worker I'd called had even tried. But each time he'd gone back to the school or a foster home, he'd been back out on the street in a week.

While some folks wouldn't understand, in our neighborhood we knew what the foster care system did to a child. He'd bolted from his last foster home after an incident he wouldn't speak of, and not one of us had had the heart to make him go back. It wasn't an easy choice. Maybe wasn't even the right choice, but instead, he'd become a neighborhood child of sorts, and we helped him where we could. Where he could let us, that was. He didn't miss a meal, had clean clothes most of the time, and, more nights than not, had somewhere warm to sleep. We'd even gotten him the cheap cell phone so we could reach him. And he guarded it like he tried to guard us when we were around.

"I need that stuff now, not later, okay? Just go to the market down the street." Jason had a tendency to wander and accept other jobs while he was doing yours.

He grinned and was out the door. Next, it was time to see if I could find Ms. Tyka Guibert. So I filed my trepidation away for pondering another time and hit the third speed dial button on my phone. Number one was Dad and two was Darryl, since I'd removed Mom's disconnected phone number.

"Wassup, Mambo?" Tyka's voice carried an early-morning edge.

"You still asleep?" I asked.

"If you mean was I asleep before your ass woke me up? Yeah."

I sighed but hoped she didn't hear it.

"I heard that shit." Tyka definitely sounded awake now. "*You* called and woke *me* up. Coulda waited to a decent hour. Heard folks that was raised right had manners. I can't say myself, but that's what I heard."

"I'm sorry to wake you up so early, Tyka." There was no arguing with her when she was like this.

"If this ain't some emergency shit, can you hit me up later?"

I heard a cough or a mumble in the background. I wondered if it was her dad or someone else. I'd never seen Tyka with a boyfriend or girlfriend, and she wasn't one to discuss her love life. She had let me know she didn't approve of my relationship with Roman, though.

"I just need your help a little later. Okay if I come pick you up about three?"

"A'ight."

And she hung up.

Some people couldn't stand to be idle. I was not one of them. I loved my city and loved my home even more. Now that it was purified again, I was content to sit and relax and turn things over in my mind. The kitchen was my sanctuary, despite Darryl's claims that I didn't know what I was doing in there. And my shop was the best workspace I could have ever imagined. But the couch that sat in front of the picture window at the front of the house let the morning sunlight fall on you with just the right intensity. So that was where I decided to lounge.

I stretched out and pulled the soft throw blanket up to my chin, inhaling the lingering scent of sandalwood incense. My eyelids fluttered closed.

If you'd asked me at the moment when I heard banging at the front door, I would have sworn that only ten minutes had passed. But when I got up and checked the time on my phone, it was just shy of an hour later.

I walked to the front door and saw a grinning Jason standing there holding up two bags. I let him in without a word, and he trudged a few steps before he stopped himself, turned, and kicked his tennis shoes off by the door. I hadn't even needed to raise an eyebrow. I followed him to the kitchen and watched as he unpacked everything and put it away.

When he was done, I handed him a twenty. "Did you get something for yourself?"

He nodded. "I ate the Snickers bar on the way here. I couldn't wait."

"Did you get any *real* food?"

He looked at me as if I had sprouted a goiter from my neck. In his world, every bit of food he could get his hands on was real food. "Go around the corner and pick up a soul food dinner when they open." I handed him another twenty, realizing with a guilty pang that I was nearing the end of my cash on hand. I'd been shirking too many appointments. My bank account, as usual, was on life support again.

He took the twenty. "Thank you, mistr—"

"Reina."

"My granny told me not to call grown folks by they first name."

I didn't argue that. "Thank you, Jason, and don't forget to get some food and eat the vegetables."

"Okay," he said, and I followed him to the front door. "Oh, I forgot. This lady said to give you this."

He reached in his back pocket and pulled out a piece of paper.

"What lady?" I asked, unfolding the sweat-dampened note. It was a photocopy of an obituary for one Gus Darby. Survived by . . . his son, Alton Darby. Roman's partner. Now what did this mean?

"Don't know her. Guess she ain't from around here." Jason slipped his tennis shoes back on and was gone again until next time.

How was Detective Darby involved? Someone was trying to tell me something, but I had no clue what it was. After I kept my promise to Salimah and found Rashad, I'd do some more digging.

CHAPTER TWENTY

I was always hesitant to ask about Tyka's methods. Doing so would have forced me to condone something I may not have been comfortable with. Until this business with Sophie, she had helped me locate only late-paying clients who'd dodged my attempts to collect.

This was my first time involving her in something as serious as a murder investigation. She hadn't batted one of those long eyelashes of hers. It dawned on me fully, then, that I *was* conducting an investigation. Whether motivated by pride or ego or an unhealthy sense of curiosity, it felt like the right thing to do.

I knocked on the door, surprised that Tyka and Eddie had been in one place for what must have been months now.

"A little something for your father," I said, handing her the Tupperware container.

Tyka set it on the kitchen counter, lifted the cover, and jabbed a spoon inside. She gobbled down that bit and went in twice more before replacing the cover and sliding the container into the refrigerator, shoving aside a bag with a big unmistakable yellow *M* plastered all over it. I hoped that, aside from what Darryl and I forced on her, this wasn't all she was eating.

She folded her arms and leaned against the counter. Her hair was done up in lovely Bantu knots. I couldn't help wondering how she slept. She clapped her hands together and rubbed her palms. Ready for orders.

"We need to find Salimah's cousin, Rashad." I didn't tell her about my trip to the police station; nor did I dare mention the tryst with Roman. "She hasn't seen him since the day she was arrested. She's concerned."

Tyka unfolded her arms and nodded. "Either he scared or feelin' guilty 'bout somethin'." She grabbed a bottle of water perched precariously on the edge of the bed and came up beside me where I stood at the door. She didn't spare me a glance as she opened it and walked out.

"Don't you want to lock the door?" I called as I trotted out after her.

"Ain't none." She kept right on walking. "Strutting" was actually the better word to describe Tyka's sure gait. "'Sides," she said, waiting by the driver's side door, "nobody dare go in there but Eddie, and it's early—he won't be good and drunk for another few hours."

I nudged her away from the driver's side door with my hip. With an annoyed sigh, she went on around to the passenger side. She sucked her teeth when I asked her to fasten her seat belt, but she did it anyway. And in between directions to the Lower Nine, we sang along to an old Marvin Gaye song about bad times.

~

News of Virgil Dunn's murder at Voodoo Real was still fresh as the morning dew on the streets, so after asking only a few people about Rashad's whereabouts, Tyka and I found out he'd last been seen at an off-and-on-again girlfriend's house near Bayou Bienvenue. Tyka called someone she knew in that neighborhood, and sure enough, he'd spotted Rashad. She asked him to keep an eye out until we got there.

We took the Claiborne Bridge over and crossed the Industrial Canal, navigating some still-fractured streets. A decade after the storm, vegetation, wildlife, and packs of abandoned wild dogs and cats had reclaimed much of the area. Locals weren't surprised, though. The land here was fertile. Weed and tree-root attacks and beat-backs were a way of life. It took years to tame the growth into something that could coexist with the houses and businesses that returned.

The low-lying marshland was really unfit for people to live in, but population booms were fodder for questionable political maneuvers.

When, after a half dozen missteps, the city had cleared away the debris and growth, those with even a little cash could buy a plot from this most devastated part of the city. Most had moved on and set up new lives, and few wanted to return, but for those who did, bargains could be had.

Newer homes and tree-lined streets dominated the area now. Only a few empty lots remained, some converted to community gardens maintained by students from the high school that the Black Mardi Gras krewes had worked and campaigned and fundraised to build. The Big Chiefs and their clubs had returned, intent on reclaiming the city. So far, they'd succeeded.

"You sure this guy knows what he's talking about?" I asked as we turned down Lamanche at North Rocheblave.

"Nope." Tyka picked at something beneath her fingernails. "But I asked him to call me if Rashad left. Phone didn't ring."

No guarantees. One of my father's favorite sayings.

"Right here," Tyka said and then sat up straight just as someone—a man—emerged from a field of waist-high weeds. How he sat scrunched there with whatever vermin lived in that field, I didn't know and didn't care to ask. He threw up a finger and walked over to the passenger side of the car.

He looked inside the lowered window and nodded at me; I returned the gesture. Then he and Tyka spoke. I caught snatches of the slang I was finding it increasingly hard to keep up with. Tyka passed him something I hoped was money, and he stood and disappeared back into the vegetation like a wraith.

"Rashad gone," Tyka said.

"I thought your, uh, camouflaged friend over there was supposed to call you if he left?"

"Can't call on a phone with a dead battery."

I gripped the steering wheel and whispered, more to myself, "What do we do now?"

"We wait," Tyka said. "If this brotha tryin' to be on the down-low, he ain't gone too far. He'll be back here 'fore too long. Lean back and catch a nap, Mambo."

"You go ahead," I said and then moved the car a little farther away, to where I could watch the house but not be so obvious about doing so. "I'll keep watch for a while and wake you up if I get tired."

The house was probably one of the first new ones built in this area. The small yard was clean, and there was real patio furniture, not a battered couch on the concrete slab that passed for a front porch. But the flower bed was in need of tending.

Tyka reclined the car seat to almost a sleeping position and leaned back. I wondered how in the world she could rest her head on those Bantu knots, but with practice, much that we didn't think was possible, was.

"What's up with Sweet Belly?" Tyka asked. Her head was turned to the side, facing the window, so I couldn't see her face when I glanced over at her.

"He's still breathing." I tried to keep the smile from my voice. I'd never seen two people work so hard to pretend they didn't care about each other while it remained so painfully obvious to anyone else that they did. "Spending too much time at the Lemon Drop, but I don't think he'll have it any other way."

"Cool." Tyka pulled my jacket from the back seat and wrapped herself up in it. She didn't say anything else, and soon she was snoring softly.

I checked my phone's time every few minutes. I cracked the window. I wanted to stand and stretch because my butt and back hurt, but I didn't want to wake Tyka. My crotch was wet and not in a good way: the unusually warm spring getting the best of me. I hated this, and if this was what being a detective entailed, I emphatically declared this to be my first and last case.

I listened to make sure Tyka's breathing was slow and even, that she was still asleep. I accelerated the sweat, funneling out all my body's excess moisture. The cooling effect was small at first, but growing. Armpits, hairline, even the wet spot above my upper lip, all cooled and dried. I dared not draw too much. I was cooler but ridiculously thirsty now, and I reached for the water bottle in my bag. I chugged half of it in a few gulps.

An hour and a half had passed, with just my phone to help me fight off the encroaching need for sleep. Something told me my companion needed the rest, so I let her be. I didn't want to think of how many nights she'd gone out in search of a father who sometimes was too drunk to make it home on his own. I'd witnessed it myself more than once. I supposed, with the loss of her mother, she was going to do everything she could to keep her father, no matter what shape he was in.

Just when I was about to call it a day, I saw someone hurrying down the street, looking back over his shoulder. A bundle of nerves and guilt. I'd seen Rashad only a couple of times, but the slender frame and hunched shoulders marked him easily enough.

I shook Tyka's arm. She snapped alert so fast that it scared me. No bleary-eyed mumbling or grogginess. Her eyes fixed on Rashad, and a smirk (or a snarl) curled her lips. "That's our boy," she said, and her breath filled the car with an odor that could be subdued by only a toothbrush or an Altoids mint. I had neither.

"That's him," I agreed, and I was grateful that I'd soon be able to get out of the car. After Rashad had cast a last, furtive glance over his shoulder, I moved to start the car. Tyka put a hand on the wheel. "Don't want to scare him away. We can walk."

She was right. We walked down the street—thankfully empty—and in a few steps, we were at the front door. Tyka placed her thumb over the peephole. I knocked.

In the movies, when someone knocks at the door, the soon-to-be victim flings it open without a thought. Reality, as is usually the case, was much different. That meant the chances that Rashad or his girlfriend would open the door were slim.

"It's Mambo Dumond," I called out in a bid to increase our chances. "I'm here about your cousin Salimah."

Silence. Tyka shrugged.

"Who?" a male voice said. "Who's got their hand over the hole?"

I gestured for Tyka to move her finger. Another moment or two passed, during which my patience grew thin. A series of locks clicked, and the door swung open. Rashad glanced between Tyka and me but made no move to invite us in.

He looked a little worse for wear. At least a few days' uneven stubble covered his face in the spots acne hadn't claimed.

"Something wrong with Salimah?" he asked, and there was genuine concern in his expression. Before I could answer, though, Tyka moved forward a step.

"Ain't you got no manners, boy? Don't nobody wanna be standing out here on the porch talkin' personal business."

Rashad was timid by most male standards, however arbitrary, but he was still a man and wasn't prepared to back down so easily. "Who are you? I don't even know you to let you in here." He tried to puff out his chest a bit, which took him from parakeet to somewhere in the neighborhood of cockatoo. He even glared. I was about to intervene when Tyka began to laugh. First in short, incredulous bursts, then full bellied. She'd probably wrestled men like Rashad in kindergarten.

"Rashad, please," I said, trying to suppress my own laughter. "I just need a few minutes of your time." There. I'd provided him a way to save face.

He stepped aside and held the door open. "Can she wait outside?" He moved to close the door on Tyka.

Wrong move. She used her forearms to barge in, causing Rashad to stumble back, barely able to keep his feet. He and Tyka stood huffing and glaring at each other.

"Tyka, that's enough." It took her a moment to acknowledge me, and when she did, anger and hurt smoldered behind her eyes. "Both of you," I added to soften the blow. "We're here to try to help Salimah, that's it."

Rashad seemed to shrink in on himself at the mention of his cousin.

"You can sit down," he said. Tyka remained standing as always. A book and a notepad sat on the coffee table. A fleeting glance at the title told me it held secrets related to running a successful business.

The house was a new take on the traditional New Orleans shotgun. It was a bowling alley: one long, rather narrow space with, a few doors down, a hallway leading to likely bedrooms and a bathroom. After our extended stakeout and downing that bottle of water, I needed to use the facilities something awful but feared if I left Rashad and Tyka alone right now, she'd hurt him.

The room was sparsely furnished, but what I saw was neat and clean. I heard a toilet flush from somewhere down the hall, and my bladder seized up. I took a seat on a black leather sofa to stall it, and Rashad sat opposite me in a recliner.

"Your cousin is okay." I left out the bruised condition I'd found her in. No need to get him any more upset than he already was. "But she's worried about you. Were you arrested?"

There was a sharp intake of breath, and Rashad rubbed his palms against his thighs. His jeans were intentionally ripped in a style that, though inexplicable, had survived decades. He tapped his socked feet.

"Those assholes," he said, earning another giggle from Tyka. He didn't look at her, but his lips thinned. "They kept me down there all day and half the night. Asking the same questions over and over. Nothing to eat and brown water that was supposed to be coffee."

Salimah had been right, but at least he'd been released. "Is it possible that you or someone else in your family can retain an attorney for her?"

Rashad's features twisted. "I don't have that kind of money. And Salimah ain't been able to turn a real profit on the shop yet. Can't y'all do something?"

By "y'all," I suspected he meant the vodouisant community—namely Lucien Alexander. I didn't want to tell him that I had, in fact, tried to get Lucien to help but had been rebuffed.

"Not likely."

Rashad threw up his hands. "What am I supposed to do? I don't have money for no lawyer." He leaned back and ran a palm over his face. "I knew that white dude was bad luck. I just couldn't put my finger on it. And that Sophie. Little Miss Sunshine she is not."

I couldn't argue with him. And my bladder's protest was at a dangerous precipice. "Do you mind if I use your bathroom?"

Rashad blinked; then his gaze flickered over to Tyka. "Second door on the right."

"And can I have some water, please?" Tyka's request sounded every bit a demand.

As Rashad sheepishly did as he was told, I gleefully relieved myself. When I came out, the urge to snoop around overwhelmed me as much as the smell of a good barbecue. I checked the first room next to the bathroom. It was empty save an old but well-kept brass bed and a colorful rug.

I plastered an ear to the last door and, hearing nothing, stepped into what turned out to be the master bedroom, painted a shade of red that would have kept me up all night. The other surprise? Sitting on the bed, surrounded by stuffed animals, bobbing her head to whatever music flowed from a pair of over-the-ear headphones was, most likely, Rashad's girlfriend.

"You that voodoo priestess, right?" she asked. She set down her phone and removed the headphones, setting them on a knick-knack-filled nightstand. Even with the dowdy gown she wore, she was an attractive girl. Plump. Hair cut in a bob that looked like it had been done with a razor. She seemed oddly unfazed by my appearance.

I smacked my forehead. "I'm sorry. I was looking for the bathroom."

She pursed lips slick with a glittery gloss and lined with a dark pencil and chuckled. "Heard you flush a minute ago."

It was then that I noticed her headphones covered only one ear. Liars had three options when caught: spin another, more impressive tale, admit it and accept the consequences, or keep their trap shut and see how things played out. My choice was clear.

"You over here snooping around, trying to help Salimah, when I wouldn't doubt for a minute she killed that man. She ain't who you think she is. I bet she the one that tried to put the cops on Shad."

"What? She asked me to come look for him; she was worried—"

"Worried about losing that store over in the Quarter. That's all she cares about."

When I stood there with my mouth open, she continued.

"Shad been reading up on all these ways to build up the business. But she won't listen. I bet she didn't look like she shed any tears over that dead man, did she?"

"But she wouldn't use . . ." I let the thought trail off. If the girl was prepared to talk, why not let her?

"And that should have been Rashad's shop in the first place." She stretched out her legs.

"What do you mean?" I took the liberty of stepping fully into the room and noticed a dragon figurine on the nightstand. Another interesting decorating choice.

"It was Shad's daddy that put up the money for it; he should be the one running it." She paused and shook her head. "He don't even see it, though. She may as well be his mother, and he won't go against her for nothing. Don't matter what I say."

"Well, maybe now he'll get his chance," I said.

She nodded her assent. "He's studying up with that priest out in the swamp too. He gonna be ready soon."

Priest in the swamp, I thought. Before I could ask who she was talking about, the sounds of a scuffle interrupted us.

First, I saw the water bottle on the floor. Water splattered on Rashad's chest. He faced me, wide eyed and sweating. He jerked and clawed at Tyka's forearm where it was wrapped around his throat. Damn it!

"Tyka, let him go!" I marched into the living room. Tyka did manage to look sheepish when she released him. But Rashad swung around and caught her with a right cross to the cheek before either of us registered the movement. He looked nothing like the timid man who'd met us at the door.

Tyka stumbled and I raced forward to separate them, Rashad's girlfriend right behind me.

Tyka rushed in on Rashad, blocking his ineffectual blows, then brought her right elbow up and connected with his chin.

Rashad went down. "You need to be grabbing him," Tyka said, straightening her clothes. "He was the one talking shit about you."

I grabbed my friend and dragged her out of there. But not before I registered the look that Rashad shot at Tyka's back. It was a look of pure menace, one that sent chills up my normally steady spine.

CHAPTER TWENTY-ONE

All that glitters ain't gold. Manman said those words to me every time I pointed out a shiny new bike or the fancy dress another girl wore. It was her way of telling me that despite what you saw on the outside, you never really knew what was going on in somebody else's house.

Granted my visits were few, but when I'd crossed Voodoo Real's threshold, I'd found what I'd thought was a family business, united. Instead, cracks had begun to appear in that facade. Salimah, at least, would resort to questionable practices when it suited her and, if Rashad's girlfriend was right, may have come by ownership of the shop at her own cousin's expense.

The real revelation, however, had been that Rashad, bless his heart, was training with a priest. That business book I'd spied on the coffee table made sense. He was hoping to make a go of running the shop until his cousin's legal troubles were over. Nobody knew a child like their parent, and it was crystal clear that the boy's father didn't think he had what it took. Nothing I'd seen of him had convinced me otherwise.

Though Papa didn't advertise it and would often flat-out deny it, he still took on the occasional student to supplement his income. What had happened in Haiti had scarred him—he had vowed to anyone who would listen that he'd never practice again, and he hadn't. At least not openly.

If I only marginally believed it possible that Rashad was training with a priest, I had no misconceptions that Papa would take on an apprentice that green, but maybe he knew who in the area would.

Doubt about the whole scenario lingered, but it gave me a good excuse to go and visit my father. So I found myself heading north on I-10 toward the Manchac swamplands he called home. On a good day, I could get there in an hour and a half. Today, I made it in just under an hour and fifty minutes.

I crawled through narrow streets peppered with houses so hidden by trees that I could barely make them out. Long, winding driveways, some paved, some not. Colorful flowers. It made me feel as if I were a world away from the noise and lights of New Orleans. If the pace there could be described by outsiders as slow, Manchac—Akers to some—was downright lethargic. In the best way possible.

Verdant, prismatic greens as far as the eye could see. A luscious springtime humidity just shy of eighty. The scent of the place, earthy and mossy and still.

The only marker for the long road that led to Papa's house was an unpaved patch in an otherwise unbroken sea of grass. I eased down the path, crowded on both sides with towering cypress and tupelo trees.

Low wails emanated from the sparse weeping willows, their branches heavy with the grief of the spirits taking up temporary residence there. When they were ready, they'd move on and make space for others in transition.

Two curves lay in the road ahead, one leading left, toward the swamp, the other to Papa's house. I glimpsed left and caught sight of a group of people, all dressed in white. One man supported another, smaller man. With each step, the smaller man straightened and seemed to grow stronger. I did not wonder long who had helped him.

My thought was confirmed as I neared the house. A goat grazed nearby, payment. Papa loved and cared for goats better than he had our childhood German shepherd. I parked next to his ancient truck and took in the tree branches draped with straw bags. Offerings for Atisou.

I stepped out, and midstretch, my skin tingled in anticipation. Just then, a swarm of butterflies alighted from nowhere and everywhere. They flittered out of the brush, swooped down from overhead. I didn't move, wasn't afraid, as they came and inspected me. One by one, it seemed, each touched my hair, my arm, my nose. I inhaled their scent, at once pungent and sweet.

The butterflies flew as if they were a flock of seagulls and landed on the tree nearest the edge of the porch. A few of the lower branches were bare and weakened. Slowly, starting from the tip and working back toward the trunk, the branches began to heal. Leaves sprouted, color returned.

Their task complete, the butterflies swirled up, took the shape of Atisou's vèvè, and then shot up like a slingshot into the sky. When I looked back down, my father stood before me.

"*Bonjou, pitit fi m.* What brings you out to the swamp?" Papa towered over me, clutching his red staff in one hand. He wore cutoff shorts and a Southern University sweatshirt that had to be at least a decade old. The cheek he leaned down and offered for a kiss could have used a shave.

"You had to make a show of it, didn't you?" I said, heading for the house.

Inside, I grinned at his raised eyebrow, took off my shoes, and put on the slippers I left here for my visits. I also left a pair or two of pajamas, a change of clothes, and a toothbrush just in case.

The aroma of something deliciously spicy filled the air.

Once my mother was gone, Papa had taken to doing all his works in the house, especially since he had few visitors. The dining room table was a playground of vials and plants and powders. All tools of the master of healing's disciples. "What are you working on?" I asked.

Papa beamed. "Ain't perfected it yet, but it's a new healing spell. Come look at this."

A thin willow branch sat on the table, along with a few bottles, what looked like a jug of holy water, and white candles.

"Light the Guardian Angel candle for me," he said. I went to the kitchen and got a pack of matches from the drawer.

"*Respire.*" At Papa's command, the leafy sprigs lifted and began to sway as if dancing. He held up both palms then, fingers splayed. Papa was like a conductor in front of an orchestra.

He curled in a thumb on each hand, and the sprigs snapped off the branch, wiggling over and writhing in front of us. I was transfixed.

Papa whispered again, and the willow sprigs jumped into a pot on the electric two-burner he had plugged in.

"Ten leaves from a caranday palm tree." He lifted the bottle labeled PALM and dumped in some without measuring. I could never do that. Not yet.

"All right, pour in two cups of Florida water." I turned to go to the kitchen again and look for a measuring cup.

"You don't need no cup." I did. I really did. But instead, I picked up the jug and started pouring.

I started out with a trickle.

"Don't act like you scared of it. Get to it."

I splashed in some more and stopped.

Papa peered at me. "Told you. Now add in a drop or two of yours to make up for that quarter tablespoon you shy."

I grinned and cringed at the same time. I'd stick to measuring cups. I graciously opened my pores and allowed a bit of my sangswe wine to drop into the pot. Papa was the only person alive who had ever seen me do so. When I finished, he turned on the pot and handed me a cup of water to replenish myself. He set the burner on the lowest setting.

"May as well grab a bowl of jambalaya and come on out back to the porch while that cooks up."

It was still breakfast time, but with Papa, there were no timetables for food. Growing up the way he did, you ate whatever you had, whenever you could. Bowls in hand, we went to the screened-in back porch. It was more like another living room than an outside space. A couple of lumpy sofas, a television, a ceiling fan, and he even kept trays for us to eat on. I sat beneath his glass-encased machete. A near mirror image of my own, it was the one he'd trained me with. Those sparring sessions had been epic.

Between mouthfuls and passing the time talking on his overall health, I started. "When is the last time you took on an apprentice?"

"Poukisa ou mande?" He scraped the last of his bowl and downed a glass of water. He wasn't going to answer without an explanation.

I inhaled and exhaled a deep breath, ready for the lecture. "It has to do with the murder."

Papa's spoon clanked loudly in the bowl where he'd tossed it. *"Avan ou monte bwa, gade si ou ka desann li."* He rattled off the warning in Haitian Creole. "Why are you still poking around when I told you plain as I could to drop it?"

Eyes closed, I searched for words to make clear what I'd already said. A sharp retort poised on the peak of a mountain, with only one way down. "Because nobody else seems to care if an innocent woman goes to jail for murder, Daddy," I huffed.

"You best watch your tone," he admonished. "And how do you know she is innocent, huh? Tell me that." Dad folded his arms and leaned back like he'd just scored a goal.

"That's the thing. I don't know anything for sure," I admitted. "But I'm trying to find out."

He stared at me and didn't have to say anything. While Manman ranted and raved, Daddy's silence was always the worst punishment he could dish out. And he wielded it like the most complicated of magics.

Eventually, he spoke. "You know when me and your grandpa used to go fishing, things never turned out the way we expected. We went in looking for blue crab and came out with yellowfin tuna. And you know that tuna brought out them bees something fierce. One time those bees were on my fish and I was determined to swat them away, but when I did, about four or five of them little bastards bit me."

"I know what you're saying—"

"Mind you do." His voice was like a door closing.

Papa and I sat together on the back porch, meal finished. Nursing our bruised feelings.

"Salimah, the vodouisant they arrested. Well, I heard her cousin was training with a priest in the swamp."

"I ain't the only priest doing some teaching out here."

"I know that, Papa." My goodness, things were never easy with him. "Have you heard of anyone coming out this way? Youngish, bird chest."

"Would this here young man have any skills?"

"None," I said. Rashad had less skill than a first-year apprentice.

Papa shook his head. "Not that it's any of your business, but I did take on an apprentice a while back. But this young man is fierce, confident. Knows how to shake a hand and look a man in the eye. He got some propensity about him too. I don't take on no amateurs. But I'll ask around about this *jèn bray* you talking about."

It was a long shot. But at least I'd had a chance to check on my father. It was time to head back home, and I told him so. I hadn't noticed it before, but a picture of him and Manman a long time ago sat on a stand in the living room. It hadn't been there the last time I was here. I stopped to pick it up.

"You still miss her," I said.

Papa's face changed then. The anger was there, but for once, the pain shone through. "Despite what you think, I loved that woman. You don't stay married to somebody for that long if you don't."

Not for the first time, it tweaked me that he spoke about her in the past tense. "I know that, and no matter what you think, she knew it, and, in her way, she loved you too. It's just this"—I gestured around the room—"it was always too much for her. It took us away from her, and she felt like there was no place for her to fit in."

Papa nodded.

"Hard to believe we never heard anything about her," I said.

His expression dulled like a worn knife. "That's the thing. I didn't hear anything; it was what I saw."

I could get mad at him. I *was* mad at him. But then, I'd never shared Manman's last text message with him either. It was just too heart wrenching, and I suspected he was trying to protect me, same as I did for him. But I was ready to hear it now.

"Tell me."

"Before they bulldozed the house, I searched it, before you. A suitcase was missing. And a few other things. Things she loved, that she cared about, I mean. It looked like she packed."

This again. She didn't just up and leave us. "Looters, Papa. Anybody could have taken those things."

"That's why I didn't tell you."

It was dark outside by the time I summoned the courage to leave. The talk with Papa had been raw, and I didn't want to leave him. He'd retreat for a while, if I knew him. Talk about Manman did that to him. He'd need some time, and so would I. Human beings reserved their most potent venom for the ones we love. Vodouisants were no exception. I was a woman, full grown with a string of mistakes trailing me like a piece of soiled bathroom tissue hanging from my shoe. But right now, I wanted my mother. And I realized that, at least in part, her disappearance drove me. If I couldn't solve her mystery, I'd solve someone else's.

Back home, I showered in a fog, ignored my rumbling stomach, and crawled into bed. The day's dead end robbing me of rest. After several hours, I finally drifted off.

I awoke many times and finally gave up just after the sun had crept beneath the edge of my curtain. My calendar would be a medley of works, thanks to yesterday's cancellations and today's regulars. It was going to be a long one.

CHAPTER
TWENTY-TWO

In search of solace and a good cup of tea among a friendly face or two, I headed over to the Lemon Drop after my last appointment. I parked, hauled the casserole dish out of the car, and slung my purse over my shoulder.

Dusk draped itself over the block and turned pedestrians and vehicles into shadows. A black and white sedan caught my eye. Whether by design or accident, even in the dark, the shape of a police car was hard to miss. It sat alone near the corner, as if the other cars had purposely given it a wide berth. I couldn't tell if anyone was inside. Curious.

Darryl always said that a drink doesn't know or care about the time of day, so I was unsurprised to find the bar already overflowing. Howls and snorts of laughter greeted me at the door.

"Hey, Chicken. Where y'at?" I squeezed into a spot between him and another customer.

"Arite," he said, with his gaze fixed someplace neither he nor, I suspected, anyone else could discern.

Darryl was stationed at a table with a trio of younger men, falling all over each other laughing. I desperately wanted in on the joke.

"Sounds like you had a real interesting visit over to Lafayette," Chicken said. I didn't detect any rebuke in his voice, only an invitation for a story I wasn't willing to dole out.

I set the casserole dish on the bar, and in midsip, Darryl shot me a murderous scowl. I lifted the container to show him nothing had dripped and dirtied up his precious counter. Wasn't he the one who'd demanded I produce these occasional recipes for his evaluation? Though the scowl was gone, skepticism remained. A bar owner with a clean streak the length of the Mississippi. How's that for irony.

"Ran into a few challenges." I turned back to Chicken. "But a necessary trip, and I thank you for the tip." Chicken held my gaze while that hung in the air for a moment. In that glance were measurement and acceptance. Luckily, no more questions.

I considered asking after his family, but I didn't even know his wife's name. I quickly discarded thoughts about quizzing him on his work as Darryl came over and told me Chicken thought of work as something he did for money and not something worthy of discussion in polite company.

Chicken didn't seem to have a hobby I could focus on, either, so in the end, we sat there, comfortably shoulder to shoulder, and I felt a certain peace in his stability. Knowing that on any given day, he'd be right here in this spot. That he'd be Darryl's friend no matter what. That beneath that veneer of quiet probably lay a man of infinite substance.

In time, Darryl approached with a teacup in hand that he slipped across the counter to me. "Do I call you Detective Reina or Mambo Reina nowadays?"

Chicken snorted.

"Just think of me as a mambo taking up a temporary side job," I said. "I'm fully capable of doing more than one thing at a time." I was a bit more indignant than I cared to admit. Was I one of those gritty, seasoned PIs out of the movies? No, and I didn't claim to be. But it seemed to me I was putting in a hell of a lot more work than Salimah's public defender *or* the cops.

"Don't get all touchy on me," Darryl said with a smirk. "You believe this here girl, Chicken? Work one little case and can't take a joke anymore. And I know she was raised better."

"Believe so," Chicken muttered and then pushed his glass forward with a finger. "I won't make mention of another lil' taste to the missus if y'all won't." A bottle materialized in Darryl's hand, and soon the glass was refilled.

I rolled my eyes at the both of them while Darryl broke into one of his full-bellied laughs. Chicken joined in. My cheek twitched. My mouth wanted to stay clenched, but soon I was chuckling too.

The sound of the bell on the door cut Darryl's laugh short. I turned around—too fast.

In walked Detective Roman Frost and his partner, Alton Darby. Whoever it was in that squad car must have tipped them off.

The cacophony in the Lemon Drop dropped ten decibels, and an uncomfortable hush descended. I stared at Darryl, wide eyed. Chicken didn't budge. Not too many people could shake my friend, but he recovered nicely as always.

"Always good to see the NOPD grace the halls of the Lemon Drop," he said, gesturing around the bar. "Can I get you fellas a table?"

I turned to glare at Roman. He locked eyes with me, and it was as if I were a stranger. There was no recognition. I wasn't ashamed to turn away first. After our little rendezvous the other night, he hadn't called, and to be fair, neither had I.

"Mr. Boudreaux—" Roman began.

"Sweet Belly to my friends," Darryl cut in smoothly. Chicken hadn't so much as sniffed when the detectives came in, but now he coughed audibly.

From the mirror behind the bar, I saw Roman move aside his tailored jacket and stuff a hand in his pants pocket. He moved to within a few paces of me, but I refused to turn around again.

"All right, Sweet Belly. You have a permit to serve food in this establishment?" He gestured at the waiter who had just emerged from the back with a tray of food in his hands. He froze, his wary gaze flickering from Darryl to the detectives and back.

Detective Darby detached himself from Roman's hip and strode over to the poor young man. He lifted the fork from the tray and raked over the plate's contents. He shoved a portion of rice and smothered chicken into his mouth. He must have been impressed because he took the plate, brushed his elbow at the patron sitting next to me, and plopped down to finish his meal.

Darryl looked stumped. "I been waiting on the city to come through with that permit goin' on a year. Everythang in order in the back. You can take a look." He shot an unreadable look at Detective Darby. "Don't seem like your man here got a problem with the food."

Roman tsked. "So you don't have a permit, then," he said, feigning sadness. "Maybe I can talk to the folks downtown and see if I can help move things along. No guarantee, of course—you know how slow things can be down there. May take a while, and who's to say? You never know when an inspector's calendar might clear up."

A few more folks who hadn't already run from the bar when the two detectives came in scurried out at that. And I'd had enough. I felt the pull of the water in the pipes, all that I could gather. I spun around.

"What the hell do you think you're doing?"

"You need to show an officer, especially one that overlooked your little stunt at the police station, some respect." This from Detective Darby.

"Doing my job," Roman said. "I'm a cop with the NOPD. I stay in my lane. I do police work. Maybe you should learn something about staying in your lane, particularly out of Lafayette."

"I heard you." Darryl tossed a to-go container on the counter next to my casserole dish. "Your partner here can take his food with him, and both of you can get the hell outta my bar."

"You don't have to stand for this," I said to Darryl. My blood was swirling, the sweat breaking out on my brow. At that moment, Chicken, who'd said nothing up until now, placed a hand on my forearm. He yanked away quickly, probably because of the heat. But it worked. I realized what I was about to do and the irrevocable damage it would have caused.

"Stand down," Darryl whispered.

Roman grinned and shrugged in mock innocence. He motioned at Detective Darby, who gathered up his plate—ignoring the to-go box—and they left. I was surprised at Darby's participation in this little stunt. Taking the plate? That was a Roman move if I'd ever seen one.

"Corrupt muthafuckahs!" Darryl slapped the counter. "You sure done pissed that man off. I told you not to get involved with no cop in the first place. Didn't I, Chicken?"

"Sho' did," Chicken said.

My father's story came to me then. The bees. Roman and Darby, they were the result of all the fuss I'd been kicking up. He was willing to hustle Darryl to stop me. How far would he go?

With the detectives gone, low murmurs from the few remaining customers returned, while my friends and I sat fuming.

Darryl took off the apron he was wearing and tossed it beneath the bar. "I got to go dig up this paperwork so I can call the city in the morning."

He disappeared behind the swinging doors to the back, barking directions at Jimmy.

"You gotta either drop this or come up with something fast," Chicken announced. He slid off his stool, clapped me on the shoulder, and headed for the door.

I sighed. Roman wanted me to drop the case. That all but guaranteed I wouldn't do it. In stooping this low, he'd just proved to me that I needed to keep going. My other choice: help Darryl get the permit. That may not stop the harassment, but it could stall it.

And there was one person I knew who was on friendly terms with politicians.

~

If Roman knew me at all, he should have realized that his little stunt at the Lemon Drop wouldn't scare me off; it'd only make me angry. My parents didn't raise a quitter, and I was never one for being bullied, so if I hadn't already made up my mind, I did now.

If a police detective with a caseload likely the size of a small river had sunk down to the level of harassing my friend, then I must have hit a sore spot. Now it was time to poke it a bit more. I'd been putting it off after our last visit, but with what I'd learned in Cajun country, and the business about Darryl's permit, it was time to pay Lucien Alexander another visit.

After checking with his office, I was unsurprised to learn that he was performing yet another of his high-priced private ceremonies. The man loved being in the public eye when it suited him, but from what I guessed, his private ceremonies raked in the money. Whispers of fees in excess of $1,000 weren't uncommon.

Through my small but reliable network, I knew that Lucien had several local government officials as clients, and it was only for this select group and the celebrities both local and national that he made house calls. They all came to New Orleans, though, since Lucien didn't fly.

My first call had told me he was out of the office. Unsurprisingly, the person on the other end of the phone wouldn't tell me where. It was time to try again. A male voice answered on the third ring. "Thank you for calling Alexander Spiritual. How may the lwa serve?"

I pitched my voice an octave higher. "This is Angela, calling from Councilwoman Moore's office. Has the houngan already left for his appointment? I'm afraid she needs to cancel."

There was a slight hesitation before he responded. "Houngan Alexander doesn't have an appointment with the councilwoman today."

"It's right here on the calendar," I said.

"I'm telling you he has another appointment—you're mistaken."

"Can you double-check, please?"

After a loud exhale, I heard pages flipping, followed by keys tapping. Lucien preferred a paper calendar—didn't want anything sensitive about his clients getting out on the internet—but his staff still used an electronic version. "I told you," the man said after a moment. "It says so right here. One o'clock with Senator King."

"You know, you're right," I said. "I'm on the wrong month. Sorry about that."

I hung up and grabbed my phone and keys. Some people would call what I'd just done social engineering. I called it good old-fashioned common sense. I was getting good at this whole detective thing. If only somebody were paying me for it.

Despite how discreet you were, sometimes details about your client meetings inexplicably got out. I'd heard that Senator King was into having spiritual baths before his normal readings. That meant that Lucien had met him either at home or at the well-known apartment he funded for his mistress. A secret about as well kept as the bribes he'd taken.

I guessed if he was going to be out all afternoon, he was probably going to spend some time with the mistress in a kind of two for one. I guessed right. Lucien's driver had parked the overlarge SUV just outside the four-story building.

Some people were surprised to learn that spiritual baths were indeed just baths. What made them special was the magic.

Regular old tap water was enhanced with potions and works tailored to address the client's troubles. Mostly, baths removed all forms of negativity, anything that could adversely affect the soul. They cleared out bad luck, healed certain illnesses, and even opened the doors to opportunities seen and unseen.

I wondered what type of bad luck would befall one of New Orleans's most corrupt politicians. Whatever it was, Lucien had done a tremendous job of keeping it at bay. Despite many allegations and accusations, not even a rash could stick to Senator King.

I got out of the car and couldn't help admiring my surroundings.

This building, like many others in the area, was part of the ongoing revitalization projects, tastefully done in the traditional New Orleans style. No high-rises here. Flower boxes decorated every window, and the iron Juliet porches were a nice touch, even if they weren't for sitting. There was parking on the street for the public and an alleyway out back that led to residential parking.

My coming here would make Lucien angry. Angry people didn't think straight. They slipped up, and sometimes, amid the nonsensical babble and insults, you got that nugget you needed. That's exactly what I was after.

The building had what I'm sure the builder had thought was a security door, with its fancy-looking digital lock, but it was glass on either side, easy enough for someone to break and slip a hand through. And just as I approached, someone was coming out. Security flaw number two.

He didn't hold the door open for me, though. Didn't need to, as my foot wedged in before it closed. Once I'd made it inside, my gaze floated past walls painted a soothing shade of beige and up a cherry-wood staircase.

There, at the top of the stairs, wearing an expensive charcoal-gray suit, a crisp white shirt, and a striped tie, stood Lucien Alexander. The look on his face had such fury that it almost made me take a step back—almost.

Lucien ground his jaw, and his fingers clenched around the bag he was carrying. He glided down the stairs so fast it was like he'd evoked some of Agassou's magic.

"I'm not even going to waste my time asking how you found me. But let me make this clear for you—you listening?"

I stood my ground, though he crowded me, and nodded.

"Don't you ever show up at one of my clients' homes again. You hear me? You want to talk to me, you can make an appointment and pay my fee like everybody else. If you can afford it. Now what the hell do you want?"

"I need a favor."

Lucien drew his eyebrows together and sighed. He stepped outside, and I followed.

"The cops are hassling Darryl about a food permit. I need you to use the influence we both know you have and speed it along."

He eyed me impassively, considering for a moment. "Done," he said finally. "But next time, just pick up the phone." It was hard to dislike Darryl; not even Lucien could manage it.

"And one more thing," I added. Lucien's expression hardened. "If you covered up something for the police, then why do they still target us—target you—every time something goes wrong that looks a little out of the ordinary?"

Lucien's eyes grew a centimeter wider. The only sign that I'd hit a nerve. He turned his gaze back toward the building and touched my arm, gesturing for us to move farther away. He didn't want this conversation to be overheard. And that made me wonder: If Lucien had so many friends in high places, why couldn't somebody handle the cops for him?

Sacrificial lambs.

It came to me as I was hustled down the walkway and to Lucien's awaiting car. It was like the arrangement that cops had with some of the local drug lords—hell, probably the drug lords in every city. They got to arrest a few and knock a few heads, but the larger business was generally ignored unless the drug lords went too far.

When Lucien's driver got out of the car, he waved him away.

"You don't know what you're talking about or the waters that you're wading into. But I suggest you backtrack. Now. Head back to your little backyard shack and dole out some more hoodoo."

"You're willing to give Salimah up as long as the cops look the other way for whatever enterprises you have going?"

"Do yourself a favor. You've got some talent. And Erzulie, I can tell she lives strong in you. Rely on that and stay out of my way. Stay out of the police's sights. I'm telling you this for your own good."

"What aren't you telling me?"

Lucien banged twice on the hood of the car, and his driver sprang up like a top. He nearly ran around to our side and held the door open for Lucien.

"It's what I *am* telling you that you need to worry about," he said as he handed the driver his bag. He slammed the door shut and spared me a last, pitying glance. After the driver had hustled back in place behind the wheel, Lucien waved his hand in a forward motion. They wove into traffic. I was left standing there while the car trailed off down the street.

My phone chirped. Shit, shit, shit! I'd forgotten about an appointment.

CHAPTER
TWENTY-THREE

For the first time since I'd opened my practice twelve years earlier, I was going to be late for an appointment. Because of the nature of her work, my client was rarely on time anyway, so there was still a chance that my record would remain unbroken.

I peeled around the corner, ready to ease into my always-available space. Screech. I sat there with my mouth agape. A little yellow Mustang sat bold as ever in my spot. Right in front of my house. Did it have a sign proclaiming me as the rightful owner? Not exactly. But everybody knew it just the same. Same as how the space right behind it had unofficially belonged to Roman back when he frequented these parts. That he was a police officer visiting the neighborhood mambo kind of sealed the deal.

I crawled along at a snail's pace, but as I neared the end of the street, every inch of curb was occupied by other cars. Cursing loudly, I turned right at Orleans Avenue and North Rendon, completed the circle around the block, and cruised down the street again. I was in no mood to wait any longer.

I backed up and stopped in front of my house; no use for pretense. I removed a satchel from my purse. The disappearing spell was a relatively simple, though often requested, one. A handful of regular old table salt, dried onion, and shredded bits of a red candle that had been dressed in castor oil. It made a thing—and it had to be a physical object—disappear only inasmuch as it caused someone to move it for you.

I let down the window and voiced the incantation.

"Orevwa."

I blew the contents of the satchel outside in the general direction of the car. The pouch went back in my purse. When funds were low, nearly everything became reusable.

This spell wouldn't do anything to the car; I wasn't a genie. Instead, it sent a subtle urge to the owner that it needed to be gone. The mind created its own story as to why.

Before an ounce of impatience could knit my brow, a woman I didn't recognize came racing out of the house across the street and hopped into the Mustang. In less than a minute, I'd reclaimed what was mine.

I'd stepped out of the car, still muttering about lack of respect, when my phone chirped again. Tyka. I shouldn't have looked: my foot slipped between the curb and the pavement. Sharp, charged pain cleaved my ankle and branched up my leg.

Shit. I let the expletive fly as I limped-ran to the house. Chavonne wasn't on the front porch, so I hustled around back, where she sometimes sat on my little yellow bench before she came in for her appointments.

The backyard was empty and once again cleared of negative energy, though I'd forgotten to add the protection spell. Tomorrow. I limped through the back door and kicked off my shoes. I padded into the living room, where I sank down onto the couch. I hit the button to check my voice mail and then read the one-line text from Tyka. 'Sup, it said. I smiled.

She hadn't spoken much after we'd left Rashad, and knowing her like I do, I knew it was because she thought I'd taken Rashad's side. I just hadn't wanted her to hurt him. But if she was mad at me, apparently she'd gotten over it. I tapped out a response, My hackles, and added a smiley face.

Though the threat of soon-due bills loomed before me, the idea of a hot bath with some soothing candles ushered that sense of urgency right out of my mind. My ankle was loosening a bit as I gingerly made my way to the bathroom. I went to start the water and scoop in a bit of cleansing salts. Something to unknot the kinks right along with the puzzle pieces of this case.

I had one leg out of my jeans when the doorbell rang. Just that quick, I'd forgotten my client. Salimah, the murder—this whole mess had me flustered. Already I'd put Darryl in jeopardy and annoyed my father. I'd have a lot of making up to do when this was over. I must have looked like a fool, standing there half-clothed, wondering whether to turn off the light and pretend I wasn't home.

Duty and the mortgage prevailed. I slipped my jeans back on and went to open the door. I peeked outside, and there my client stood.

"Sorry I'm late," Chavonne said. I was always struck by just how much she favored Kiah. Cousins were like that, sometimes looking more like siblings than, well, siblings. "I tried out back first. This dude walks into the barbershop ten minutes before closing and dangled some extra bills in front of me. Hate it when they stream in at the last minute, trying to avoid the crowd they just create later on."

Chavonne worked at a fairly upscale shop called the Gentleman Barber. One of Tremé's few remaining after the storm. Word had it that Chavonne was the best barber there, and she had the clientele to prove it. She'd been known to cut a man who tried to rob her, curse the ground a nonpaying customer walked on, and also cry at the sight of an injured dog.

Chavonne *always* paid and *always* tipped. Plus, everyone knew that barbershops and beauty salons were safe havens. Sort of community hubs. Though it wasn't always reliable, more entertainment than truth, all the latest gossip could be had, and Chavonne never failed to deliver an interesting story.

"Come on in." She was one of only a handful of clients I allowed to cross my front door.

"You sure it ain't too much trouble?" She said this while simultaneously walking inside, with her shoes on.

"Might want to check your feet," I said with bite that I intended.

"My bad," she said. "You think I could remember that." Chavonne slipped off her tennis shoes and placed them by the door.

"Have a seat. I'll only be a few minutes."

Chavonne whipped out her phone and sat on my couch cross-legged. I raised an eyebrow, but at least she didn't have on her shoes.

I tied on my red headscarf and opted for a T-shirt and loose cotton pants that tied at the waist. This was as good as she was going to get, being an hour late. Guess I was late, too, but technically speaking, I *had* still beaten her here.

Chavonne worked long hours, frequently without stopping. She was only a few years younger than me, but young or old, that kind of thing took its toll. I wondered if this was her first break today. "You want something to eat?"

Chavonne considered. "I didn't have time to eat nothing but a bag of chips today, so yeah. But this thing is on my mind. Can we eat after?"

"Suit yourself," I said. Chavonne went to grab her shoes and followed me out the back door. Inside, I flicked on the lights and let her settle in while I whispered an offering. "And what brings you here today?" Chavonne had left that field blank when she'd completed the online appointment. To my clients, privacy was often very important.

Chavonne studied her fuchsia-colored nails, filed into the rounded points that were so popular today. I couldn't do it. One wrong swipe and I'd put my own eye out. I'd keep rocking my old-school look, thank you very much.

My client clasped her hands together, lowered her head, and then peered up at me sideways. Still, though, she didn't speak. I was hoping this would be quick, but every second that Chavonne sat there with her tongue glued to her lips was another moment I imagined the warmth slipping from my awaiting bath.

But to my customer, my expression remained cool, patient. The look of a woman unconcerned with silly things like time and hot baths. Here I'd sit until she was ready to talk.

In the minutes that passed with her worrying her hands, her shirt, her hair, she'd chewed off the lovely coral-colored lipstick. "I need help making a decision," she finally said. She blew out a breath after the words had tumbled out of her mouth.

"I have just the spell," I said and then pushed my chair back to gather what I needed.

"Wait," Chavonne said. "Can I talk to you about it first?"

"Of course," I said. Sometimes it seemed that works and spells were the smallest part of what my clients needed. An ear, someone to talk to. Most people just needed to be heard. "You don't even have to ask."

Chavonne ran her hand over her neatly done curls. "I know that. I just need to speak the words out loud first. So, I don't, you know, embarrass myself with them."

Our talks always ran long, and I'd be too tired to draw another bath. I'd have to settle for a shower, then. Fine. "I'm all ears."

More fidgeting and more reluctance. Just as I was about to call on the lwa to give me some patience with this girl, she spat it out.

"I don't want to be a barber."

Interesting.

"I want to learn to code," Chavonne continued. "I mean, I can already. A little. I've been playing around on my own and I understand some, but I think this is what I want to do with the rest of my life."

"Chavonne, I think that's awesome." I was actually really happy for her. But like everybody, fear was preventing her from doing what she probably already knew she wanted to do.

"I'd have to move," Chavonne continued. "Maybe someplace like Austin or San Francisco. Ain't no really good engineering jobs here. And I've got scholarship offers for the fall in both places."

"Seems to me like you don't need my help at all," I said, and I wished I hadn't been so honest. I needed the cash.

"But I do." Chavonne's eyes turned really serious. "My whole family is here. Like everybody. Even my boyfriend. And he says he won't leave his mama. I'd be walking away from everything I know. A job I'm good at too. I got lots of customers. And what if folks won't hire a Black woman that learned to code at thirty-two?"

I nodded. "Now I see why you came. While I've certainly got an opinion on what you should do, mine isn't the one that counts. That's up to the spirits. Let's get started."

At that, my client exhaled. I was going to call on the lwa Elegua. The master of keys to the past, present, and future would help Chavonne with her indecision. I thought she should go: her family would be here, and if that boyfriend of hers was worth anything, he'd go on this adventure with her. But the spirits may have felt differently from me; they often did.

This wouldn't require herbs or candles or anything I had here. I gave Chavonne a pen and held a small pad. "You'll burn this afterward?"

It was a question that required a verbal answer, and I held the pad until a nervous Chavonne answered: "Yes."

"See to it that you do. This is important, Chavonne."

"I hear you," she said, a bit too curtly for my taste. I gave her a side-eye to make sure my point got across. "You'll need three pennies—shiny ones. Hold them in your right hand and tell them your problem. After that, switch the pennies to your left hand and tell them the solution most prominent in your mind."

I continued, "Then cup your hands together, keep the pennies in the center of your palm, and ask Elegua to help you decide. You can put the pennies in your pocket or purse after that. Take a walk, exactly three blocks from your house: not four, not one and a half 'cause you're tired, three—"

"I understand," Chavonne said, interrupting me. I hated it when they did that.

"Stop at an intersection where four corners meet, like they do at the corner of North Galvez and Esplanade. Then walk that square, taking care to stop at each corner. When you've done that, walk diagonally through the crossroad. Lastly, at the center, toss the pennies over your left shoulder."

Chavonne held up a hand this time before speaking. "But what if there's no intersection like that when I reach three blocks?"

"I was getting to that," I said. "Come back to your home and walk in the opposite direction. If at the next three-block stop there is still no four-way junction, then you'll need to change it up. Go with a two-corner intersection. Switch the pennies to the opposite side of your body and walk that path between those corners four times. Then come back to the center and toss the pennies."

Chavonne scribbled the last few words and then looked up at me expectantly. "And then what?"

"Nothing," I said, rising. "Elegua will arrange things so that the answer is crystal clear to you."

"And how long will that take? The semester starts in August. That's only five months from now."

"He knows that and will get you the answer you seek in time to do whatever is necessary. If you stay, the when won't matter; if you're meant to go, you'll do that too. Don't fret about it. Let it go and go on with life. Now," I said, pushing back from the table. "Make another appointment if you need something else."

Chavonne looked as if she was considering hugging me. Luckily, she didn't. Instead, she pulled out a wallet from a front pocket and counted out the bills. I cautioned her, as I had before, about walking around with so much cash.

"Now let's see about getting you some dinner."

—

"Kiah mentioned the French Quarter murder," Chavonne said between bites of leftovers I'd cobbled together for her. "Heard your name come up too. Let's just say it wasn't in a complimentary tone."

Chavonne knew my history with Kiah. Knew that the man had never gotten over the fact that I'd stood up for him. And since becoming Lucien's watchdog, things hadn't gotten any better. So far, we'd been able to keep the fact that she was my client a secret.

"Ain't no way a mambo could have done it, though." Chavonne blanched at the glass of water I set beside her. "This all you got?"

"No. But it's what you need." With the one taste I'd covertly drawn from her pores, I could tell she was precariously dehydrated. Something I'd warned her about before.

"I heard something in the shop too," Chavonne said after she'd taken a sip.

I perked up, pulled out a chair, and sat down. Chavonne's stories were always the best. "Do tell."

"It was a few nights ago, after closing. You know how it is—we'd closed down, and I was finishing up this afro. Mr. Chambers's last client had left an hour earlier, but he was still there, hanging out. You know that just means he's waiting for one of his more exclusive clients. Guess who comes strolling in."

Being an upscale shop, that could mean anyone from a professional sports star to an actor. "Beats me," I said.

"My cousin strolls through the door, looks around like he's checking for rats or something, and then comes up to me and asks if I'm about done."

This was taking an interesting turn.

"I was just dusting off my client's face and removing the drape, so I told him so. He goes back out. I head to the bathroom, and when I come out, none other than Lucien Alexander is sitting in Mr. Chambers's chair."

I knew that Lucien frequented the barbershop. He came in after closing, probably so he wouldn't have to rub shoulders with anyone he felt was beneath him. And I guessed he paid and tipped handsomely enough for the owner to accommodate him.

"What'd he do this time? Demand to bless the clippers before his cut?" Lucien had a reputation for being quite particular about the implements that touched his head.

"Girl—" Chavonne stumbled. "I mean, Mambo."

"I'm Mambo out back; 'girl' will do just fine in here," I corrected my client.

"Girrrrl." Chavonne chuckled and then went on. "Lucien done gone and bought his own clippers, scissors, razor. E'ry damn thing. I half expect him to drag in his own barber chair next time."

"You'd think he'd want a barber to come to him," I said.

"I think he gets off on all the deference. You know," Chavonne said.

"You definitely got him pegged," I agreed.

"Anyway. I was sweeping up and tidying my station. Kiah's talking to me about some family nonsense when the houngan gets a call. I don't hear most of what he's saying, but I did hear him mention something about somebody not keeping his mouth shut."

That got my attention. "What else did he say? Tell me everything you remember."

Chavonne bit her lip and looked up in the air. "Now I think about it, he said the word 'detective.' Then he went on talking about lemons or lemonade. Whatever it was, I couldn't make sense of it because my beloved cousin notices me tuned in and holds up a hand for Lucien to stop. Lucien looks over at me like he's seen me for the first time and puts the call on hold."

"He was waiting for you to leave?"

"You know it. And what does Kiah do? Offers to walk me to my damn car."

"I take it you didn't hear anything else," I asked. "A name?"

"No, he clammed up."

Chavonne went on talking about other gossip and finished her meal. I murmured my outrage and laughed where appropriate, but I was only half listening. Soon she bade me thanks and good night.

I undressed and climbed into the shower, positively melting beneath the warm water as I considered Chavonne's words.

It was possible that Lucien was working to help Salimah behind the scenes and, for some reason, didn't want to let me know. But Lucien was an orchestrator. He did things for a reason. If this call wasn't about a pardon on a parking ticket, his help would be in his service, and his alone.

Now there were many detectives on the force, not just the two I happened to be . . .

Wait.

Someone talking too much. An informant? A source? Lemonade . . . lemons. The pieces rattled together in my head like a gate slamming shut. Steam threatened to erupt from my ears. A confrontation was on the horizon, but it would have to wait. It was long past the time for rest.

I turned out the lights in the kitchen and went to make sure everything was locked up in front. When I got to the parlor, I found an envelope poking through the side of the door. I picked it up.

I tore it open and found inside, one page, handwritten in block letters:

I'M AN EX-COP. IF YOU WANT TO KNOW WHAT HAP-
PENED TO VIRGIL DUNN, MEET ME AT THE PAVILION
IN BEHRMAN PARK IN ALGIERS. TOMORROW AT ONE.
ALONE.

CHAPTER TWENTY-FOUR

Though Tyka and I seemed to be back on good terms, I was making this trip by myself. Some might've called my decision to go meet someone who knew where I lived, but about whom I knew nothing, unwise. And I wouldn't have argued with them. But I knew how to take care of myself.

The source—I wasn't committed to the idea that they were former police—was taking me out of the comforts of New Orleans proper and luring me across the long Crescent City Connection to Algiers. Despite how long I'd lived in New Orleans, I'd never made the trip.

Even before I reached the Mississippi, the pull of the river was strong. It sang a lullaby from behind a veil of late-morning morning mist, tempting me to curl up within the song and drift off into an endless slumber.

I made do with a few moisture-laden, deep breaths.

The only Orleans Parish community located on the West Bank of the river, the Fifteenth Ward was still predominantly Black, though over the last few years a nice influx of Mexican Americans had also begun to call it home.

I rolled past the dens where the krewes constructed their Mardi Gras floats and up through Aurora to the park. What little traffic there was slowed to a trickle as I turned at General Meyer Avenue and wound my way through the web of roads to the pavilion, wondering if this was all a hoax orchestrated by Lucien or Kiah just to annoy me. Or something worse.

At least whoever it was had picked a place at once public and private—Behrman Park.

After a couple of laps, I found the pavilion. Two aisles of parking spaces lined a single-lane driveway. I chose a safe but not too obvious spot three cars over from a blue Chevy. I noted the license plate, just in case.

Another car took up two spaces in the aisle behind me, thumping a tune with a distinct flugelhorn loud enough to rattle my windows. I scanned the area. No one sat beneath the pavilion, and besides the amateur disc jockey, I was alone.

For the third time, I checked my purse. A few satchels were snug in their specially sewn compartments. Like any tradition, Vodou had its rules. Erzulie, the lwa, they were not servants. They were spirits, and they existed in a realm that kept them occupied with matters that concerned them. A wise vodouisant remembered this and, when in need, employed the knowledge and tools they provided us instead.

I got out of the car and decided to leave it unlocked in case I needed to make a quick exit. Eyes on swivel, I headed toward the pavilion. A few joggers ran along the gravel paths designed for such things, eking out some midday exercise. No children played, likely in school.

With each step, the state of disrepair encroached like a slow-moving rash. The blue paint was dull and peeling in spots. The benches and tables were weatherworn in spite of the covering. Concrete cracked in a few places. I didn't even want to think about the horrors in that roped-off bathroom.

The sound of a car caught my attention: a newer one, judging by the purring engine. The driver pulled up in the back row, next to the music thumper. The car ran for an interminable amount of time before the engine died. When the door opened, I held my breath. A tall woman wearing jeans and a windbreaker stepped out. Before she took a step, she scanned the area, gaze catching like a snare as it passed me. Recognition.

I'd assumed I was meeting a man.

She walked over to the noisy car and banged her hand once on the hood while peering in at the occupants. In a moment, the car pulled away. Her gaze settled on me again, and she lifted her chin. I raised a hand in greeting.

"Ms. Dumond?" she said while she was still a few feet away. Her voice was rich and weighty and sad. It was a sound that poured into your ears, worked its way to dormant heartstrings and plucked.

"Officer." I stood and went to meet her.

"It's been a while since anybody called me that." The woman offered me her hand. Her handshake was firm without overdoing it, and the fact that she even offered it was an unexpected courtesy.

Her hair was short and styled in neat rows like someone had spent hours tending to each hair with a quarter-inch-size curling iron. Her jeans were more boot cut than skinny. The unzipped windbreaker revealed a crisp white button-up and a black belt.

We sat in the middle of the pavilion, not so close to the parking lot as to be easily seen but not all the way at the back either. She, of course, faced the lot. Nobody would be sneaking up on her.

"Did you get the obit?" She held my gaze for a moment before turning to scan our surroundings again.

I'd guessed that she was the one who'd given Jason the obituary for Darby's father. I never advertised my address, so she'd probably trailed him to my house so she'd know where to deliver the second letter. I'd have to have a talk with Jason. A lesson in observing one's surroundings, including all the people in it, was in order.

"I got it," I said. "But why don't you tell me what it means."

The officer reached into a jacket pocket and took out a pack of cigarettes. After she'd tapped one out and lit it, she spoke. "Why are you even bothering with this?" She didn't blink, and there was no anger in her tone, only curiosity.

"I'm a fully ordained Vodou priestess, a mambo." I didn't know why I felt the need to justify myself, probably because she'd neglected to do so. I shook my head at my own vanity. "That is what I do and who I am; the two are inseparable. I'm doing this because a friend—someone needs my help."

"You know that's the problem some people have with y'all, right?"

When I didn't answer, she took a drag on the cigarette, thankfully blew the smoke over her shoulder, and continued. "You notice the rest of us when it suits you. The only reason you're here is because they got one of you on lockdown. And because Vodou was implicated in my partner's—my ex-partner's—murder."

Virgil had been her partner. My mouth opened, and a retort that would've made me look more defensive than anything was poised to roll off my tongue, with a bit of fire on the back end. I held it in with effort. She was right. I didn't want to think of the number of people who had been wrongly convicted in this city, and that meant there were even more, besides Salimah, in the same predicament. And I hadn't given it a second thought, other than the typical momentary outrage whenever the picture of an innocent and newly released prisoner was plastered across the news.

"You're absolutely right," I was surprised to find myself saying. "It's selfish interests that got me involved with this mess, and if I had it my way, I wouldn't even be here talking to you right now, but here we are."

She tapped ashes on the ground. "I can't speak on who did or didn't kill Virgil, but I can tell you why he was killed."

That hung in the air for the full minute that I studied her face. The pain squinted her eyes and pursed her lips.

The officer looked left and right again before she spoke. I could tell she was barely holding it together and was mad at herself for showing the vulnerability. "It seems like everything that went wrong with this city started after that damn hurricane."

I wanted to correct her and tell her that no, the trouble, in fact, had started long before, when the first slaves landed on the shores of the West Bank of the Mississippi. That more trouble ensued when our language and gods were ripped from us. When our religion was ridiculed, and worse, when we became the perpetrators of that ridicule. But that was a discussion for another time.

"We weren't part of the squads, but—"

The sound of a silencer was something I'd heard only in movies. And they'd been wrong. Instead of the whisper of a blade unsheathed, the blast was only slightly dampened. Blood flowered at the front of the officer's shirt before she slumped over sideways and tumbled to the ground.

I tried to get up and tripped all over myself. I tumbled backward, nicked the back of my head on the bench behind us, and cried out as my back slammed onto the concrete.

Terror turned my insides to liquid. I coaxed myself out of the ball I'd curled into and spotted the perpetrator. Covered in black from head to toe, gun still in hand as he stood there watching me. The figure had come from the taped-off bathroom: the one place neither of us had expected.

I snatched a pouch of blurring powder from my waist, opened the ribbon, and tossed it all up in the air. I closed my eyes and let the potion settle over me. It wasn't like I would disappear, but I'd blend in, becoming blurry enough to not be seen. It wouldn't stop the perp from shooting in the general area and finding his target, but it would buy me some time.

The shooter advanced, then changed his mind and took off running in the opposite direction, disappearing back behind the bathroom.

I cried out for help, but there wasn't another soul in sight. I clambered around to the other side of the bench and found the officer slumped awkwardly on her side. I checked her pulse and felt for a heartbeat. Her eyes were open, her face slack. There were two bullet holes in the back of her T-shirt. I sighed with relief that the bullets hadn't traveled through her and killed me.

Whatever she was going to tell me had died with her. A thought—a risky, unwanted idea—sprang into my mind. There was a way to still get the information I needed. But time was of the essence. The soul hung around for only so long before it embarked on its journey. I snatched my phone and called 911, opting to not leave my name.

How long before they got here?

There were spells, works that Papa had explained but warned me against using. I knew I shouldn't, but my mind was already made up. With a quick glance around to make sure the area was still abandoned, I scurried back over to grab my purse.

I didn't have everything I'd need, but I had to try. A pinch of goat hair, ground in with the remains from a freshly killed blue lizard, a dead toad wrapped in dried sea worm, itching pea vine, and the reproductive organs of a puffer fish. You had to be careful not to get the latter on your hands while it was fresh. It was poisonous.

My resolve wavered. I'd been hauled in and unceremoniously fingerprinted like a common criminal last year over those burglaries. If I left even a sliver of a print behind, there was no doubt that they'd try to tie me to this murder. But it was a chance I had to take.

I sprinkled a pinch of the concoction on her heart, over a patch sticky with blood. The rest, I rubbed up and down her arms. Finally, I opened my pores and released a bit of sangswe wine onto her forehead. Then I waited, listening for sirens.

It wasn't like I'd ever done this before, so I didn't even know if it was going to work, but I sat there crouched down next to her, sweating and wondering at the same time what doing such a thing would mean for me.

I stumbled backward when the officer's willowy soul materialized. Her eyes rolled around before settling on me.

"I won't hold you for long," I said to reassure her, and myself.

"I should have checked the bathroom," she said. The words were spoken slowly, spaced out and tentative. She felt her chest and blinked at the contrast between the mess on her body and the clarity of her soul. "Rookie mistake."

"Miss," I began and then realized she'd never given me her name. "If you can tell me why you brought me here, I will send you on your way. Your time here will be done."

She blinked and moved her limbs as if testing out her new form. "This feels so weird." She looked off into the distance then. An expression on her face that wasn't fear, but wonder.

"What were you going to tell me about the storm? Did something happen then? Is it related to why Virgil Dunn was killed?"

Her gaze settled back on me, and there was a hint of anger there. She was ready to go; matters of the earth were no longer her concern.

"The death squads," she said finally.

The rumors were true, then.

"Me and Virg weren't even on the force yet. Everybody had gone crazy," she continued, her gaze fixed on a spot in the sky. "Looting, murder, assaults. There was no time. No place to take them. They killed people. Some of them innocent. When Virgil found out, he told me. Wanted to go public. I resisted at first, but we couldn't live with it. Not anymore."

I couldn't believe what I was hearing. The stories were true. Virgil Dunn apparently had died for having a conscience.

The officer's willowy form began to tremble. My mind raced. Was there something else I was supposed to do? An ingredient I'd forgotten?

The trembling increased, and her face began to twitch. "I got to go. You got to let me go."

"Do you know who killed Virgil?" I didn't add that this person had made her his second victim.

"No, but that priest might. I don't know his name." The officer looked away again, longing in her eyes.

"Go on home," I whispered.

She hovered there, face tilted skyward. Her arms raised overhead, like a newborn soul anxious to embrace ancestral parents waiting in the next realm. She spared me a knowing smile, a glance lightened by relief, and her soul drifted up and away until it was no longer visible. I got up then and ran, ran faster than I had since I was a teen track star, back to my car. I hated to leave her there, but I couldn't be found with her either. She was gone. An ambulance would find her soon enough.

Though the informant had unburdened herself and now she could take her place with the ancestors, I would have no such luck.

I had no idea what the consequences would be for what I had done. I nearly upended the contents of my purse searching for my keys, my fingers tree-trunk stiff. Somehow I got into the car, but when I looked into the rearview mirror, my eyes went watery and I howled at the blood spatters on my face. I grabbed a tissue from the glove compartment and raked it across my face as I started the car and zoomed away. I knew that I would never do anything like that again. And if Erzulie saw fit to forgive me, I would dedicate the rest of my life to using my gifts to *sèvi lwa yo*. To serve the spirits and the people.

But first, I had to figure out what the death squad had reaped and what a Vodou priest had to do with it. The more answers I got, the more questions appeared in their place.

I careened through traffic, unafraid of drawing a cop's attention because they were all headed in the opposite direction. The direction where they would find the body of one of their fallen comrades. An ex-cop was still a cop. The rearview mirror may as well have been taped over because there was no way I'd even chance a look behind me.

Only after I'd crossed the bridge was I able to unclench my jaw. A herd of elephants still thundered in my chest. I let down the window and sucked in gulps of thick, humid air that brought me no enjoyment, no relief.

Erzulie and Papa crowded my thoughts. She was eerily silent. Hadn't even warned me at the park, which meant that either she was busy, up to something with the other lwa, or I'd never been in any danger in the first place.

Papa had warned me. Told me to drop the case. If he got wind of what happened, he'd rattle off a string of I-told-you-so's. Chastise me for dangerously skirting the rules and generally unleash a lecture for the ages. But no way this would escape from my lips.

I sped around a car whose driver apparently thought Sunday afternoon would be a good time for a leisurely drive. A car horn, no, multiple car horns, blared behind me. I had trapped a soul that should have been on her way to the ancestors and held her to answer my petty questions. I was forgetting myself, my training, and my oath.

At that moment, all the adrenaline that had fueled my escape drained away like a stopper had been pulled. I navigated to the nearest empty parking spot, pulled over, and rolled up the windows. Didn't bother glancing around to see who was in earshot. Fists clenched, eyes wide open. The elephants in my chest came rumbling out in the form of a scream. Twice more I screamed and didn't stop until my throat and vocal cords were as raw as a hunk of meat.

I rested my forehead against the steering wheel and allowed my breath to slow. I prayed then. I prayed to anybody who could grant me reprieve. I prayed that the officer's soul had found its way home and for forgiveness for being selfish enough to delay her.

Until the day I'd shown up at Voodoo Real, murder was something I'd watched on the news or read about online. My existence was that of a houngan's sheltered only daughter. But seeing all this convinced me as I hadn't been before. I would see this case through till the end. There was no way I could turn back now, too much already lost and too much still at stake. And from now on, I'd do so within the confines of the rules of my practice, using my own special brand of magic.

Erzulie's watery agreement infused her subtle warmth flooding through my veins.

It was clear that I was getting close. The killer had wanted to silence both Virgil and the officer at the park.

She hadn't finished her thought, but I was certain of one thing. The death squads were real. We'd been warned about the approaching storm, but having survived so many, few had bothered to heed the warnings and leave. So, when the water came, the police weren't prepared. Nobody was. For some, it had been easier to kill than to file a report.

That meant there were others. How many? Dead or alive? Still on the force or gone to Houston a decade ago with the rest of the transplants? For many looking to escape the state, Houston had been a sanctuary, first offering hotel rooms, food, and other accommodations. In the end, many stayed.

Before I realized it, my phone was in my hand and I heard my girl's voice: "'Sup, Mambo?"

I was settled by the casual certainty of the strength in those words. It pulled me back from a place—a weak and pitiful place—that I didn't want to see again anytime soon. "Tyka, I need you to get the word out about something."

"Now I'm back on the case, huh? You shouldn't have taken that dude's side over me. I'm still kinda mad at you."

I didn't have time for this. "I didn't take his side—I was saving his ass. And for the record, I was never mad."

The sound of silence frayed my nerves while my friend pondered whether I was being sincere. "I'm listening," she said finally.

I relayed to her that I needed her to drop a word, casually, that the lady mambo detective had evidence that would point to Virgil Dunn's killer.

"Is it that girl? Sophie?"

"Well, I said to put the word out. I didn't say I really knew who the killer was."

"Trying to fish somebody out?" Tyka's voice held a note of concern.

"Not that I'm certain it'll work, but yes."

"Consider the word spread," Tyka said.

"Okay, I'll call you later."

"Sweet Belly said you ain't answering your phone," Tyka said before I could hang up.

The mention of his name stirred something. *The obituary.* "I haven't even checked my phone. I need to have a word with Mr. Boudreaux anyway." I recalled what Chavonne had overheard at the barbershop. Lucien. Lemons. A terrible suspicion turned my stomach.

"You sound like you got a bone to pick." Tyka actually chuckled. She had the demeanor of a person who made toughness an art form and the giggle of a five-year-old girl.

"Touché." I had no further argument.

"I'll see you at your house," Tyka said. "You 'bout to stir up some shit."

She hung up before I could thank her.

CHAPTER
TWENTY-FIVE

I had stopped home to clean up, unable to bear the sticky tang of the officer's blood any longer, and by the time I reached the Lemon Drop, it was early evening. The car's air conditioner was losing the battle against the spring heat. But that wasn't what plastered my shirt to my back against the seat. It was fury. Sweat poured from my body, and though I knew it wouldn't do any good, I cranked up the air a notch.

And the car sputtered.

It didn't cut off; that was just its way of letting me know that it was doing its best and that I shouldn't ask any more of it. I obliged, dialing down the airflow. The car lurched its way into a parking spot a few doors down the street.

The music on the jukebox didn't stop, but everything else did when I stepped inside. I knew that energy was real, even if I couldn't see it with the naked eye. And my energy screamed my outrage. Eyes grew wide. Jimmy almost dropped a plate of food. My friend, my not 100 percent honest friend Darryl, came from the back and took in the whole scene.

"What?" he said, looking at me like I'd stolen something from him. "Did Jimmy sneak a Lipton tea bag in your cup?"

We glared at each other before I turned my heated gaze on everyone who was staring at me. They turned back to their plates and drinks. Conversations resumed. I sped right past Darryl on my way back to his office.

"You must got the devil in you. What the hell is wrong?" Darryl squeezed behind the too-large desk and stood there. He didn't sit, and I ignored the little love seat where I hated to admit I'd slept more than one night.

"You lied to me!" I sounded like a child, but I couldn't help it.

"I ain't never lied to you. Not one day. And—" He stopped midsentence. He gestured with his chin. "Why don't you sit on down. Seem like this is gonna take a minute."

I took my place on the love seat. My feet were hurting anyway. "You don't get a treat today. You get a chance to tell me what you didn't when you earned your last box of chocolates."

"You gon' be specific? I got customers waiting, and it look like you done gave poor Jimmy the fright of his life."

I huffed. "Darby is your source," I said. "Or one of them anyway." Chavonne had overheard a few things: "lemon," "detective," and the need for somebody to keep their mouth shut. The ex-cop had given me Darby's father's obituary and said the priest—probably Lucien—knew something. Darby was the detective; he'd blabbed something to the neighborhood news broker and proprietor of the Lemon Drop. Darby, apparently, had been talking too much.

Darryl deflated a bit. One of his precious secrets was out in the open. "That ain't got nothin' to do with you."

"A cop? Roman's partner?"

"Me and the boy's father knew each other since we was kids. Even worked together back when I painted."

That part was true. The obituary had said Darby's father was a painter and carpenter.

Darryl looked down, fiddled with his fingernails. "'Fore he died, I promised to look after his son."

"And you never thought to tell me?"

"What I did tell you was to stay away from this mess. Not to take the case. Not to get involved with that damn detective of yours. Try to do some Black folks a favor that come back and slap you in the face for ya trouble."

"I don't want to hear it."

"Didn't want to tell it."

I jabbed an index finger at him. "You know what I mean."

Darryl crossed his arms and leaned back. "Don't 'spect I do."

I let magic sparkle between my fingers while I pondered how a man so obtuse had become my best friend.

"I'm going to ask you some questions, and you're going to give me some answers," I said. "And leave out the part where you try to protect me."

"This ain't Burger King, and you don't get to have it your way—"

"Darryl!"

He held up his hands. "Don't even get a penny candy and you come in here makin' demands." He rested his hands on his small paunch as if pondering the size of the offense in not having something to satisfy his insatiable sweet tooth. "Ask on, then."

"Lucien did something to help the police cover up what happened with the death squads. Did you know about this?"

"Heard a thing or two, but never nothin' concrete."

I nodded. "So Roman wasn't even on the force then. I assume he's covering up for somebody else. Do you know all the people who were involved?" There had never been any prosecutions, no arrests. The whole thing was swept away like the debris that had been carried off after the storm. But they couldn't sweep away everything, and bits and pieces, reminders of the devastation, remained. I guessed it was the same with the squads. Something remained, something many people didn't want to dredge up. But that still didn't explain what this had to do with railroading Salimah.

"You remember that cop got killed a few years ago? Found at the crack house?" Darryl stroked his chin and got a faraway look in his eyes as if remembering the story.

"I think so. He was one of them?"

"That's what I heard. Seems he might have been getting loose lips. Conscience creepin' up on him. They say the whole thing was staged. He liked the women in the crack house, but nobody had heard anything about him taking drugs before that."

"And you don't know any of the others? Was there somebody related to Salimah somehow?" I was grasping at straws. It seemed the connections were there, just dying to come together, but I couldn't see them.

"That I can't help you with. Salimah ain't even been here that long."

Darryl was watching me. I knew there was concern there, but I wasn't over being mad at him. "Don't keep something like this from me ever again," I said as I stood up. "You're about the only person I can count on here. And not telling the whole truth is just as good as a lie."

"Fair 'nuf," Darryl agreed. "Got some ribs if you want 'em."

For the first time ever, I declined his offer of food because I knew, more than anything, that would hurt him the same way he'd hurt me.

CHAPTER TWENTY-SIX

As soon as I pulled up, I remembered that I'd forgotten to lay down another protection spell. I didn't think lightning would strike twice—a mistake I'd never make again.

Every cell in my body tingled with awareness. Erzulie. Her presence was like the rush of a tidal wave cutting through my veins. One that lit the skin and singed the bones. She fired my senses. Another soon-to-be-sorry soul had dared to darken my doorway. Tense, sweaty minutes passed while I considered whether this might've been the work of the officer's spirit. Had she somehow found her way to my home to exact some kind of revenge?

I got out of the car and charged up the stairs. This time, I wouldn't be taken by surprise. I drew on the water in the air and a bit from the soil. The water crashed against my skin, buckling for release. I spun a storm between my palms, mixed in some of my sangswe wine. I stepped inside.

The house was untouched. I reached out with my senses. They drew me through to the kitchen and out the back door.

I found Tyka tiptoeing around the backyard. The water ball retreated back into my pores, temporarily sated. My friend spun around at the sound of my approach, ready to attack and eyeing me suspiciously.

"What the hell?" I hissed, coming up beside her.

"Saw somebody shoot down that way like a rocket, soon as I knocked on your front door." She pointed down the side of the house, the blue and white pavers. One knocked out of place. "Didn't know if somebody else was waiting around."

Then, a slice of moonlight cut through the murk. My gut felt as if I'd been hit by a sledgehammer. The door to my Petit Temple Vodoun looked like it had come out on the losing end of a standoff with a police battering ram. The frosted glass like callous little snowflakes dusting the grass.

"Wait here," Tyka and I both said, echoing simultaneously. Any other time it might have been comical.

We positioned ourselves on either side of the doorway. I held up a hand to stay Tyka and stepped inside. Le Petit Temple Vodoun. My sanctuary. The place where I practiced my sacred tradition, where I conducted my healing practice, was in shambles. The wail that escaped my throat was reminiscent of a wounded and dying animal. I sank to my knees, ignoring the pain of flesh meeting unyielding concrete.

Tyka was beside me before I could blink away the rage carving rivulets of grief down the sides of my face.

"Damn," she muttered. The mini altar was littered with trash. Bolts of precious fabric cut to shreds. My table, a gift from my father upon opening my practice, looked as if someone had taken an ax to it. The pressed white tablecloth, covered in dirty boot prints, lay in a tattered heap. All my hard-to-find powders and potions and dried remains scattered on the floor like hay in a barn.

This was no robbery. It was another warning from a weak and scared coward. Two potential culprits came to mind, one more unlikely than the other.

Tyka took me by the arm. "Come on," she said, tugging gently. "Get on up now."

I grudgingly allowed her to haul me to my feet and waved off the balled-up tissue she tried to press into my hand. I wanted the feel of the hot, angry tears on my cheeks to remain. To fuel what I had to do next.

Tyka had already collected the pieces of my table and set them outside. When she came back, I hadn't moved. Outrage rooted me in place like a statue.

"You need another minute?" Tyka grabbed my tablet and tapped on it, probably to see if it was salvageable.

I went outside and made a phone call. When I came back in, she'd picked up my tablecloth and was using it to try to sweep away some of the debris. "Leave it," I said, then took a moment to straighten Papa's machete on the wall—luckily that hadn't been smashed along with everything else. "We've got somebody to go and see."

Even Tyka was surprised when I took her up on her offer to drive. I'd never done so before, and it had been a running joke with us. But I needed the time to think, and I didn't trust myself behind the wheel. Vaguely, I recalled Darryl playing the dutiful father figure and taking her to get her driver's license at sixteen, but I wondered if she'd ever bothered renewing it.

She'd glanced over at me a few times already. I ignored her, content to seethe and plot.

"What you did back there at the house." She was rolling down the street, a good ten miles over the speed limit, and watching me at the same time.

"Eyes on the road," I said. I knew what she was going to say and didn't want to talk about it. Nobody outside my family but Lucien had ever witnessed me using water magic.

"You went all watery," she said, gesturing with her own hands—off the steering wheel—to mimic what I'd done. "I lived in this city my whole life. Seen some weird shit. But that?"

Erzulie's power, any of the lwas' powers, weren't to be discussed with noninitiates. "You're mistaken."

Tyka drove silently down the street, following my directions. After an uncomfortable silence, she said, "Be that way, then. Got a secret or two of my own."

That's one of the things I loved about her. Unlike other people, she knew about and respected boundaries.

I'd asked Roman to meet. Thankfully, he hadn't suggested his office, so we were meeting in a parking lot at the waterfront. His voice had betrayed nothing. Guilt or innocence masked beneath years of on-the-job deception.

"I'm meeting Roman. Don't get out of the car," I told Tyka. "I need to talk to him alone."

"What you bring me for if you just want me to sit in the car?"

"Would you rather I didn't bring you at all?"

Tyka cut her eyes at me, and I held her gaze. She shrugged. When I caught a glimpse of Roman pulling into the lot, I got out. Before I closed the door, she unbuckled her seat belt. "Don't get in his ride—talk outside."

⌒

Roman had barreled toward us in his fancy SUV, not his police-issued sedan. All black and sleek, the vehicle rolled to a stop directly in front of us, not alongside us. The man lived to make a show of things. The engine died, and he sat staring daggers at Tyka and me.

When I grew tired of this game, I got out of the car and walked around back to my trunk. He'd have to come to me. Eventually his door opened and slammed shut. After an exaggerated exhale, I heard Roman's heels clacking against the concrete, and in a moment, he stood before me.

The man wore a suit like a leopard wore its spots: naturally, beautifully, confidently.

He flicked his head in Tyka's direction. "Still dragging your charity case around with you?"

Before I could open my mouth, from the two-inch gap where she'd slid down both windows, Tyka shouted, "I ain't nobody's damn charity case! Mr. Detective . . . sir."

That girl and her mouth. One day.

Roman ignored Tyka and scanned every inch of the deserted corner of the parking lot. After what had happened in Algiers, I found myself doing the same.

Inspection completed, he turned to me. "What's with all this? What couldn't you say over the phone?"

Or at your house, his eyes said.

"You listen best in person," I said. "Why are you hustling Darryl?"

"Why did you bring me all the way out here?"

"Did you have somebody pay me a visit?" I knew he wouldn't stoop to doing something like that himself, but that didn't mean he hadn't heard something about it.

"I don't use messengers," Roman said, his eyes smoldering in the slow-gathering dusk.

"Did anything the police got tangled up in after the hurricane have something to do with Virgil's murder?"

I sensed a breath held. His gaze averted as if a shield had sprung up between us. "What was our agreement?" That tone in his voice, a fluttering of another time.

The agreement had been one of two conditions on which we agreed to date much too soon after all the vodouisants had been cleared in the home-invasion case. First, we'd keep our religious beliefs separate; second, I wouldn't ask him about his work. The state of our relationship spoke to how well we'd kept to those promises.

"Those rules were for two people who were in"—I had to stop myself before I said the word "love"—"in a relationship. We aren't."

"Your choice," Roman said.

I crossed my arms. "Your insecurity."

Roman's face took on that mask. The mask police used when they were trying hard not to convey any emotion. He'd used it on me many times before. "When's the last time you been out to Algiers?"

My mask was nowhere near as practiced as his, but I slid it over my features nonetheless. "How many other crimes have you covered up?" Even if he hadn't been involved in the aftermath of the storm, he, like so many others, hadn't done anything about it.

Roman's face twisted with rage. He grabbed me by the shoulders.

"Get off'a her like that."

I yanked away as Tyka cracked her door and warned Roman. I turned and implored her to stay put.

"Don't get your ass outta that car if you don't want what goes with it," Roman said. "I won't take you to jail—I'll just kick your ass out here and let you bleed out."

With him distracted, I slid my hand to my waistband and pulled out a pouch.

"Take that gun off—we'll see." Tyka was out of the car.

"Tyka, please get back in the car," I said.

"All right." Roman was pulling off his jacket. "Let's see what you got, Grip. I'm gonna show you that wrestling shit don't work on grown men."

Tyka grinned.

"Can the both of you even pretend to be adults for one minute!" I slid in front of Roman, keeping myself between him and Tyka.

"Tell that to old one-nut over there." Tyka thrust out her chin.

No. No she didn't.

Rarely had I been able to get Tyka to sleep at my house, and the one time she had, she'd overheard Roman and me talking about his accident.

The one that had left him with one . . . well. I could've strangled her for bringing this up.

Roman's arms went limp and hung at his sides.

And in the gaze that Tyka shot between us, it was clear that even she knew she'd gone too far.

Roman tilted his head from side to side, cracking his neck, then slapped his hands together, wrestler-style. "Eddie didn't teach his little alley cat any manners, so I'm gon' have to do it for him."

They were circling each other. Part of me wondered how the fight would go. Roman would take her eventually, but I had no doubt that Tyka would let him know he'd been in a fight. I had to do something.

The only time Roman had broken his second rule, when he'd positively blathered on about his latest case, was when he'd returned home after a night of heavy drinking with his fellow officers. When he was good and drunk, he sang like a stool pigeon.

Magic, they said, was the art of using the forces of nature and its symbols to manifest a desired change in people or things. There was a spell. A fickle, iffy, depending-on-which-way-the-wind-was-blowing spell. And I absolutely should not use it on Roman, had promised I never would do anything like this.

Dancing between them, I reached out and tasted a sliver of moisture in Roman's body to see if there was any liquor there to make use of. There was. Being drunk was only a matter of not being able to break down the alcohol in your system fast enough.

A little ground kava root evoked an amazingly similar effect on the body to alcohol. I ripped the pouch open and flung the contents up as high as I could.

"Back in the car!" I shouted at Tyka. And for once, she complied.

I held up my hands, fingers splayed. Blood-red mist flowed from my pores and activated the root powder as it fell toward us. With a breath, I urged it on its way, infiltrating Roman's eyes, his open mouth, his nose. He sneezed, once, twice. He shook his head, blinked as if trying to clear a sudden fog.

The wait was a short one.

Roman's body relaxed. He took a step forward, swayed on his feet, and stumbled toward the car. His eyes became glossy. "What the hell did you do to me?"

"What is your mother's middle name?" I needed to test how well the spell was working. He was ashamed of his mother's middle name, and few people alive today knew it. He'd be extra pissed that, assuming we made it out of this, Tyka would be one of them.

His jaw worked and his eyes widened first in alarm and then a vivid, blooming anger. "Jemima," he blurted out.

Tyka's girlish giggle was all it took to send Roman through the roof. He fired off a string of expletives at both of us. The drunken spell would loosen his tongue, sure enough, but my hold over him wouldn't last for long.

He stumbled forward again, landed against the car, and sank to the ground, where he sat, his head lolling from side to side.

Mentally, I ran through the most important questions and settled on the first. "Who killed Virgil Dunn?"

"How the fuck should I know?" Roman's eyes went so wide I feared that they might fall from his skull. I was only slightly surprised at his admission. A street kid was as much of a suspect as Salimah or anyone else. They didn't know and didn't care who had killed that man. "What is this, Reina? What the hell did you put on me?" He struggled to move, but the potion held him firm. "I can't believe you used your shit on me."

"Mambo!" Tyka interjected. "You been with the woman for a year. Seem like you'd show her some respect."

"Tyka—"

"You shut your mouth," Roman said, charging right over me.

I sighed; maybe it was a mistake to bring Tyka with me. "Next question," I began before Tyka could retaliate. "Why was Virgil killed?"

Sweat was pouring down Roman's face. A sign of the effort he was putting into trying to fight me. I felt the slightest tingle of admiration. Slight.

"Him and his partner. They were going to break the code."

That much I knew.

"Do you know who broke into my shop?"

At this, he looked quizzical. "When? Again?"

I'd assumed the police had gotten someone to ransack my place to try to intimidate me. If not them, then who?

"Is the murder investigation active, or have you all just stopped looking?"

"A-ask your friend. The big shot."

Lucien.

"Reina, you better be gone real soon. 'Cause I don't know what I'm going to do when I come out of this."

Great, I was losing him. Already, he was flexing his fingers. The spell was weakening.

"This didn't harm you," I told Roman. "You'll be fine. Just don't drive for a few minutes."

I turned to go, and to my back, Roman said in a voice brittle with the wound of my betrayal, "I won't forget that you did this. I'm done. Finished. I won't protect you. I don't love you, and now I don't even like you. All that bullshit talk about only using your powers for good. All of you are full of shit. And your ass is going to hell. Whatever happens next is on you."

My heart collapsed at his words. He had every right to be done with me. What I'd just done was selfish, unforgivable. Everybody had been right. Papa, Darryl, Tyka, even Ms. Lucy had told me that cops saw too much, carried too much pain. That Roman had a problem with my faith. That our attempt at a union would end badly. The part of me that would have told him to spare me the fire and brimstone was silent. I didn't turn around, couldn't face him. "I'm sorry, Roman."

I didn't hear his retort for the roar of the engine as Tyka took us away from the pier.

CHAPTER TWENTY-SEVEN

Though Tyka wanted to help, I sent her on her way. I didn't like people touching my things, and she would just be associating her essence in with the lingering negative energy. Later—after a good cleansing—she'd be welcome; the others who'd trespassed would not. I'd make sure of it.

The cleaved remains of my beautiful red oak table tightened the corners of my mouth. It was irreplaceable, not just for the workmanship, but also for the sentimentality that Papa had always cautioned me against applying to people or possessions. Perhaps it could be repaired.

My money was reserved for necessities like supplies and food, not new tables. One at a time, I took them out—these pieces of my life, my practice—and set them in a metal bin that was left over from a failed koi pond experiment.

Spells, magical works of any kind, really, could have unexpected consequences. This was the vodouisant creed, and one of Papa's most ardent lessons. My encounter with Roman had done nothing to dispel this rule. I'd expected answers, confirmation of what I'd thought I already knew. And, in part, that was the case. But he'd reintroduced another probability: Lucien was somehow involved.

What happened after the storm wasn't some urban legend.

People had scrambled onto rooftops, crowded into attics. Far too many drowned. Pillaging and violence ensued. For some it was sport, but for most, it had been their only means of survival. The NOPD, in their haste to restore order, had set about finishing off the job of the real estate investors who had been plotting for decades. Got rid of people in certain neighborhoods. The official word was that they targeted the criminals, the looters. But two police officers were going to change all that.

Of course there'd been whispers. At the Lemon Drop, barbershops and beauty salons, backyard barbecues. Sanctuaries of Black truth. Murmurs and speculation about innocent people gunned or beaten down for the crime of not dying with the first devastating waves. The surge that buried the areas below sea level, including the Lower Nine, where my mother lived.

"I figured the only way you gon' learn how cook a respectable gumbo is for me to show you." I turned and found my friend Darryl "Sweet Belly" Boudreaux sheepishly standing at the door, balancing a cardboard box on his hip. Tyka had obviously already told him about what had happened. I tossed aside the rag I'd been using to wipe down the counter.

Darryl had lied to me for years. Concealed a relationship with Darby, Roman's partner, of all people. That sat in my gut like a stew left to ferment on the stove for a month. Partners spent more time together than they did with their families. They talked. About everything. My imagination assailed me with the intimate details of my rocky relationship with Roman that Darryl may have chuckled about behind my back.

I was still angry, but I walked over and inspected the box to see what he had brought in the way of a peace offering. "What's all this?"

"Your roux has to be done right. Everythang flows off'a that. We gon' start there and make you a real nice gumbo. Since you can't sit still long enough to follow simple written directions, I'm gon' have to oversee it."

I handed him the key. "Go on, I'm almost done here. I'll be in in a few."

Darryl understood my tone without asking. I didn't want his help here. He took the key and strode—no, limped—off toward the house. I also noticed a shiny black handle protruding from the waist of his pants. He rarely carried his gun outside the bar, and I was sorry that I'd put him and everybody I cared about through this. But it wasn't to be helped now.

Most of my herbs and tinctures had been destroyed. Scattered in the yard and on the floor. Vials smashed, dolls ripped to pieces. Whoever did this wanted to send a message, and they'd succeeded—in making me more determined. With the drawers and cubbies clean and back in place, the floor swept and mopped, I'd figure out how to replace everything later. My credit card payment terminal, though, was in the trash. Cash would be king for a while.

The last task was to purify my place.

I'd be able to do the job only halfway with the stash I had from the house. I kept some things in the top kitchen cabinet just in case of emergencies, and this certainly constituted one.

A metal bowl. Essential oils of rosemary and frankincense. One sizable bay leaf. Substitute thyme for angelica oil and the skin of the near-rotten apple stuck in the back of my refrigerator for the mandrake root. That one would be tough to replace. I savored a glass of water, then loosed my pores, allowing a bit of my sangswe wine to seep into the bowl. I ground up the mixture by hand.

With the index and middle fingers of both hands, I coaxed the darkly tinted oil from the bowl. The mass of liquid floated between my fingers, and like a symphony conductor, I guided the oil onto the entryway, the doorknob, and a little outside as well. I poured the excess into one of the few glass vials still intact.

When I stepped through the back door, Darryl was seated—
seated—at the kitchen table, chopping an onion. He always stood
when working in the kitchen. He paused to pop a piece of candy in his
ever-ready mouth, balled up the plastic wrap, and . . . left the wrapper
sitting right there on the table. Even more unlike him. I swept it up and
dropped it in the trash.

"All right," I said. "What are you waiting on? You got some teaching
to do—let's get to it."

Darryl pressed his hands against the table and stood with effort.
Was it his knee?

This was difficult to do without him knowing, but I surreptitiously
reached out and siphoned just a trickle of water from his blood. The
moisture crawled along my exposed arms and sank beneath my skin
with a barely audible sucking sound.

If I knew my friend, he suspected I was up to something but remained
silent as I tasted the moisture, checking for any sign of what ailed him.
Aside from the fact that he was a bit dehydrated, not unusual for someone
living in such a humid climate, I couldn't discern anything useful.

"What's wrong?" I asked, even though I knew he wouldn't tell me.
"Why are you limping?"

"What kinda oil you got?" Darryl was opening and slamming cabinets. My question went unanswered.

"You have oil right here." I held up the bottle of Crisco from the
box he'd brought with him.

"I know my own oil when I see it," he huffed. "Ingredients is everythang. I'm looking for yours 'cause I need to know where you goin'
wrong."

I opened the cabinet beneath the sink and pulled out what I had.
The look of pure affront on Darryl's face spoke volumes.

"The hell is that?" He snatched the bottle from me. He studied the
labels, front and back, and then stomped over and deposited the whole
container in the trash.

"Hey!" I said. "That was still half-full."

"Crisco or Wesson. That's the only kinda oil you want."

"Fine," I said. I took everything else out of the box, noting where I'd gone wrong with many of my other shopping choices. "It was Tyka, wasn't it?"

Darryl was rinsing a large pot and set it on the stove before he replied. "That lil' old gal strolls up into the Lemon Drop, eyeballing Chicken like the poor man minding his business on his stool bothered her. Yeah, she told us."

I could only laugh. The three of us spent a lot of energy trying not to tell each other things that one or the other always did anyway.

"I had her old man holed up on the couch in the back too," Darryl added. "Got into a fight with somebody on the street. I didn't see who, but he was messed up pretty bad. She took him on home. Didn't want me to see that look in her eye, neither, but I saw it. That drunk bastard is goin' ta be the end of her if she ain't careful. The man same as he was when we was boys in the Lafitte. Ain't gon' change either."

There were many things that could get Tyka into trouble, her mouth being foremost in my mind, but it was clear for anyone who cared to look that her father really hurt her. Neither of us could do anything about it.

"That's Tyka's cross to bear," I said. "And she won't let none of us help her carry that load. We've tried."

"All right, then, let's get on with it. Quit stallin'. Hand me that flour. I don't even want to see what kinda mess you got in that canister over there. And how long it been in there anyway?"

Darryl took the flour and waved off the measuring cup I tried to offer him. *Just like a cook—or a skilled Vodou priest.* He fired up the stove and heated the oil. He followed by drizzling in the flour and whisking.

"How they break through your defenses?" Darryl didn't look up from the pot. Probably trying to conceal the worry that clouded his features but was still in his voice.

"I hadn't set them back up," I said. "After the incident with that customer."

Darryl looked up then. "Second time, huh?"

"And the last." I peered over his shoulder and observed the beautifully browning concoction in the pot.

"What kind of case is Salimah's lawyer building up?" Darryl asked.

"I don't really know," I admitted. I could only hope that he was doing everything he could.

"Now drop them onions in the pot." He pointed at the bowl on the table and then went over to cut up the sausage he'd brought.

"Sophie, Rashad, the cops . . ." I didn't dare tell anyone else about the officer in Algiers. But if I knew Darryl, he'd find out sooner or later. I just couldn't talk about it now; the whole thing still had me rattled. I pulled out some chicken breasts that I had in the refrigerator and set them on the counter. Darryl looked at me as if I'd just proposed we use day-old shrimp. "What?"

"What you plan on doin' with that?" He pointed at the chicken container like it was poison.

"I like chicken in my gumbo."

"I don't, and I damn sure ain't puttin' that in here. Who knows how long you done had that laid up here? That's your problem: everythang need to be fresh."

Effectively chastised, I put my chicken—and it was only two days old—back in the refrigerator. I watched as Darryl put in the sausage, fresh crab, and shrimp the color of the lake. He gave everything a good stir and then plopped down at the table. Another piece of candy found its way into his mouth.

"Suppose ain't no use stopping now," he said as soon as I'd slid into the chair opposite him. "So what you gon' need to do is to stay outta the crosshairs of whoever you got riled up."

"It's not the police," I said to the unanswered question.

"Guess it's somebody got more juice than you. Lot of priests and priestesses in these parts. You got your eye turned to one in particular?"

I did. "I suppose any of them could do it, but the only one I think has some incentive to do it is Lucien."

Darryl stretched his neck back and whistled. "Cops put on a show every now and again about hustlin' him. But word is he got somethin' on 'em."

"Maybe it's the other way around," I said.

Darryl's eyes went wide. "How you figure?"

"If he's behind the break-in, he had to be doing it for them." I explained what I'd learned about the death squad.

"Ain't like we didn't suspect it," Darryl said. "This seems low, though, even for Lucien."

But not Kiah, I thought to myself.

My friend and I sat in a companionable silence for a while after that. Me waiting for him to say he was sorry, and him feeling like by showing up, he already had.

Darryl made to get up but made the slightest trace of a wince. "Go on and stir that pot. It ain't gonna cook itself."

I got up and stirred. Then I groped around in the back of the cabinet for a general pain concoction I'd whipped up for a customer. I returned to the table with the bottle and pushed it toward him with a tentative finger. "Add five drops to your sweet tea or water, twice a day," I said.

He didn't look at me and didn't argue but clasped the bottle between his fingers and averted his gaze. "Can I take some now?"

And that, more than anything that had happened to me in the last week, scared the hell out of me.

CHAPTER
TWENTY-EIGHT

After a day spent running long-neglected errands and chasing my own tail, I rounded the corner and slid into the parking spot right in front of my house. This time, the space was open, just as it should be. I was halfway to the front door, lamenting the fact that Lucien was running a game of his own and had no intention of letting me in on it, when I heard a voice both familiar and unexpected.

I turned and marveled when, for the first time ever, I saw Chicken someplace other than the corner barstool at the Lemon Drop. He opened the hatch on his pickup truck. Metal scraped against metal, and he set a toolbox down on the ground.

I walked over, and he promptly shoved a crate into my arms. "Sweet Belly said you was in need of some things."

Next, he hopped up into the bed, hoisted what looked like a table onto his shoulder, and jumped down beside me. For a man who was about as wide as my thigh and wore at least a week's worth of stubble, he was surprisingly spry.

The words of thanks I wanted to convey mixed with the part of me that wanted to say "No, I can't take the handout" and clogged my throat.

I stood there with a silly grin on my face, willing myself not to cry for a few deep breaths before I finally muttered something: "Chicken." I had to stop to breathe again. "Thank you—"

He swooped up the toolbox with his free hand and said, "Getting heavier by the minute."

"I mean it." He was as uncomfortable with my thanks as I was with accepting the gifts.

Chicken couldn't echo my thoughts, but he didn't need to. I thought then of the man who bound us all together, Darryl. There were many places one could pass the hours in New Orleans if you wanted a good drink. The Sazerac was just okay and the food was good, but nobody was fooled. Darryl was the reason everyone came, and he was the glue that held us together.

I walked toward the back of the house, and without another word, Chicken followed, waving away my offer of help. I had my hands full anyway.

The table was beautiful. Round, highly polished, and reclaimed with a love as deep and beautiful as New Orleans's African roots. He didn't complain as I had him move it around a few times until it was positioned just right. I got the chairs that were against the wall and slid them back under my new table.

"Your daddy told us what to get." He pulled off his cap and gestured at the crate that I'd left by the door. I didn't bother to try to stop or wipe away the tear that slid down my cheek. Papa had thought of everything: candles, dried herbs, oils. It was a veritable Vodou priestess starter kit. Nearly everything I'd lost replaced in an instant.

I didn't go through the polite formality of offering Chicken money. I didn't have it to give, and even if I did, he wouldn't take it. It was one of the things tourists to New Orleans sensed but never quite understood.

Like in Haiti: once you were accepted as part of the community, you were family. And family was there for the good times and bad.

I did get Chicken a bowl of the gumbo Darryl and I had made the night before. We ate on the front porch.

By the time I'd taken our bowls back inside, it was already dark. I walked Chicken out to his truck. I struggled with whether to even bring it up, but finally I gathered my courage. "Is Darryl all right?"

Chicken stopped walking, then turned around after an interminable moment in which I died a thousand times. His expression didn't change, but he shifted his toolbox from his right hand to the left and back again. "He won't say."

My heart dropped as Chicken climbed into his truck, fired up the engine, and threw up the peace sign as he pulled away.

In addition to being a duly initiated mambo, I was now a detective. I would find out how to help our friend.

I'd just closed the door when my phone rang. I darted into the kitchen, where I'd left it on the table, and answered on the fourth ring.

"I'm over in the Quarter," Tyka said. "You know somebody done changed that shop's name. Got up a new sign and everything."

Had Salimah somehow sold the shop? "You sure it's Voodoo Real?"

"You insult my intelligence, Mambo," Tyka chuckled. "There's a light on. I'm gonna check it out."

"Tyka, wait—"

She'd already hung up.

I sat in the parlor anxious for a return call. None came. To keep my fingers busy, I tidied up a bit, then checked the time. Ten minutes. I called Tyka back.

Voice mail.

I texted. What's going on???

As the minutes ticked by, I paced, checked my phone's battery and bars—all three visible—a knot of worry twisting my stomach.

By the time I'd hit "Redial" three times more without an answer, I was already outside, halfway to my car. For reasons I didn't understand, I turned, ran back to my shop, smashed the machete case, and took the weapon with me.

Twelve minutes from my front door to the Hotel Royal in the French Quarter. I got out of the car and said a silent prayer that the valet—a brother whose aunt was a longtime client of mine—was here. I tossed him my keys.

He took in the set of my jaw and said, "I'll keep it close by."

I nodded and sprinted down Royal Street, turning the corner onto Dumaine, maneuvering around a couple snapping pictures and a lone man walking a dog. I slowed as I approached Voodoo Real.

From across the street, probably the vantage point Tyka had called from, I took in the dark storefront. No movement. Eyes on a swivel, I scanned both sides of the street and darted across.

I tried the door. Unlocked. I glanced over my shoulder and stepped inside.

Much of the mess the police had left had been cleaned up. But the overturned box, a torn piece of clothing, blood droplets—all signs of a more recent struggle. I knelt, stamping down a whimper, and reached out a finger. The blood was fresh.

I whipped out my phone and called Tyka again.

CHAPTER TWENTY-NINE

"Saint Louis Cemetery Number Two." The slimy male voice on the other end uttered the words almost like an invitation—or a dare.

I stood there with the phone in my hand, fingers going numb from the iron grip I held. Each of the next five hysterical redials went directly to voice mail.

I raced through the city, daring the cops to stop me, a trail of curses and angry horn blares in my wake. I careened around the corner at North Claiborne and North Robertson and skidded to a stop at the cemetery, with the moon slowly making its way to its peak.

The gate was locked. I reached for my purse, and the few potions I had left there, and my stomach dropped. They were back at home.

Machete tucked into my waistband, I'd wedged my foot into the fence and was hoisting myself up when Kiah's voice snared me.

"As much as I would like to see you try to climb that fence, that's far enough. Come on down from there."

I dropped back to the ground and turned around slowly. Half of Kiah's face was hidden in shadow. The long jacket, though, and the gleam of a nine-inch machete in his right hand, were all too clear.

"I was right," I said, advancing. "You here? Now? Lucien is somehow behind all of this."

"Stay right there and drop that blade before you cut yourself." The tonal squeal of a nearby streetcar punctuated his command.

"I'll stay right here, all right." I reached behind my back and brandished my own machete. "But I'm not dropping anything. Make your move." He took a step forward, as did I. "How did you find me? You into tapping phones now?"

"For some reason, you think you're some kind of detective," he spat. "But you don't even know when somebody's on your tail. Been following you since that day at the Lemon Drop."

"That looks like a Bowie." I raised my own weapon and pointed.

"And I see you favor a panga."

He knew his weapons. "You skilled in the art of *tire manchèt*?"

"Haitians don't have no patent on that dance."

"I just have one question for you, and then you can take that and go find those bullies you need to settle up with."

He sneered. I'd plucked that old nerve like a harp string. "I'm listening."

"Where's Tyka?"

Kiah rushed forward. I backpedaled and raised my machete in time to meet his downward stroke.

I pivoted left and swung down from the side, but my opponent was quick and blocked the blow. I sliced at his middle; he dodged. Our blades met overhead, and I landed a kick that sent him stumbling backward. In the back of my mind, all I could think about was Tyka. We continued trading this way before I noticed that Kiah wasn't coming at me as hard as I knew he could. I stopped and lowered my arm.

I backed away, toward the gate. Curiously, Kiah stood there watching. He tilted his head as if listening for something. I chanced making a dash for the fence. After a few hacks with the machete, the rusty chain and the machete gave way. I dropped the broken pieces and ran inside.

I didn't turn back. No footsteps pursued me. The realization hit me then. That hadn't been Kiah's voice on the phone. Something or someone else was in play here.

The pathways were empty of the living, but the dead were out in force. They never lost their interest in the living. Ghostly murmurs from behind a quickly gathering mist.

"Tyka!" I howled and screamed like a thing wounded. Only the echo of my voice returned. Stupid. I'd probably just alerted whoever was waiting for me.

The feel of magic was thick in the air and rank as rotting meat. It was a twisted, ugly magic. It writhed and struggled under the will of an unpracticed and dangerous hand.

Shadows deepened with the quickly descending night. The moon advanced on the horizon, silently obscured by clouds. A voice called out to me, more whisper than bellow. It drew me onward as more souls drifted from their tombs. They crowded beside and behind me. They wouldn't interfere. Wouldn't come to my aid or harm. They'd observe my victory or demise with the impassivity only the dead could master.

The crowded tombs gave way to a grassy clearing. I gasped at what I saw at its center. Standing atop a sheet, one side green, the other black, split and sewn together, was Rashad. He was cloaked in a white robe with a large green number 3 on his chest.

A ghastly smile drew up the corners of his mouth.

On the sheet lay things that shot an arrow of fear through me. An image of Saint George sat behind offerings of rum and tobacco. A rooster strutted untethered. It pecked at what I knew instinctively to be the goat horn Rashad or whomever he'd employed had stolen from my shop. And beside them both, catching a glint of starlight as the clouds billowed past, a saber.

At the edge of the sheet nearest to where Rashad now stood watching me was a three-legged cauldron. It shone with the hint of a recent oiling. Inside would be things of metal: blades, chains, screws.

And today was Tuesday. Each lwa had days that were significant, days when their powers were at their peaks. It all pointed to the spirit that Rashad was calling on to end me. One of the Seven African Powers.

Ògún, the God of Iron. The Architect . . . the Wild Man of the Woods . . . the One Who Feeds on Blood. The Dragonslayer.

"Ògún méje logun mi," he chanted. "My Ògún manifests in seven different ways."

My blood roiled, Erzulie building power within me.

The spirits that had been trailing me murmured and rasped. They fanned out, enclosing us in a seemingly impenetrable circle of souls.

As I watched Rashad, the pieces rushed together all at once. He'd heard Virgil and his partner planning to speak out about the death squads, and he'd used it. He knew the cops would want the case to go away as quietly as possible and wouldn't look too far for the culprit. "Did you really kill a man to get your hands on your cousin's shop?" I asked, moving away from his direct line of sight. "We could have saved you the trouble and taken up a collection to get you your own place, if that's all you wanted."

Rashad's stare was intense, cold, but he hesitated. The souls, as perplexed as I was, flitted their vacant eye sockets back and forth between us. When he found his voice again, it was unsteady. "Your pops turned me down, you know. Just like my daddy did. But Salimah's ass landed

236

on our doorstep after our mamas died in the wreck, and what did that muthafuckah do? He lit up! Treated her like some Black-ass princess. Gave her everything, trained her. And me? I didn't exist. Like it was my fault for living. Don't think he put together a handful of words for me since."

"Your father saw something. He saw this." I gestured at the grotesque display before him. "He saw you for what you are, and he was right not to teach you. We won't let you get away with what you've done. You must know that."

Rashad laughed, a good full-bellied laugh. "Really? Because you and Lucien are supposed to be some big-time Beninites?"

I didn't answer. Didn't need to.

He stopped laughing. "When's the last time you talked to your sidekick?"

I went rigid as a petrified branch.

"Not for a hour or so, huh?" Rashad paced back and forth along the sheet, careful not to let a foot fall outside the square cloth, where I needed him to be.

I couldn't speak. As bulletproof as Tyka seemed to be sometimes, not even she could stand against the powers of our craft, especially twisted as it appeared in Rashad's hands.

"Cat got your tongue, Mambo?" Rashad began to radiate a sickly, muted green—the color of a dying forest. "I'll spell it out for you. She tried to put up a fight—I'll give that to her." He pointed to his cheek. "Clocked me right here with one of her pointy-ass elbows. Was going in for one of her famous choke holds when I got her."

"If you—"

"Don't worry. She's alive. Well, I guess she's alive, but probably not for too much longer. She'll wake up in enough time to scream herself silly, clawing and scratching at her coffin until her air gives out. Fitting end, wouldn't you say? Her drunk daddy won't even have to worry about burial expenses."

237

I shook with rage and fear. "What have you done?"

"What needed to be done. If you hadn't brought her into this, she'd be creeping around boosting a car or whatever the hell her felonious ass does all day. *You* got her killed. And now you'll go to join her. You want me to put you beside her? Nah, you probably want to have your body buried out there in the swamp beside your pops when I get through with him."

I struck.

~

My arms rose steadily. At the point where the moisture from the rain-dampened earth climbed in rippled undulations, the motion edged into the supernatural dominion of the goddess Erzulie, emerging from her slumber as if riding in the tail end of a storm. I stirred it up, drank it all in, and drew down what I could from the sparse clouds cloaked in the night sky.

I surrendered, feeling as if I'd crossed into a viscous ocean, breathing and seeing as if through a shroud. The goddess called to her partner, the lwa Damballa. Indignation and outrage became the waves on which we rose and fell as we wove the Sky Father into being.

The length of a felled tree, the width of a stream, coiled and ready for battle, Damballa manifested as a great serpent.

Simultaneously, Rashad called on Ògún. Groans and creaks filled the air. Stray nails, bolts, remnants of the chain I'd smashed—everything metal within the cemetery flew toward him. I dived and crouched to avoid being hit.

He condensed it all, kneaded the mound like a metal loaf. Soon, a swirling iron ball of death hovered in front of him.

With one hand, Rashad held the metal globe in front of him. With the other he reached out and ripped the cemetery gate from its hinges. I spun around as it hurtled forward, slicing the wind in its wake.

The gate was closing in: ten feet . . . five feet. I drew on Damballa and flattened the serpent into a liquid barrier wall. I braced for impact. The wall stopped the gate, but the force flung me backward, tumbling feet over head, about ten paces closer to Rashad. A spray of water and iron showered down.

The metal globe. Just as I was stumbling to my feet, Rashad launched the mass at me. I reformed the serpent. This time I sent it slithering ahead at lightning speed. It shattered the mass, but one piece found its mark. An iron finial struck me in the chest.

Struggling to maintain concentration, I urged my creation closer. For the first time, Rashad's calm visage faltered. He ran to the edge of the sheet and snatched up the saber. Again and again, where he hacked at the serpent, it regenerated.

The weapon moved with inhuman speed. I'd already sunk to the ground, but I kept my will fixed as the cycle of destruction and rebirth continued. Through my connection with the serpent, I sensed the force of the hacks subsiding. Rashad was weakening as much as I was.

Unsteady on his feet, Rashad stumbled. It was enough. The serpent rose up to its full height, surged forward, and wrapped itself around Rashad's neck.

"Wait," I moaned. I was losing control of my creation. It couldn't kill Rashad yet. I needed him to tell me where Tyka was.

But fueled by Erzulie's rage, the serpent persisted, sapping away precious liters of water from Rashad's bloodstream.

I held both my hands aloft, fingers splayed, battling for control as I crawled forward. The dead crowded in closer.

"Tyka!" I screamed. "Where is she?"

My veins bulged. My eyes felt as if they were ready to burst from their sockets, every muscle in my body on the verge of snapping. My chest ached where the finial remained lodged in my flesh. My breath was a misfiring engine.

"Go ahead and kill me, witch," Rashad sputtered through the terror in his eyes. "'Cause if I get out of here—"

I inched forward, my arms burning with the effort to remain aloft.

"You can go easily or the hard way. Tell me where she is." I didn't lament the note of pleading in my voice.

Rashad glared at me. His hands worked, still trying but failing to call on the iron spirit. "This isn't over."

As the serpent circled, applying more pressure, Rashad's facade crumbled.

The Rashad I knew resurfaced. Fright bucked his eyes as the serpent's head was poised in front of him, ready to claim its sacrifice.

"Get it off!" Rashad gasped, turning his face away from the horror. "I'll tell you. Just get it off!"

I slowly turned my left wrist, beginning the sequence of moves that would unravel my creation. The serpent turned to hiss its disapproval and outrage at me, but it uncoiled one ring and, ever so slightly, loosened its grip.

"Where?"

I trembled all over with the effort to hold the power I'd unleashed. I glanced down at the shard of metal inches from my heart. The blood . . .

I shouldn't have looked down.

As Rashad opened his mouth to speak, the water serpent took advantage of my momentary distraction. It opened its mouth wide, wider than even its natural cousins, and consumed a wailing Rashad.

"No," I whimpered. The fight didn't end so much as it dissipated, like a drop of blood in a bowl of water, with a residual metallic taint that remained.

Once the serpent was sated, it slithered over to where I'd collapsed, one hand still ineffectually held high. The water serpent set its head on my stomach, satisfaction lighting its bejeweled eyes. With an angry flick of my wrist, it sizzled and popped and disintegrated into splashes of water and torrid mist.

I greedily sucked in those spent droplets and regained a small measure of my strength. I screamed Tyka's name, and it reverberated against tombs stoic and silent as sentinels before crashing back to me. I lay there on the ground and bawled like a child.

"Think!" I commanded myself through the pain in my chest and then stumbled to my feet. Sirens roared, still distant, but closing. Black spots clouded my vision, and I was drenched in a sticky combination of blood, sweat, and water. Only Erzulie kept me alive.

My mind replayed everything I'd seen since I entered the cemetery, everything Rashad had said. I had no clue as to where Tyka was, and I—she—was running out of time. Did I start trying to blast my way into every tomb?

"Where is she?" I kept repeating as I paced. Finally, my mind returned to me. I was in a cemetery, after all. If Tyka was indeed here, then she'd be the only body that still held moisture—if she was still alive. I combed the area, stumbling and sending my senses out in search of water reserves that could only be found in great quantities in a human body.

Painful minutes ticked away. How much time had I wasted with Kiah and Rashad? Had Kiah been working with—

There.

I stumble-ran back a few steps, trailed by the dead. Near the entrance at a pyramid tomb. A spot that looked freshly tilled.

I set to that dirt like a madwoman, only vaguely aware that the sirens had gotten closer. I clawed and tore at the earth, channeling the last bit of life I had in me to seep in moisture to make it easier to tear away.

I had no idea how much time had passed before my torn and bleeding nails scratched at something hard.

And then I saw a pair of golden eyes. The same ones I'd seen on a priest king in a New Orleans East warehouse years prior.

The leopard's form peeled away from the shadows and coalesced before my fading vision. I could only croak the word "Tyka" and point to the hole. Feline forepaws tore and clawed at the soil as I felt myself drifting away.

CHAPTER THIRTY

Beeping and snoring. The scents of antiseptic and roasted meat and . . . flowers. A hushed murmur of voices. And pain that bloomed like a rose in my chest.

Tyka.

I opened my eyes and bolted upright.

None other than Darryl "Sweet Belly" Boudreaux sat nodding off in a chair pulled close to my bed.

"Whoa," he said upon waking up. "Just hold your horses. You wanna open that back up again?" I followed his finger and glanced down at the expertly stitched wound in my chest.

"Where is—"

"She's fine," he cut in. "Heard that little old gal cussed something awful when they brought her in. Yanking out tubes, threatening everybody. They had to hold her down and give her a sedative. Soon as she woke up, though, she hightailed it outta here. She'll resurface when she ready."

I lay back, satisfied that Tyka was all right. *And* that Rashad was gone. I marveled at how blind we'd all been. How he'd fooled his cousin, me, the police. I then noticed a beautiful bouquet on the table next to my bed.

"Your Creole detective brought 'em," Darryl said.

So Roman had been to see me too. I wasn't ashamed to admit to myself that it made me happy.

"And my father?" I chanced.

Darryl looked away, pursed his lips. "He knows you'll be fine."

Papa hadn't come. I hadn't really expected him to either.

"Where are my clothes?" I swung my legs over the side of the bed. Winced. It felt like a ten-pound barbell sat on my chest.

"Uh-uh." Darryl shook his head. "You gon' lay right back down there and wait till the doctor come back around."

I'd always hated hospitals. The way my mother told it, a few hours after I was born, I damn near dragged her out of the maternity ward and only stopped wailing once I was settled at home in my own bassinet, next to her and Papa.

Plus, once they got back the results from the bloodwork I suspected they'd already ordered, I'd have to answer some uncomfortable questions about my physiology.

I held Darryl's gaze, and he huffed but went over and got my things out of a closet. Helped me dress too. When I felt strong enough to stand on my own, I had him sneak me out of there. Left their flimsy robe on the bed.

I could care for myself better at home with my own works anyway. I didn't need to battle all the germs and infections that lived and thrived at that supposedly sterile place.

As soon as we got home, I collapsed on the couch and was out.

"Got you some macaroni and cheese and some smothered chicken in there. Greens is on—you just need to check 'em in a half hour," Darryl said when he heard me stirring. He fussed around me, fluffing pillows on the couch and rearranging a blanket. I'd refused his command to hole up in my bedroom all day.

I waved him off. "I can check the greens. You get on back to the Lemon Drop. You know Chicken can't finish his drink unless you're there hovering over him."

Darryl was dubious, probably still unconvinced of my cooking talents. "He'll be all right. I'll just wait till them greens is done; then I'll get out'cha hair."

I didn't argue. Wouldn't have mattered what I said. I wanted nothing more than time alone with my thoughts, but I got the feeling I'd have plenty of time waiting for my chest to feel like someone hadn't driven over it with a Hummer.

Darryl sat in the wingback chair and winced when he lifted his leg over his knee. He saw my raised eyebrow and waved it off.

"You need to quit gapin' at somebody every time they tweak an ankle or eat too much boudin."

"Which is it?"

"You know my sister-in-law is a nurse at the hospital, right?" Avoidance was one of my friend's many talents.

I raised an eyebrow. "Did she tell you to make an appointment with a doctor too?"

"She worked the emergency room when they carried Tyka in. 'Fore she snuck out, she peeked her head in your room. That Lucien fella was there. She took that as a sign to leave, satisfied that you was breathing and all."

So she had come by. That's all that mattered. When she was ready, when she got over the embarrassment and whatever tangle of emotions she felt after nearly losing her life to someone she thought she should have gotten the best of, she'd be back around.

"Wait." I just realized what I'd heard. And I recalled the now obviously fake battle with Kiah, and the sight of Lucien's eyes in the shadows at the cemetery. "Did you say Lucien was there?"

Darryl nodded. "Ain't no mistakin' him. Yeah, he was there."

I pondered what this meant and must have drifted off into another impromptu nap, because soon Darryl was shaking my arm.

"Food ready when you want to eat." My friend set a tray of food and a cup of hot tea down on the coffee table. "I'm headin' out."

It took me three days to polish off the food Darryl had brought me. In that time, I nursed myself back to reasonably good health. I ignored the calls from the hospital chastising me for leaving and demanding that I come in to be checked out. I dreaded the slow death that would be coming in the form of trickles of bills from this doctor and that one.

I was ready to get back to being what I was, a mambo. I had clients waiting. The detective work would be left to the experts.

And almost as if I'd called it, I heard an authoritative knock on my door. I moved the curtain aside and saw the unmarked sedan parked behind mine.

When I opened the door, Roman's gaze locked onto mine, and in it I saw the man who used to love me. Who listened intently to my thoughts and opinions. Who snuck up behind me in the mornings while I made tea and planted a kiss on my cheek. The twang of morning breath I imagined smelling like cinnamon.

He pushed past me into the living room. He did have the good sense to remove his shoes. He handed me the flower arrangement I'd left behind.

"I think you forgot this at the hospital."

"Who ratted on me?"

Roman smiled his smile. That smile. The one that had silenced many arguments.

"Cops and lawyers and journalists—" he said, beginning the familiar refrain.

I finished it for him. "Never reveal their sources."

I padded past him into the kitchen, and he followed. I was careful not to wince at the lingering pain I felt in my chest. I set a mug in front of him and started the water for some instant coffee.

"Sit down," he said.

I watched him move around the kitchen, getting the milk and sugar and spoons with the familiarity of someone who'd spent many days here. He also found the cake that Darryl had left and cut a piece for each of us.

I hated how self-conscious I felt. My ratty robe was less than flattering. My hair was standing on end in some places. And I hadn't had the strength to even slather some coconut oil on my ashy self.

"You're looking well," he said as he poured and then sat down across from me. My smile was just shy of a blush. "That stunt you pulled down at the marina?" He whistled and shook his head. My breath quickened. "I decided right there while I watched you and that girl drive off . . . I realized I could never see you again. 'Cause if I did, I'd either arrest you or strangle you."

I appreciated the confession and in truth had expected much worse.

"But here you are." I didn't add that he'd automatically sat in his favorite chair. The one that gave him a view of both the back door and the window with the herb box over the kitchen sink. "And I want to say I'm sorry," I added. "I shouldn't have done what I did. It was to help someone, but it was still wrong."

"Seeing you with that thing stuck in your chest. All that blood . . ." Roman's gaze left mine and drifted to the window. When he didn't continue, I asked what I'd been dying to know ever since I'd heard the sirens at the cemetery.

"How'd you know where to find us?"

Roman slurped his coffee and chewed a piece of cake before responding. "What did I just tell you?"

"Sources," I repeated. "Right."

Two names came to mind: Lucien and Kiah. Somebody not on the force. Secrets were still plentiful in this relationship. Wait . . . what relationship? No, definitely not a relationship.

"We let her go, you know." Another bite of cake. Crumbs fell to the floor. I'd sweep them up later. And another spoonful of sugar, a slurp. He'd used the same spoon that had already been in his mouth. My mama would have cried scandal.

"Salimah?"

He nodded. "Couldn't find Rashad, but once we get DNA results back from the scene, that'll confirm he was there. He won't get far. We'll catch him. For what he did to Virgil, to you." He paused. "And to Tyka."

I couldn't tell the good detective that he would not, in fact, ever find another trace of Rashad.

"All this so that he could steal her business from her?" I said.

"This is why I didn't talk to you about my cases. The gore was one thing, but crime often doesn't make much sense. Greed is powerful. It's just that simple."

"You just couldn't believe me when I told you, huh? Left that woman in jail for no good reason other than laziness." I hadn't touched my tea.

"Do I look like the chief of police to you? Maybe the mayor? You don't know shit about what it means to have a boss. But let me tell you something: It means you don't get to make up the rules that suit you. It means that sometimes, hell, most of the time, shit ain't up to you. You follow orders."

I regarded Roman for a few moments before I spoke. "And your orders were to keep this case quiet. To cover up the fact that Virgil was going to come forward about the squads."

Roman drained his cup and went to refill it. "Like I always say, I can't stomach a dumb woman."

"Or one who doesn't believe everything you do."

I knew as soon as I clasped my big mouth shut that I'd said the wrong thing. It always amazed me how well couples, family, those closest to us knew what buttons to push and pushed them at will. And how readily, like clockwork, the offended party clapped back.

Roman didn't take the bait, though. Sometimes, people actually used their innate ability to change. Sometimes.

"Does it still hurt?" He gestured at my chest.

"Just a little," I said.

Roman slurped his coffee, and I gulped down my tea. He took out his phone, likely scanning the news the way he liked to in the morning. I in turn watched him and the bird at the feeder sitting outside my kitchen window. In time, he brought us each another piece of cake and refilled our cups. Our manner was smooth and familiar as Mardi Gras come spring.

CHAPTER
THIRTY-ONE

Weeks passed before I was able to go and see Salimah, my mind and body in need of healing. Plus, my practice had picked back up. With Mardi Gras in full swing, finding a parking spot would be next to impossible, so instead of driving, I called one of those bike taxis. The pedaler took the new waterfront route and, as I was no tourist, kept his chatter to a minimum and allowed me to enjoy the view of the water and revelers. The drunks and serious partygoers wouldn't be out until much later.

The pedaler dropped me off at the corner of Royal and Dumaine. I couldn't help recalling when I'd come here to return Sophie's thumb ring. Instead of tourists and beads, police cars and anxious onlookers had crowded the street.

The Voodoo Real sign was back in its place. I still cringed at the spelling. Though the tenuous relationship between our religion and capitalism allowed us to profit from the tourists, I also saw it as our responsibility to educate them in the process.

It was an edict that even I didn't always live up to. Accordingly, I set those feelings aside, opened the door to the sound of a light chime, and stepped inside. The air was chill against my sun-warmed skin.

The mambo stood behind the glass case filled with books and jewelry and other items for sale.

She looked up at me and didn't smile, but she didn't frown either. A few open cardboard boxes lay along the side wall. In the search for evidence, the police had most certainly destroyed her place as thoroughly as Rashad had destroyed mine.

"Mambo Grenade," I said.

"Mambo Dumond." There was a hardness to her features that hadn't been there before her ordeal. Even a line or two around the eyes that perhaps I just hadn't noticed before. Tastefully applied makeup covered any lingering bruises.

But it was her manner that had changed the most. Before she had been quiet, more introspective than aloof. Now her manner was of defeat, mistrust. Being unfairly accused of a murder, one that took place practically in your own shop, committed by a jealous relative? I'd have run for the hills. The fact that Salimah was here, right where it had all begun, told me I'd misjudged her.

"You closing up or stocking up?" I asked, gesturing at the boxes.

Salimah sighed before answering. "I was going to go back to Houston. But there's nothing better waiting for me back there. Truth is, since the murder? Folks are clamoring to get in here. I can't keep them away. They're buying everything in sight and asking all about what happened. You know, I even thought about opening up that little room upstairs for tours. I'd be a millionaire inside a year."

Salimah perched herself up on a stool behind the counter. "No, I'm staying right here."

She didn't offer me a seat . . . or a cold drink.

"Look, Salimah, I'm sorry about everything that happened."

She crossed her arms and pursed her lips. "Rashad isn't coming back, is he?"

I shook my head. "You've been to the cemetery?"

"And I found some books in the things Rashad's girlfriend dropped off. He was trying to call on some tricky spirits, and he had no goddamned idea what he was doing."

"Greed does strange things to people."

"Rashad wasn't only greedy," Salimah countered. "He was something a whole hell of a lot worse—weak. I probably had a hand in it, though. That boy was a taker if I ever seen one. And it was never enough. If he'd ever tried to learn anything the right way, this spot would have been his. But he always thought somebody was supposed to give him something just for being born and for being a man."

I didn't want to pile on. Rashad was her cousin, not mine.

After a few moments, she continued. "What are you?"

My eyes narrowed. "What do you mean?"

"Bullshit," she said. "You ain't nothing like me. This Beninite thing is more than I thought. You made him disappear. And I know you didn't bury him. There are traces of his essence there. But he's dead. I can feel it."

She was right, but there was no way I could tell her that. "Rashad killed Virgil Dunn. He tried to kill me and set you up. He didn't visit you in jail—I did. He didn't do anything to try to clear you—I did. I would think a thank-you would be in order, not an interrogation."

"You know, I never liked you," Salimah said.

"And I don't need you to."

After a begrudging minute, she finally said, "Thank you for what you tried to do for me."

I nodded and turned to leave. There was nothing more to say.

"There is just one question, though," Salimah said to my back. I stopped as I wondered if she was thinking the same thing I was.

"There's something that doesn't add up."

I turned around.

"Lucien, the cops, Sophie, and Virgil. There's a connection."

A puzzle piece still missing. She was right. "It's not like the cops are going to tell us a thing. Somebody wanted this covered up. And they may have killed one of their own to do so."

Salimah reached beneath the counter and slipped her purse over her shoulder. "Let's go pay Houngan Alexander a visit."

Noting Lucien's car and driver outside, Salimah and I barged through the door and glared at the lackey who looked, for just a fleeting moment, like he was going to raise a hand to try to stop us.

There was a mirror on Lucien's desk, a lamp tilted directly on his face. It was the slightly off tilt of the toupee that set off Salimah's laughter. The perfectly coiffed, cut-at-a-barbershop hair was a likely very expensive bought-and-paid-for piece. For most men, this would have been a nonissue, but for a man whose middle name was Vanity, this was huge.

Salimah and I exchanged a glance filled with knowing and a little mischief. The first I'd seen on her face since the first time I'd met her. Lucien composed himself and stood glaring at us.

"What the hell is wrong with you two? Barging into a man's office like you don't have a damn bit of sense. Get out!" He waved his long-fingered hand in dismissal.

At this point, the lackey appeared. It was clear that the man didn't know what to do but felt that he should at least make a show of doing something.

I tossed my head at the lackey. "I guess we should talk to *him* about the hurricane and the police?"

If Lucien's evil eye alone could have cut us down, we'd be long dead and buried. But after what Salimah and I had been through, we barely batted an eye.

Without an invite, Salimah sashayed over and sat at the little settee, not at his desk. Smart move. I followed without complaint. Lucien would have to come to us, and not hide behind his perceived authority with that ridiculous desk.

He came over and mumbled something to his employee, probably calling in Kiah, then sat opposite us. We weren't offered refreshments.

He steepled his fingers and crossed his legs. "What is it you think you know?"

"I know that the squads were real," I began. "Virgil and his partner were going to come forward about it. I also know the police had help—our kind of help—in covering up their crimes—"

"And," Salimah said, breaking in, "I know that you let me, a fellow vodouisant, sit in jail, barely lifting one of those manicured fingers of yours to help me." She was leaned forward, nostrils flared. "I called you. Reina tried to come to you for help, and your self-serving behind turned her away too. And you did it to protect them. All that stuff you did at the end wasn't enough."

Lucien held up a hand, but I wasn't finished.

"Rashad killing Virgil was an unfortunate inconvenience for the cops. They didn't care that he was dead. In fact, they were probably relieved. But they couldn't let a lengthy investigation uncover what some of their ilk had done. And you were willing to sacrifice one of your own to save them. And you sent Kiah to the cemetery to stall me. You were there. I still don't know what that was about. Whether you were trying to help or hinder remains to be seen."

Lucien sighed heavily. Salimah was on the edge of her seat, seemingly seconds from leaping over the small table and tearing out his throat. I put my hand on her forearm to still her. Lucien was silent for a long time, his gaze drifting over us and out the floor-to-ceiling windows. When he looked at us again, there was what I thought was genuine contrition in his eyes. Silly, in hindsight, how I expected an apology.

"You would have done the exact same thing in my position." He delivered this in a level tone that shocked even me. He leaned back in his chair and crossed his legs.

Salimah and I tripped all over each other's tongues, ready to unleash fervent denials.

"Let me finish," Lucien said.

We restrained ourselves, after a fashion.

"Police don't make requests of the citizens they're sworn to protect. They make demands. And if you don't comply with those demands, what they can do to you is of the smallest consequence. It is what they can do to everybody around you that will send chills down the spine."

I could have done without the preaching, but I kept my mouth shut.

"I did what I had to do, and yes, I did a little more to ensure that I, my business, my family survived. Reina, you would have done the same if it meant saving your mother, and Salimah, if it meant saving that turncoat cousin of yours, you would have too."

He did have a point.

"What did you do for them?" I asked.

"Do you really want to carry the burden of the answer to that question?" Lucien asked. "Do either of you?"

Somehow, once again, the houngan had taken the wind right out of my sails. Every time I thought I had him on something, he evaporated through my fingers. He made a show of swiveling his head from me to Salimah and then, when we didn't reply, considered the matter settled.

"So now that that's all behind us, I'm actually glad you're here. There's something I've been thinking about."

"Cleansing your soul?" I offered. Though I wondered if, instead, he was thinking about whether word would get out that he was a mere mortal, one losing his hair. I was content to wait; making Lucien squirm was an art form. One that apparently Salimah was still working on because she threw her hands up in the air while we stared daggers at each other.

"Should we have what's his name order lunch while you two try to kill each other with your evil gazes? Wouldn't hurt to have a glass of water either."

I couldn't blame her. She'd been in jail for a crime she hadn't committed. And sent there by her own cousin, just to get his greedy hands on her shop. I'd gone through my own trials trying to help her. She was right: now wasn't the time for Lucien's or my games. I was about to say as much when he uttered the words "Vodou council."

After a moment of confused silence, I took the bait. "The man who wouldn't lift a finger to help us now wants some kind of union for wayward priests and priestesses?"

"If this mess taught us anything, it's that we need to organize," Lucien said, charging ahead. A gift of his. "We need a support system."

The irony of that statement wasn't lost on Salimah. She snorted, loudly.

"You know how many vodouisants set up shop in New Orleans last year?" Lucien leaned forward, hands clasped, forearms on his thighs. "Over a hundred, and nearly as many left. It's these kinds of riffraff that dispense little more than magicians' tricks and give us a bad name with the public and the cops."

I couldn't disagree with that. "And you're saying this council would control who can practice?" I was skeptical about how we would enforce something like that without a Vodou hit squad but chose not to voice that bit.

"That's exactly what I'm saying," Lucien said.

"But who's going to stop them?" Salimah said, clearly unconvinced. "You proposing we start burning down the shops of those who don't fall in line?"

"That's why we'll make it law."

My eyebrows shot up an inch. "I'm just going to sit here and wait for you to explain how we make such a thing a law."

"We have relationships with certain members of the political scene." By "we," Lucien meant "he," but that was splitting hairs.

"You remember what happened last year? Those hacks claiming to do in-home works and then robbing the good citizens of New Orleans?"

It had been a black eye for us all. That group had even forced people from their homes while holding other family members at gunpoint, hit every ATM they could, and taken everything they could on their way out. Luckily, they hadn't seriously hurt anybody, but the damage was done in other ways. People didn't trust, and the cops had come down hard on, the entire Vodou community.

"Senator King was just talking about that, and I think he might be on board for something like this. We get a local ordinance passed. If somebody tries to practice here without being vetted by our little council, the cops take care of it, not us."

"What makes you think I want anything to do with those bastards?" Salimah said, fuming.

"I was thinking of you when I came up with this—"

"I seriously doubt that," Salimah said.

"As I was saying . . ." Lucien was on a roll. "This will keep what happened to you from happening to any of us again. The cops will know who's on the up-and-up. Who's operating rogue. The finger will always point away from us."

"I'm with Salimah," I said. "I don't know if we can ever fully rely on the cops to do what they say they will."

"We may have to make it worth their while . . ."

"Great. A payoff? A sacrificial Vodou lamb once a quarter?"

"Take the emotion out of this and be reasonable. Name me another successful religion that doesn't have some sort of organizing body?"

The words "successful" and "religion" grouped together just didn't sit right with me. But I couldn't deny that we could be stronger if we worked together. I'd have to set aside the fact that it was Lucien Alexander proposing the idea and think about this logically.

"Decisions would need to be made by the group, not by one person," I said.

"Wait a minute," Salimah said, looking like she wanted to strangle me. "We haven't agreed to anything. I don't trust him, and I didn't think you were stupid enough to trust him either. I'm done. I came here to talk about why this asshole didn't help me and what he knew about this murder, not some new voodoo club. Find another ride home."

"Salimah, wait," I said.

She leaped from the chair as if it had burned her and stormed out of the office, leaving the door open. The lackey popped his head in. "Boss?"

Lucien waved a hand. "Close the door, John."

"I see you didn't try to stop her," Lucien said to me.

"She's not over what happened to her. We can't expect her to be ready for this just yet." Lucien and I had been adversaries for much of the time we'd known each other, but I had to admit he was onto something. "I don't appreciate her calling me stupid, though. That she'll have to answer for sooner or later."

We shared the first chuckle we'd shared in forever. I didn't want to admit it, but it felt good.

"You know they're going to give Detective Frost a commendation."

I didn't know, and I had to convince myself not to care. This was all such a ridiculously macabre joke.

"There should be rules," I said to change the subject. "Rules for what constitutes a real practice and what is just television junk."

Lucien nodded. "And an educational component. I don't know where some of these new initiates are being apprenticed, but they don't know their butterbur from a maca root."

Despite myself, I was getting excited. "And dues of some sort," I added. "Nothing big—some of us don't have practices as large as yours. But a fund not only for troubles like Salimah faced, but just a general pool for those who find themselves in need."

Lucien pursed his lips. "I don't know about all that, but dues, yes. We definitely need some kind of dues."

I inclined my head.

He added, "On a sliding scale according to practice size, of course."

There was much to work out, yes, but we had a start.

"Well, I wouldn't dare introduce this until we had all the kinks worked out," I offered. "Too many opinions would mean we'd never agree on anything."

"Agreed," Lucien said. "Better you and I work out the details and then present it to the larger community. And we'll have to deal with the, shall we say, subtle differences between voodoo and Vodou. Our spellings, the saints. You know."

God dammit. There was no end to this man's needling. Just when I thought we'd crossed a bridge, he proceeded to light it on fire. But I didn't bother taking the bait. I wouldn't be distracted. "When do we get started?"

Lucien thought for a moment and stood. "After Mardi Gras."

There was one more thing to discuss, and I waited to see who was going to broach the subject.

"He wasn't going to hurt you, you know," Lucien said.

"Figured as much," I admitted.

"I didn't know about the girl, your friend, until after. Not until I saw you digging up that grave—"

"And you took over when I passed out," I said.

Lucien nodded. "Kiah was only supposed to delay you a bit. Through means of my own, I discovered Rashad was behind it all, probably about the same time as you did. I was trying to get there to help you, but looks like you managed exceptionally well on your own."

Was that a compliment? "Thank you," I said. "For what you did to help Tyka. And . . . for calling the paramedics."

The houngan looked as if there were more he wanted to say. Something about his expression betrayed a war within. Whatever it was, it remained unsaid. He pressed his lips together, stood, and returned to his desk. "I'll be in touch about the council."

Lucien was arrogant, hypocritical, self-serving, and the most brilliant vodouisant I'd ever met besides Papa.

I hated him.

CHAPTER THIRTY-TWO

Salimah had left me without transportation, so I had to begrudgingly accept Lucien's offer to let his driver take me home. I hoped that in time, Salimah's wounds would heal. It seemed that her business, at least, was already well on the road to recovery.

There was another thread yet untangled. A girl whose visit and forgotten thumb ring had set me on this path. Like that day that drew me to the Quarter, I found myself called to see her one last time.

I thanked Lucien's driver and hopped into my own car. I had no idea if Sophie would be at the house where Tyka had found her, but it wouldn't hurt to try.

This time, I'd be making the trip without my friend. However comforting it would have been to receive one of her infamously curt text messages, one had yet to materialize. Rashad had hurt her. Worse, he'd probably scared her. She hadn't been able to protect either of us, and for someone like her, death wasn't worse than what she had to live with now—fear.

Love could make many demands on us. Today, love would require me to make the first move, let her know the door was open and that no judgments or rebuke awaited inside.

I spotted the moving van as I was driving down the street. It backed up against the curb in front of the house. No doubt who it was here for. Two men hoisted a sofa and dragged it up the ramp and onto the truck.

The door was open, and I found Sophie leaning against the living room wall, thumbs dancing across the screen of a phone that looked more like a tablet in her hands.

"Looks like I caught you at a bad time," I said.

"Mambo Dumond." Her voice sounded sturdy, solid, devoid of mourning.

One of the movers had returned. She pointed to a cluster of boxes on the floor and then turned to me. "Let's talk out back."

We went through the kitchen and out to an overgrown yard. Her roommate—Alicia, if memory served—was nowhere in sight.

"No need for pretense," I began. "I suspected you were involved in Virgil's murder."

At the mention of his name, that unfazed veneer warbled, threatened to shatter. Sophie yanked at her cutoff jeans and wiped at her eyes with the heels of her palms. "He didn't deserve what happened to him."

"He didn't," I agreed.

"That he died that way. So, so . . . horribly. And that you, that anyone, thought I could do something like that?"

Just like the first time I'd met her, Sophie's moods swayed to and fro like the tall grasses in her backyard.

"They say Rashad killed my Virgil. But they still haven't found him. He could be out there anywhere just waiting to pounce."

That wasn't going to happen, but I couldn't tell her that. "There won't be any place for him to hide. They'll find him."

With the corner of her T-shirt, Sophie wiped away her tears and her grief. "All over money?"

Apparently, she hadn't lived long enough to know that in one way or another, money, along with its partner in crime, ego, was behind almost every vile thing that ever happened.

"Where you heading?"

"I can't stay here," Sophie said. "I'm going back to my mama."

Cajun country. Papa always said that a fish pulled from the river longs to return. Those brothers of hers might never let her out of their sight again, and maybe that was for the best.

"Wait here," Sophie said and then ran back into the house. She returned and said, "You're the one that figured out who killed Virgil. You got Salimah off and kept them from looking in my direction. You deserve a real detective's fee. The police, they took up a collection. It's guilt money, and I don't want it."

Sophie handed me an envelope. I looked inside at the small collection of bills. Aside from what I made from my practice, this was the first time someone had paid me for something since I'd abandoned my corporate job. "Sophie, I'm no detective. I can't—"

"You can cut through there to get to the front, Mambo Dumond. Thank you." With that, Sophie turned and jogged back into the house. The sound of her voice barking orders at the movers flowed outside.

"Take care, Sophie," I said aloud, even though she wasn't there to hear me.

⟋

As I sat in the car watching the movers pack the last of Sophie's things, I sent two texts: one went to Tyka, the other to Darryl. One, of course, was returned immediately. The other one was a wild card.

With the influx of cash I'd just received, a feast was on tap.

Though we'd known each other for years, rarely had Darryl, Tyka, and I been in the same room together. It was hard to drag Darryl away from the Lemon Drop, and Tyka . . . well, a part of her life was lived completely separate from us. It kept her away for stretches, and when she was around, sitting in one place for longer than an hour was a challenge.

I left Gentilly in my rearview mirror and decided to do a traditional soul food dinner. Something I should have been able to pull off by myself. A quick trip to the market, and I had catfish, chicken, an unhealthy amount of cheddar cheese, and a fresh batch of green beans. The smoked turkey wing at home in the freezer would have to do, though my friend and mentor would scoff at me not using ham hocks.

By the time I got home, a nice cool breeze battled the sun-warmed concrete and brushed my exposed skin, sweet as baby's breath, in the crook of the neck. I'd avoided passing Saint Louis Cemetery No. 2. It would be a while before I felt comfortable thinking about that place, let alone driving past it.

Both Tyka and I could have died there. I shivered again just thinking about it. Despite what he'd done, Rashad was a human being, and I'd taken, or at least unleashed, the force that had taken his life. And that was something I feared would never sit quite right with me.

Back at home, I preseasoned the meats, then covered and left them in the refrigerator. I'd clean the beans and start on everything else tomorrow afternoon. Dinner was at six o'clock. Darryl had grumbled about leaving the bar, but more and more, Jimmy was proving himself worthy. I'd never say that to Darryl's face, though.

As evening descended, I stepped out back. I paused on the last step of the porch and listened. Absorbed the vibrations and energy. Aroma of cooking, cool and moist earth. Humidity thick in the air. Children playing in the street with cars zooming past them way too fast. Ms. Lucy's German shepherd barking, probably at both.

For the first time in what felt like much longer than the last several weeks, during which all that mayhem had unfolded, nothing felt out of place. Nobody lying in wait. No twisted magic fouling the air. Red brick dust remained undisturbed.

Though a small rueful smile played at the corner of my mouth, there was still one thing missing.

I strolled to my newly restored Petit Temple Vodoun and entered with relief. Vials and bottles in their places. Dolls and gris-gris bags perfectly aligned. Candles on the shelves, unlit.

Risk of loss aside, I felt the familiar tug to pull out the water-gazing bowl to search once again for my mother. I was at the cupboard, hand on the handle, when instead I sat down at the table, feeling like a full-fledged detective.

CHAPTER THIRTY-THREE

One mystery was solved; another remained. If it were in my power to reverse the outcome of the two, to abandon another mambo to have my mother back, I was only slightly ashamed to admit I would. Using magic to search for Manman would cost me a memory. Time, and likely Papa, would reveal which. But what would happen when he was no longer around?

I was cleaning up, tossing things in a junk drawer in the kitchen, when I saw the pen and paper I used to make grocery and herbal supply lists. Inspiration struck. For my plan, I'd need a notebook. Something nice. I'd fill it with the few pictures I had of my mother and write down everything I knew about her. It wouldn't be the same as a real recollection, but one day, it might prove to be all I had left.

The water.

A decade later, Hurricane Katrina was never far from our thoughts, her destruction still evident in so many places. Another storm could wash the notebook away, but Erzulie couldn't.

Whispers in the Vodoun community laid the blame at the hands of an angry spirit rumbling to life over the Atlantic Ocean before slithering south to the gentle waters of the Caribbean.

My patron lwa was a healer, and she watched over those who didn't know how to do it for themselves. But she was also the goddess of water and love and knew a thing or two about storms. Katrina was the abomination of another master of storms, his fury growing more every year. He didn't know or speak the language of the Haitian pantheon.

The days leading up to the storm were sleepless wreckages. Between the news and what I could discern from the tools of my trade, I knew its trajectory had changed and, despite my prayers, it was headed straight for us.

Governor Nagin had called for evacuations. I sat stuck in traffic for hours trying to get to my mother, but with streets as impassable as a clogged drain, I traversed all of three blocks. I abandoned my car where it was and ran back home. On the crackling, dying phone line, I cried, pleaded, and cursed, but Manman refused to leave her home. I was dizzy with panic when she phoned back and said she was leaving. The calm terror filling the staticky gaps between her words: *"I . . . I think I'll try to get to—"* That was the last time I heard her voice. The text message had come an hour later.

The streets were empty—in all the wrong parts of the city. Those who lay in the direct path had hunkered down to wait it out, while those in the outlying areas had made use of every mode of transportation and swiftness of foot to escape. We'd survived other storms. New Orleans sat below sea level; such things were expected. And to continue to call this city home, most of us were willing to pay the price ten times over. It had a soul that couldn't be found in any other part of the country. We wouldn't give that up without a fight.

The only way to save my mother and everyone else was to stop the storm.

I'd somehow made my way to the site where the news and the lwa had told me the storm would touch down, Saint Tammany Parish. Worried eyes had peeked out at me from behind curtains and hastily nailed wooden planks, trailed me down a web of streets and alleys.

The city had fallen behind an impenetrable curtain of darkness when I planted my feet on the shore of the Mississippi River. Hurricane-force winds and rain lashed my face and pummeled my body. Sometimes, I could still smell the evil taint on the water that day.

Head raised; eyes closed. The roaring ceased. Only the taste of the vile ocean spray on my lips remained. I knew a normal human body was 60 percent water. But I'd ceased being normal on the night of my initiation into the priesthood.

There, at what felt like the edge of the world, Erzulie and I met the storm. Puddles of muted light punctured the dark. The storm had inhaled, cut off my air, suspended time. A heartbeat later, it gathered its strength and flexed its muscle.

Pain. A pain that sliced the skin like a red-hot machete burrowed inside and feasted on muscle and tendon. Pain that Erzulie swallowed to keep me on my feet. I ingested that storm's bile, my lungs and body swelling near to bursting, but I held it while Erzulie set to work battling the storm. At the point where I felt so drunk on rain and my own tears, and the certainty of drowning was choking off my short convulsive breaths, Erzulie streamed the deluge from me. My pores erupted with shoots of steam and mist.

And the cycle of opening the door to death's grizzly sneer and slamming it shut again continued.

I channeled that water, thick and rotten like curdled milk, balanced on that precipice between my end and all possible futures that night and into the next day. At some point, when the water threatened to overwhelm us, I fell.

I'd awoken the next day, sprawled in the middle of a rain-slicked road, and I looked up at a sky the color of green tea. My clothes redolent of sweat. The fire in my bones replaced by a frigid chill. The only signs of the storm were a few broken branches and wind-battered debris. I came to my feet and thanked Erzulie.

And then the levees broke.

I survived, drowning an impossibility for me, but too many others did not.

Papa was still angry that Manman wouldn't move to the swamp with him, so he seized the opportunity to suggest that she had abandoned me too. Only I knew she was still alive—just out of reach.

The friends, the makeshift family I did have, wouldn't replace her, but I treasured them no less. And tonight, I'd gather them together and hold them close.

I was more than ready to get back to the business of being a mambo. After this dinner, of course.

The green beans went on first, and soon their musky aroma permeated the house. I heaped obscene amounts of cheese and heavy cream into buttered macaroni noodles and slid the baking dish into the oven. My two deep fryers, where I'd drop the chicken and fish before my two favorite New Orleans natives arrived, were set up on the back porch. Precooked chicken would send Darryl into a fit like no other. "Fresh everything" was his motto.

Though he preferred smothered chicken, I wasn't afraid to admit when I was in over my head. If he wanted gravy, he could make it himself when he got here.

While I waited for my guests, I had time to think about Lucien's idea for a Vodou council. Not the least of which would be how we'd spell the word. Despite myself, I was warming to the idea. Lucien would make noises about fairness, about being open to a vote, but I had no doubt that he'd end up leading things—an inevitability that gave me pause. Still, if we structured the group properly and governed according to rules everyone agreed upon, this would be a good thing for vodouisants.

Neither Salimah nor I had attempted contact after she'd stormed out of Lucien's office, but in time, I was sure she'd come around. Our obligation was to the lwa, not any petty human-level differences. My guess was that we'd meet again in a few weeks, and I found myself looking forward to it.

A knock at the door, a full half hour early, let me know the Lemon Drop's owner and proprietor had arrived. I found Darryl standing there, wearing his familiar uniform: jeans and sneakers, a short-sleeve button-down shirt, and a scowl.

"'Bout time," he complained as he came inside and kicked off his shoes. He removed his slippers from a paper sack he carried. "It's hotter than a blister bug in a pepper patch out there. Ain't even May yet."

Darryl tried to hide it, but he walked as if he were afraid of fully placing his feet too heavily on the ground. A hip? Back? Something internal? Without knowing the specifics, it was hard to figure out how to treat him, but I'd consulted Papa and prepared a general wellness tincture tea that I shoved at him as soon as we made it to the kitchen.

"Good to see you, too, Mr. Boudreaux." I handed him the cup without comment.

He cocked an eyebrow at me, took the cup, and sniffed at it. "What is this mess?" He set it down on the table. "I need some iced tea. You the only one I know be drinkin' hot-ass tea all year 'round. It ain't natural."

I plodded over to the refrigerator, got an ice cube from the dispenser, and dropped it in the cup. "Drink." This time it wasn't a request, and with a sigh that made clear his annoyance and exasperation with me, Darryl raised the cup and downed it in a few sloppy gulps.

I breathed a sigh of relief while he snatched up a pot holder, opened the oven, and peered in at the macaroni and cheese. I stood on the other side, admiring the bubbling, cheesy goodness. Nearly browned to a nice crust on top. Darryl took a bit longer than necessary in his assessment, but then he had the nerve to grab a spoon and sink it into my beautiful dish.

"Hey!"

"If it ain't right, best to fix it now 'stead of waiting till everythang's on the table."

He blew and blew at the steam coming off the spoon and, after a moment, popped it in his mouth. He looked up as he chewed, smacking his lips. He swallowed. "Coulda used a pinch of that jalapeño jack, but it'll do."

Darryl closed the oven and turned his attention to the pot of beans. After another taste and assessment, finding me ever so slightly lacking in my culinary talents, he went to the refrigerator and took out the chicken and fish I'd let marinate overnight.

"That lil' old gal can't spell 'watch,' but I guess she'll make it here on time." Darryl went back to his bag—the same one that held his slippers. He pulled out his special hot sauce and unlabeled bottles of seasoning and doused the chicken and fish with them. I closed my mouth, stifling the outrage.

At a quarter to six, we went out to the back porch, where I'd already started the fryers. We dumped in everything. I wanted Tyka to be able to take some food home. Darryl and I took our seats on the back porch as our meats sizzled and popped, taking in the early-evening breeze.

By six thirty, my dining room table was covered with a small but fitting feast. The only thing missing was Tyka. I texted and called. No answer. My first thought was that she'd gotten herself into trouble—or that her father had done something stupid. I played out every scenario of car accident, robbery, and other maleficence that I could think of.

Darryl? He got angry. He took a sip of his sweet tea, plunged a napkin into his T-shirt as a makeshift bib, and started piling food on his plate. "She ain't coming."

I followed suit. "You think something's wrong?"

"Pride bruised. That's about it." Darryl bit into the chicken and nodded his approval.

It was my turn to get angry. "She did this on purpose, didn't she?"

"We know different, but all that gal thinks she's got is that reputation of hers. Her feelings are hurt. That's all there is to it. We got to let her be. I'll take some food around to her. She'll come around when she ready."

Darryl may have been a particularly picky food critic, but he was indeed a wise man. Over our meal, I explained everything I'd learned about the case. And as I did so, I wondered if the police informant in his back pocket had already told him. It would take time for me to forgive his relationship with Darby.

After two and a half plates, Darryl wiped his mouth, got up, and went into the kitchen. His wince was less pronounced. But he came back with an exasperated look on his face. "Where's the cobbler?"

I shrugged like a child caught with her hand in an empty cookie jar. "I forgot."

His mouth opened. One hand on his hip. Head cocked. "Lawd. If I ain't taught you nothin'! Make a whole damn dinner like that with no dessert. Where did I go wrong!"

The lecturing went on as we prepared plates and containers for Darryl to drop at Tyka's house—at least the last place where we'd known her to live. He'd insisted that I stay in and heal myself up.

Hours later, as I set my phone on my nightstand and lay down to go to bed, the phone chirped. It was a text from Tyka.

> If you look outside and don't see your car, don't worry. I'll bring it back tomorrow after I change the plates. I'll get up with y'all next time.

What? I yanked the covers back, marched through the house, and flung open the front door. Sure enough, my parking space was empty. But there, on my doormat, was my empty casserole dish—the one containing the gumbo I'd taken Tyka and Eddie. Inside, a beautiful abomination of an offering. A Glade candle.

CHAPTER THIRTY-FOUR

I was never one for clichés, but sometimes things really did have a way of working themselves out. A steady stream of paying customers of both the local and tourist variety kept me busy. As details of Virgil Dunn's murder flooded the airwaves, arrests and indictments followed. An anonymous tip to a reporter at the *Times-Picayune* had started it all.

News of what had gone on here after the hurricane reached the national news level. Convictions, they said, were likely.

Though I knew the time, I checked my appointments again out of habit. One of my return clients, Mrs. Evangeline Stiles, was due any minute. When we'd spoken over the phone, her voice was as weathered as a centuries-old stone, as resigned as a tree's leaves yielding to fall. During our short conversation, Vangie had alluded to needing help preparing for a difficult transition in her life.

A fear and courage ritual might be in order. But that was no more than a guess. The story often changed when I met my clients in person. Just as much was said through body language as through voice. Gesture told the tale the mouth was unwilling to. And sometimes what people thought they wanted didn't match up at all with what they needed.

This was why I hated those folks who called me occasionally from across the country hoping for a consultation over the phone. Times were changing, though, and Chavonne had already scheduled a video consultation from Austin, where the lwa had guided her to study for that new career. I'd have to adjust if I wanted to survive.

I strolled around my freshly restored and painstakingly reappointed shop, adjusting and readjusting everything. Tilting the machete case that I'd replaced up in its resting spot on the wall, rearranging the premade poppets. Placing a basket of gris-gris satchels on the counter with my new register.

I eyed the courage candle but decided to leave it in the box until I met with my client. As was customary, I'd advised her to come on around back, and sure enough, at ten o'clock on the dot, I heard a determined knock at the door.

Vangie was a full head taller than me. Beautiful streaks of gray hair that was most certainly done by a professional. Close to my mother's age, but a more conservative dresser. She clasped her purse in front of her and held my gaze, not uncomfortably, for a full minute before she spoke or moved a muscle.

She inhaled and lifted her chin. "Besides your business card, this purse holds a small jar of Vaseline, a comb, and a coin purse with three crumpled-up bills, a quarter, and two pennies. But judging from the looks of that hair peeking out from under that scarf, you in need of a good deep conditioning again."

As much as I wanted to be offended about that hair comment, Vangie was right. I hated doing my own hair about as much as I hated sitting in a salon all day. She wouldn't be paying in cash, and as usual, it didn't seem like she needed courage to do anything. I invited her in.

"Thank you for seeing me," she said. "Looks like you fixed the place up some since last time."

"I have," I responded without going into the weeds. I preferred to leave the details of the last several weeks where they belonged. In the past. "So you want to get help today with a big decision you need to make."

"Oh, I've made one already. That was hard enough. It's the next one that's got me all tied up in knots."

Vangie's hands gripped the handle of the little black purse sitting on her lap. Her expression had turned grave. Shoulders so stiff it was as if she wore a straitjacket.

"Can I get you something? A cup of tea?" She had a story to tell, a difficult one. This, and the manners my parents had taught me, said it was time to offer a soothing, warm beverage.

"Just water," she said.

I filled a glass from the jug in the mini fridge, grabbed a coaster, and set them down on the table. After a few sips, she began. "I've left my husband."

"And that was the first decision," I prodded. "What else?"

"It isn't what you think. No other woman—at least not that I know of. No, my Arthur is mixed up in one of his scams again. He ain't had a job since that hot minute he drove the city bus. You know he live on disability."

All of a sudden, there's five thousand dollars in our account. I don't know what he's up to, and he's gone all tight lipped over it. Whatever it is ain't legal, and I don't want no part of it."

Vangie was indeed wise. "You're trying to decide whether or not to go back to your husband?"

Her chuckle was full of mirth. "I've never worked outside the home a day in my life. Never had a bank account of my own. Besides the clothes I tossed in a bag, don't have more than what's in my coin purse to my name. I'm not sure if I'm going back anytime soon, but I need to have the courage to find out what he's gotten himself into. Depending on what that is, I'll think on whether or not I'll be going back at all."

"Do you need a place to stay?" I had no idea why, but for Vangie, I was prepared to freshen up my guest room.

She shook her head. "I'm with my sister over in Metairie."

I nodded and stood to gather my supplies. From the cupboard I retrieved a sparklingly clean crystal chalice reserved for just these occasions. A precut piece of parchment paper from a drawer, along with a yellow candle for clarity. And there, at the back of the new pull-out drawer that Chicken had installed, Dragon's Blood ink.

I dressed the four-inch, free-standing yellow altar candle with Clarity oil and rolled it in a spattering of herbs.

I got the glass dip pen I'd snagged from Papier Plume over in the Quarter.

I dipped the pen in the bottle of ink and wrote the word "Courage" on the parchment. Next, I filled the chalice half-full and allowed my pores to expand. I needed only five drops of my sangswe wine for this spell. Pores closed, hands dried, I dropped the paper into the chalice and returned to the table.

I set the glass in front of Vangie. I lit the candle and recited Psalm 142:

1 I cry aloud to the Lord;
    I lift up my voice to the Lord for mercy.
2 I pour out before him my complaint;
    before him I tell my trouble.
3 When my spirit grows faint within me,
    it is you who watch over my way.
In the path where I walk
    people have hidden a snare for me.
4 Look and see, there is no one at my right hand;
    no one is concerned for me.
I have no refuge;
    no one cares for my life.
5 I cry to you, Lord;
    I say, "You are my refuge,

my portion in the land of the living."
6 Listen to my cry,
    for I am in desperate need;
rescue me from those who pursue me,
    for they are too strong for me.
7 Set me free from my prison,
    that I may praise your name.
Then the righteous will gather about me
    because of your goodness to me.

"Imagine this glass represents the blood of your enemies—whoever it is that led your husband astray. Feel the strength of the ancestors around you as you confront this enemy. Repeat after me: 'I build my house on the heads of my enemies.'"

Vangie hesitated a moment before she complied: "I build my house on the heads of my enemies."

"Again," I said. "With a little conviction this time."

Her voice, when she found it, was deep, even, and commanding. I inclined my head.

"Repeat this every time you need it, and soon you'll have your answer."

"You mean it will tell me what Arthur has done?"

"No," I corrected. "It will tell you what step you need to take, who you need to help you on your journey."

Vangie stood. "That money in the account—it's yours if we come out all right on the other end of this mess."

I needed the money. Who didn't? Whether I accepted it would depend on where it had come from. "The money isn't the reason I'll help you."

Vangie stood a little straighter. "Saturday at two for your hair?"

"That works for me."

There was a lightness to Vangie's step when she left. I was glad to have her as a client.

My fingertips sought the space in the middle of my chest where Rashad had wounded me. It no longer hurt physically, but mentally, that was another thing. Time. That was all I needed.

I cleaned up, then sat down at my new table to think. I couldn't get Vangie out of my mind. She reminded me of a friend of my mother's. Her name, another lost memory. I'd get Papa to fill in that chasm and record it in my memory journal.

Vangie I could help. In fact, I would. It didn't matter if she couldn't pay. If her husband was up to something that could put her in danger, well, that just wouldn't do, now, would it?

ACKNOWLEDGMENTS

A second novel is a curious thing. You start out thinking there is no way that you will top your first. But somewhere in the messy middle, you have an epiphany: that isn't the point. Each book will be its own unique creation. Still, I am happy to say that a second novel is no less precious than the first.

A special thank-you goes out to the experts who helped birth our detective: Brianne Joseph, LPI, of Sly Fox Investigations in New Orleans, for sharing her experiences as a private investigator, and Manbo Hathor Erzulie Akunaten, for her patience and grace in helping me understand the history and beauty of Vodou as a sacred tradition. Many thanks to Dr. Jeffrey Anderson, professor of history at the University of Louisiana Monroe, and Dr. Leslie Desmangles, professor emeritus of religious studies and international studies at Trinity College in Hartford, Connecticut, for their help with my exploration into the history and origins of Vodoun.

Special shout-outs to my amazingly talented author friends Eden Royce and DaVaun Sanders for your feedback, encouragement, and cheers. And to the equally amazing Nicky Drayden. I wrote a good chunk of this book with her over shared coffee shop snacks and drinks. Even though we're no longer in the same city, our writing hijinks continue virtually.

Deepest gratitude and thanks to my agent, Mary C. Moore, and the team at Kimberly Cameron & Associates. I also have to thank editors Adrienne Procaccini and Camille Rankine for their vision, patience, and support. You make me a better writer.

I'd be remiss not to mention the city of New Orleans and its people. I'd read about it, watched television shows about it, but it wasn't until I visited that I understood. The city has a soul, a life and history unlike any other. New Orleans, you made quite the impression. Thank you.

And finally, to the team at 47North: thank you for being the most excellent publishing team in the business.

ABOUT THE AUTHOR

Veronica G. Henry was born in Brooklyn, New York, and has been a bit of a rolling stone ever since. She is a graduate of the Viable Paradise Workshop, a member of SFWA, and an Author Spotlight interviewer for Fantasy Magazine. Her work has appeared in various online publications. The author of the novel *Bacchanal*, she now writes from North Carolina, where she eschews rollerballs for fountain pens and fine paper. Other untreated addictions include chocolate and cupcakes. For more information, visit www.veronicahenry.net.